O9-AHU-047

V.C. Andrews® Books

The Dollanganger Family Series
Flowers in the Attic
Petals on the Wind
If There Be Thorns
Seeds of Yesterday
Garden of Shadows

The Casteel Family Series
Heaven
Dark Angel
Fallen Hearts
Gates of Paradise
Web of Dreams

The Cutler Family Series
Dawn
Secrets of the Morning
Twilight's Child
Midnight Whispers
Darkest Hour

The Landry Family Series
Ruby
Pearl in the Mist
All That Glitters
Hidden Jewel
Tarnished Gold

The Logan Family Series
Melody
Heart Song
Unfinished Symphony
Music in the Night
Olivia

The Orphans Miniseries
Butterfly
Crystal
Brooke
Raven
Runaways (full-length novel)

The Wildflowers Miniseries
Misty
Star
Jade
Cat
Into the Garden (full-length novel)

The Hudson Family Series
Rain
Lightning Strikes
Eye of the Storm
The End of the Rainbow

The Shooting Stars Series
Cinnamon
Ice
Rose
Honey
Falling Stars

The De Beers Family Series
Willow
Wicked Forest
Twisted Roots
Into the Woods
Hidden Leaves

The Broken Wings Series
Broken Wings
Midnight Flight

The Gemini Series
Celeste
Black Cat
Child of Darkness

The Shadows Series
April Shadows
Girl in the Shadows

The Early Spring Series
Broken Flower
Scattered Leaves

The Secrets Series
Secrets in the Attic
Secrets in the Shadows

The Delia Series
Delia's Crossing
Delia's Heart
Delia's Gift

The Heavenstone Series
The Heavenstone Secrets
Secret Whispers

The March Family Series
Family Storms
Cloudburst

The Kindred Series
Daughter of Darkness
Daughter of Light

The Forbidden Series
Forbidden Sister
"The Forbidden Heart"
Roxy's Story

Stand-alone Novels
My Sweet Audrina
Into the Darkness
Capturing Angels

V.C. ANDREWS®

Roxy's Story

G

GALLERY BOOKS

New York   London   Toronto   Sydney   New Delhi

G Gallery Books
A Division of Simon & Schuster, Inc.
1230 Avenue of the Americas
New York, NY 10020

Following the death of Virginia Andrews, the Andrews family worked with a carefully selected writer to organize and complete Virginia Andrews's stories and to create additional novels, of which this is one, inspired by her storytelling genius.

This book is a work of fiction. Any references to historical events, real people, or real places are used fictitiously. Other names, characters, places, and events are products of the author's imagination, and any resemblance to actual events or places or persons, living or dead, is entirely coincidental.

Copyright © 2013 by the Vanda General Partnership

All rights reserved, including the right to reproduce this book or portions thereof in any form whatsoever. For information address Gallery Books Subsidiary Rights Department, 1230 Avenue of the Americas, New York, NY 10020.

First Gallery Books hardcover edition September 2013

V. C. ANDREWS® and VIRGINIA ANDREWS® are registered trademarks of the Vanda General Partnership

GALLERY BOOKS and colophon are registered trademarks of Simon & Schuster, Inc.

For information about special discounts for bulk purchases, please contact Simon & Schuster Special Sales at 1-866-506-1949 or business@simonandschuster.com.

The Simon & Schuster Speakers Bureau can bring authors to your live event. For more information or to book an event, contact the Simon & Schuster Speakers Bureau at 1-866-248-3049 or visit our website at www.simonspeakers.com.

Designed by Leydiana Rodríguez-Ovalles

Manufactured in the United States of America

10 9 8 7 6 5 4 3 2 1

Library of Congress Cataloging-in-Publication Data
Andrews, V. C. (Virginia C.)
  Roxy's story / V.C. Andrews.—First Gallery Books hardcover edition.
    pages cm
1. Escort services—Fiction. I. Title.
PS3551.N454R69 2013
813'.54—dc23
                    2013011690

ISBN 978-1-4767-0698-6
ISBN 978-1-4516-5100-3 (ebook)

3 9222 03108 800 3

Prologue

"You see the door?" my father asked, pointing his thick right forefinger at the entrance of our East Side town house in New York City. "Pack your things and get out. Go on, get out," he added, poking his finger in the air repeatedly, as if he were trying to hit the invisible button that would make me disappear.

Mama stood next to him looking even more terrified than I did, her beautiful cameo face shattering beneath the storm of his rage. She was always easier to read than I was. I never showed my father fear, cowered, or retreated, which only made him angrier. In fact, my defiance usually grew stronger as the volume and intensity of his anger boiled over like hot milk. There was simply no middle ground for either of us to occupy, no well of compromise from which either of us could draw a cup of calmness. Ironically, I was too much like him.

"You think I won't?" I fired back.

"No. I think you had better," he replied with a level of determination I had never seen him reach. There was no hesitation in his eyes and nothing that suggested an empty threat. This time, there was no doubt that he meant what he had said and how he had said it.

I glanced at Mama again. She looked far more surprised at his firmness than I had ever seen her look. She confirmed his determination for me. She could see that Papa wasn't simply having one of his spontaneous temper tantrums. Her eyes were wide open now, her lips trembling. In fact, her whole face looked as if it was vibrating as she paled. She even stepped away from him. I had no doubt that throughout their twenty years of marriage, she had never confronted or witnessed such fury in him and had no idea what else he might do. We had been circling each other like two martial-arts warriors for months lately. This confrontation was inevitable.

"Yes, sir," I said, then clicked my black leather shoe boot heels together and saluted him. The proper way to salute was one of the first things he had taught me when I was a little girl. After he taught that to me, emphasizing how smart and snappy it had to be, with my palm to the left, my wrist straight, and my thumb and fingers extended and joined, I saluted him every time I saw him. In the beginning, even he was satisfied, and Mama thought it was cute, but after a while, he saw that I was really mocking the salute, doing it so often, practically every time he looked at me, and he began to be annoyed by it and eventually forbade me to do it.

Now whenever I did it, especially with my heels clicking, it was as though I had set off a firecracker in his brain. At the moment, the veins in his neck pressed boldly against his skin. Pea-size patches of white at the corners of his lips began to spread like a rash. He looked as if he had swollen into some horrid ogre who could heave me and all of the furniture out the window.

My father wasn't a terribly big man. He was a little more than six feet tall and had broad shoulders, but he didn't look like a weight lifter or a lumberjack. Having been brought up in a military family, he had a cadet's perfect posture, so he always seemed solid and battle-ready, even though he had rejected the military life and had gone into investment management and financing.

His father was General Thornton Wilcox, who was once considered a top candidate to command NATO. The gilt-framed two-by-four picture of my grandfather in full dress uniform with all of his med-als glittering hung in our entryway hall and loomed over us the way the picture of a saint might hover in the home of a religious family. The light positioned above it seemed to highlight the dissatisfaction I had no trouble imagining in his face. My father's older brother, Orman, had followed in his father's footsteps, but not *mon père*.

Even though no one came right out and said it, I knew that in my grandfather's mind, my father was a great disappointment. I knew that both my grandfa-ther and my uncle ridiculed my father's decision, treat-ing him as if he were somehow weaker than they were, and in a family where affection and emotion were con-sidered weakness to start with, his father and brother had little trouble thinking of him as an outsider.

I never saw him or my mother shed any tears at how his father and his brother treated him, but there was no question about where he stood in their eyes. Even though no one clearly had said, "You're not one of us; you're no Wilcox," the words hung in the air between them like some foul odor whenever they had occasion to meet, which was happening less and less, anyway.

So I guess that pointing at the front door and telling me I was no longer part of our family wasn't all that big an emotional leap for my father. His family had all but done the same to him. That old expression, *It takes one to know one*, probably fit him, but I'm not laying all the blame at his feet. I'm not looking for some psychological rationalization or a comfortable excuse for what I had done and what was now happening.

No, I'm not going to deny being the top choice to model for a problem-child poster. *Mon père* had threatened to disown me many times and had suggested more than once that I be sent to one of those isolated behavior camps to experience tough love, but I really didn't want to believe that he would actually reach the point where he would firmly and permanently want me out of his life the way he obviously did at this moment.

I looked at Mama again to see if she would interfere and rescue me. She appeared to be wilting quickly in the wake of my father's overwhelming rage. As if she were trying to keep her body from breaking apart, she wrapped her arms tightly around herself. She looked like someone in a straitjacket. No, there was no sign of my getting any help there. This time, she wasn't going to step between us as she had many times previously. I knew that especially lately, she was coming to believe that I was irretrievable, too.

No matter what the reason, opposing my father was one of the most difficult things for her to do. She was about as devoted to him as any woman could be devoted to her husband. From overhearing conversations between her and some of her friends, I knew that she was constantly accused of having no mind of her own and permitting my father to run her life. But I also knew that my father had convinced her that I could be a devastatingly bad influence on my little sister, Emmie, his and Mama's golden child, their *enfant parfaite*, and that possibility also caused her to stand back.

They weren't even supposed to have Emmie. After my difficult birth, Mama's doctor had advised her not to get pregnant again. I didn't know all of the medical reasons, but I did know that her getting pregnant, even nine years after my birth, was a dangerous thing for her to do. When I heard she was pregnant, my first thought was that my father wanted another child because he was so disappointed in me. He wanted this child so much that he was willing to risk my mother's life. If I had any doubts about how low I stood in his list of priorities, Mama's pregnancy confirmed it. Every time he closed his eyes in my presence, I suspected that he was wishing I had never been born.

"Norton, *s'il vous plaît*," Mama said softly. That

was the extent of her resistance that day. She came from a family in France where men were treated like kings. That's where the Napoleonic Code established the supremacy of the husband when it came to his wife and children.

"No!" he screamed at her. "No more. I want her out of my sight."

His shout bounced off the walls and rattled my spine, but I didn't show it.

"No problem," I said. "Relax. The feeling's mutual," I added as coolly and calmly as I could, and went to pack my things, sucking in my fear and shock. As I walked by him, I thought I could actually feel the heat in the air.

When I was honest with myself, I admitted that I had always expected this day would come. Secretly, I had planned for it, hoarding money, considering what I would take and what I wouldn't and where I would first go. My parents didn't know, but I had recently been seeing a college boy who had his own apartment in the Bronx. He was always trying to get me to stay overnight, and I had done so once, lying about sleeping over at a girlfriend's home. Now maybe I would stay for quite a few nights.

As I packed, I heard them arguing downstairs. Comments such as "You remember we were told that tough love was our only hope" and "Let her see what it's like trying to survive out there" floated up the stairs to my room. I could imagine my mother wringing her hands as she chanted, *"Mon Dieu, mon Dieu."* That wouldn't impress my father. Calling for God's help was something a soldier did in battle, and surely my father was thinking that this battle was over. Not that his family was very religious, anyway. To me, it seemed that they thought of churches the same way they thought of the officers' club, just another place you visited from time to time to remind yourself that you were special.

My sister, Emmie, heard nothing of this argument. She was fast asleep in her bedroom, snug under her comforter, her teddy bear dressed in a soldier's uniform beside her, its glass button eyes catching bits of light seeping through the curtains. Emmie was nearly nine years old and admittedly very bright for her age. Unlike me, she had a warm, very outgoing personality. She was easy to love. I was more like a seamless walnut, impossible to crack or get into. You had to smash me to peel off my hard shell. I trusted no one and believed that everyone was selfish like me. Even nuns were doing what they were doing solely to get themselves into heaven.

It seemed to me that my father had been complaining about me from day one, not that I could remember day one. But he often made reference to my infant days, describing how difficult and stubborn I could be. It was safe to say that my father rarely, if ever, complimented me about anything. It was as if he thought that one compliment would open a fortress, and I would rush through with all of my bad behavior. Although I wasn't particularly looking for excuses, I suppose a good therapist would say that *mon père* was at least partly responsible for how I had turned out. My father might not have chosen an army career for himself, but he certainly ran our home and family as if we were a military unit. Sometimes I thought he wasn't my father; he was just someone in charge, someone assigned guard duty.

I wasn't exactly Miss Popularity at my school, either, but I was close enough with some of the other girls to hear about how their fathers treated them, fawned over them, and, most important, made excuses for any of their failings. Some of the girls enjoyed playing their fathers for sympathy and bragged about how easy it was for them to get "Daddy" to do anything for them or let them do anything. Even the girls who came from very conservative and religious homes seemed to have more freedom and longer leashes than I had, not that I ever paid much attention to my leash.

Although I was good at hiding it, a therapist would surely say that right from the beginning, I had more fear of my father than love for him. I could recall how he loomed over me ominously when I was a little girl. There was such an obvious look of displeasure and frustration on his face. I could almost hear him thinking, *Is this the child for which my wife almost lost her life?*

I couldn't begin to count how many times he had told me about my birth and Mama's flirtation with death. Sometimes he made me sound like an infant assassin, a spy planted inside her. Mama would try to tone him down, but he was ready with his far-too-graphic and detailed description of how difficult my birthing had been. Eventually, I realized that the memories haunted him and not her. He had gotten her pregnant, so he, not she, bore more responsibility. For what had they taken this great risk? Yes, for what? I didn't need to hear him say it. I knew what he thought. They had taken it for this little monster, this *grande déception* they had named Roxy.

I believed I suffered with *mon père*'s anger more than Emmie because I was born closer to his break with his own father, not that it was in any way my fault. He had made his choice long before Mama became pregnant. He had wanted to be who he was and do what he was doing, but he couldn't escape the guilt. There was just too much family tradition haunting him. In making his decision not to be in the military, he made all of his ancestors and especially his own father and brother seem inferior and stupid for dedicating themselves to national service. Maybe because he felt so bad about himself and his family relationship, he had less patience for me. I was a perfect scapegoat.

Or perhaps all of this really is just my way of looking for an excuse. After all, when it came to finding an excuse for something I had done or failed to do, I was an expert. In fact, other girls often came to me for suggestions when they were about to get into trouble. I could prescribe excuses as easily as most doctors could prescribe antibiotics. I was tempted to open an "Excuse Stand" and charge for them.

Did I do bad things in school? There's a question that answers itself. Does it snow in Alaska? From kindergarten on, I was impossible. I hated sharing anything with anyone. I was aggressive and bullied whomever I could. By the time I was in the sixth grade, I had probably had at least a dozen fights—in the girls' room, in the hall, or on the school grounds. I could kick and punch like a boy. Some of my fights were with boys, in fact, and I didn't lose. I got a few bumps and bruises, but none of that caused me to retreat. I think my lack of fear for my own safety and of pain did more to terrorize my opponents than anything else.

Mama was trekking a path right into the concrete sidewalks between home and my grade school to have frequent parent-teacher and administrator sessions because of my bad behavior. Whenever my father was brought in, called out of his office, the follow-up was even uglier. He didn't believe in things like time-out, sitting in a corner, or losing privileges. What kinds of privileges did a ten-year-old really have, anyway? No television, parties, or movies? I could live without any of it so well that it frustrated him more. No, it was only his thick belt that gave him any hope, but I frustrated him there, too.

Just as I was almost immune to the pain that I would suffer in a good yard fight, I was also immune to my father's thick belt. Tears would come to my eyes. I couldn't stop that, but I kept my lips sealed and my tongue paralyzed. I didn't even moan. I stood or lay there like a piece of wood. I knew my skin was nearly burned off sometimes, but I wouldn't cry out. Finally, he would give up, declaring I was simply impossible. I would come to no good. It was a self-fulfilling prophecy. He expected that he would stand in our living room one day and point at that front door just as he had today. Sometimes I thought he was actually looking forward to the opportunity. It had finally come, and it wasn't because of some final straw. The accumulation was just too much. He couldn't swallow down another rule being broken, another law being disobeyed.

My schoolwork was in shambles. I was barely passing most subjects and failing a few in the twelfth grade. I had a good chance of not graduating. Earlier that year, I had been caught smoking some weed in the girls' room. I suspected a girl named Carly Forman had informed on me. A few weeks before, I had stolen away her boyfriend, Walter Martin. It wasn't hard to do. Carly was determined to hold on to her virginity. I knew Walter's buddies were with girls who were just the opposite, and he was taking some heat for his failure to score. Carly was very proud and vocal about her innocence. For me, attracting and tempting Walter was like shooting fish in a barrel. Although he wasn't bad-looking, I wasn't particularly attracted to him. I did it only to get back at Carly, because she loved spreading rumors about me and looking down on me.

Twice this month, Mama had been called and asked to come to school because of the way I had used French words to curse out my teachers. My father had married Mama in France and had brought her to America. She still spoke French at every opportunity and did so with me and even with him from time to time. I was good at picking up some curse words and creating some very nasty images, in addition to becoming quite fluent in the language. Because of the way I looked when I spoke, my teachers suspected that what I was saying was inappropriate, so they got translations that I was sure turned their faces red, especially Mrs. Roster, my science teacher. She came down on anyone who used "damn."

I suppose if I listed the mothers who called to complain about me, the fathers who spoke to *mon père* complaining about my influence on their perfect daughters, and the three police arrests for shoplifting over the last two years, I could understand why both of my parents were feeling defeated, especially when they looked back at the years of disappointment.

Five nights in these last two weeks, I had come home well after midnight. Twice I snuck out of the house when I had been "confined to quarters." Papa actually used that terminology. He had tried to keep me contained by forbidding Mama to give me any money. Once in a while, she snuck me a few dollars, but for the most part, she was more afraid of defying him than I ever was. I had a stash of money that I instinctively knew I would need someday, so I didn't touch any of it, and I was always trying to add to it.

This particular day, I got caught stealing fifty dollars out of Carrie Duncan's purse during P.E. I denied it, of course, but Carrie's father had given her a twenty with a bad ink smear on one side, and that twenty was in my possession. I was suspended again and couldn't return without both of my parents meeting with the dean. It looked very ominous. There could be an effort to have me sent to some other school or brought before a judge again, only this time with more deter-mination to have me placed in a juvenile detention center or something.

Two weeks before, I had met Steve Carson at the Columbus Circle mall. I saw him reading the cover of a novel in the bookstore. He looked very interested in it, and then he put it back on the rack. I thought he was a very good-looking guy, about six feet tall, with a swimmer's build. He had soft, wavy light brown hair and patches of freckles on his cheeks but a look in his face that gave him a more mature expression. I prided myself on always being a good judge of character and personality. I knew how to read people's eyes, the way they looked at other people, and the small movements they made with their lips. Innocence and insecurity were always easy for me to see, as was arrogance.

I watched how Steve looked with interest at other people, skimming the surfaces of their faces and bodies just like someone who knew as much about people as I thought I did. He brought a smile to my face. When-ever I saw someone who interested me, I suddenly felt very good, as if there was some purpose to being born, after all, because most people bored me.

I watched Steve walk away, and then I shoplifted the book he had been considering. It wasn't difficult this time, because it fit so well in the inside pocket of the oversize man's leather jacket I was wearing. Despite being caught at it three times, I was almost as good as a Las Vegas magician when it came to "now you see it, now you don't." I left the store right after he did, and when he stopped to look at some clothing in a window, I came up beside him and took out the book. I stood there looking at it, and then he looked at me with a smile of incredulity.

"You just buy that book?" he asked.

"Sorta," I said.

"Sorta? What's that mean?"

"Sorta means 'sort of,'" I said, and he laughed. "Here," I told him, handing it to him. He looked at it in my extended hand.

"'Here'? You want to give it to me? Don't you want to read it?"

"The last thing I read was a ticket for jaywalking, and you know how hard that is to get in New York City."

He laughed again, looked at the book suspiciously, looked back at the store and then at me.

"Don't worry. It was a clean sorta," I said, jerking the book at him. "Take it. I don't want it."

He finally took it. "If you don't want it, why did you do this?"

"I saw you read the cover with interest and then put it back. On a budget?"

"Sorta," he said, smiling.

"There you go, then. You have what you wanted at no cost."

"Yes, but why did you want to do this for me? Who are you?"

"I'm not an undercover policeman working out an entrapment or anything. Don't worry. You looked like you really wanted it. I liked your look, so I did one of the things I do best. I made some good-looking guy happy."

He laughed but shook his head incredulously. I could tell he had never met anyone like me. But then again, few people had. "My name is Roxy Wilcox," I added, and offered my hand.

He looked at it as if taking it would doom him.

"No diseases," I said.

He took it, holding it very gently, almost too gently for a man who looked as fit as he did. "Steve Carson. You liked my look?"

"Sorta," I said, and he did that smile and shaking of his head again.

He looked around—to see if anyone was noticing us, I guess. Then he turned back to me. "I guess you live in New York?"

"Right. East Side. You?"

"I'm going to Columbia. Junior. Born and raised in Rochester, New York."

"Raised? What are you, corn?" I asked, and he laughed.

"You're funny, all right. You go to school or what?"

"Mostly 'or what,' but I'm still enrolled in school. At least today."

"College or . . ."

"High school," I said. "A senior, but don't hold it against me."

He nodded. Then he looked at his watch.

"Heavy date at the dorm?" I asked.

"No. I don't live at the dorm. I took a studio apartment on Jerome Avenue."

"Oh, a loner?"

"I'm just not into the college rah-rah stuff. Can't afford to fail anything. Besides, I like being on my own."

"Makes two of us."

"So you're a senior in high school?"

"I'm old enough. Don't worry about that. I was left back three times," I added, half in jest. He looked as if he believed it and smiled a little more warmly now. I could see he was very attracted to me, not that most boys weren't.

I think that was a big part of what confused my parents and my teachers. I was, in all modesty, quite beautiful, with a terrific figure, but as Billy Barton, a boy in my class, was fond of saying, I was "hell on wheels." The contradiction probably kept me from suffering more severe punishments. Whenever I had been brought before a judge, I could see the confusion in his face. Why would someone who looked like me be so bad? Who was I, the daughter of Bonnie and Clyde? I knew how to be sweet and remorseful, too. Each time, I was sent off with warnings. Most men, especially some of my teachers, were easy to manipulate. But not my father, never *mon père*.

"So what do you want to do afterward?" he asked.

"After what?"

"High school," he said.

I shrugged. "I don't know. That's too far away to plan."

He nodded. I had the feeling I was beginning to scare him now.

"No, I don't know. I might go into fashion modeling."

"You could."

"Thank you."

He glanced at his watch again and then surprised me. "How about some lunch?"

"Lunch?"

"That's the least I could do for a girl who risked her reputation and her uncertain future for me."

I shrugged. "Why not? Only, I didn't risk my future. I reinforced it."

He laughed. "You're very funny."

"I'm better when I'm really trying to be. So where's this lunch?"

"I know this great sandwich shop on Fifty-Seventh."

"Lead the way," I said, and we started out together.

I suppose a relationship that began with a theft didn't have a good prognosis, but I was never one to care about long relationships, anyway. Maybe my mother's relationship with my father turned me off the idea. My guidance counselor, Miss Laura Gene, was an amateur therapist, and she often accused me of always looking for ways to blame my parents for anything and everything.

"One of these days, you'll have to take sole responsibility for things you do, Roxy," she told me. "That's when you'll know you have become an adult."

"Oh, I thought that was when I had my first period," I replied, and she turned a shade of purplish red.

She would definitely categorize Steve as an adult. He was obviously a very responsible person and serious about his schoolwork. He was not my idea of an ideal guy, anyway. I liked guys who weren't uptight about their futures. When he told me he was very interested in international politics, I thought he was going to start talking about current events like my father and be boring, but he had a passion for what he liked, and I was attracted to that for a while. It didn't take me long to figure out that he was not terribly experienced when it came to romance, despite his good looks. He was an only child, born to parents who had him late in their lives. Cursing, sex, drugs, and drinking were so alien to him that I thought at first he was from another planet. But he didn't prove too difficult to corrupt.

After lunch, we went for a walk in Central Park. He was going to go on to his apartment to work on a research paper. I asked him if he wanted company later.

"Later? When later?"

"I don't care. You tell me," I said.

"It's Sunday. Don't you have school tomorrow?"

"I never let something like that interfere with my happiness," I said.

He smiled, now far more relaxed. I could see he was intrigued with me, and for now, that was enough for me.

"I'm not much of a cook, but I'm good at putting out a ready-to-eat chicken with some vegetables."

"I'm always ready to eat," I said. "And other things."

"Other things?"

"You'll figure it out. You seem smart."

He smiled and gave me his address. "Six-thirty?"

"Fine," I said, and gave him a quick kiss on the lips, then hurried away. When I looked back, he was still standing there looking after me, glancing at the book I had swiped for him and then back at me as if he couldn't believe that what had just happened was real.

That was one of those nights when my father nearly took off my head, but I endured the pain and continued seeing Steve on and off during the next two weeks. As it turned out, he didn't just have limited romantic experiences. He was a virgin. That ended fast. I was able to spend that night later at his place because one of the girls at my school covered for me in exchange for an iPod I had lifted. She really wasn't much of a friend, not that any of them were. *Mon père* was on a short business trip, so I was able to pull it off.

I did begin to really like being with Steve, but I still couldn't see a long relationship with him. To his credit, he never got too emotional, never said "I love you" or even something like "I really like you, Roxy." Maybe he realized how little that mattered to me. We just had a thing. In fact, I told him he made love like someone brushing his teeth.

"What's that mean?" he asked.

"You do it like it's simply something that has to be done. You're afraid of cavities."

He thought a moment, missed the point, and shrugged. By now, he had decided not to take anything I did or said seriously, anyway. It was as if he went in and out of a dream when we were together. I really questioned whether he thought about me the day after or pushed me aside for fear he might miss an important point in political science class.

However, the night my father threw me out, I went directly to Steve's apartment. After I had packed, I stopped to look in on Emmie for a long moment. There was a good chance I wouldn't see her again for some time, maybe ever. I wondered how she would react to that. We weren't very close. There were just too many years between us, and my father did his best to keep me from doing too much with her without either my mother or him around. I could count on my fingers how many times I had taken her somewhere in the city without one of them. I wasn't to be trusted.

She didn't stir. She looked like a little doll some other girl had tucked into her bed. I thought her teddy bear was looking at me suspiciously. I touched her hair softly so as not to wake her, whispered good-bye, and then descended the stairs. Mama came to the door of the living room. She looked out at me standing there with my suitcase and shook her head. She seemed unable to speak. It was hard for me, too, but I managed.

"Have a good life," I told her, and walked out.

It was overcast and dreary, but even if it weren't, the street never looked as dark or as empty to me, even though there were people walking on both sides and the traffic was heavy. I did feel a little dazed, but I wasn't hesitant. I walked with determination to the corner and hailed a taxi to take me to Steve's apartment building. When he opened the door and saw me standing there with a suitcase, he looked about as amazed as anyone possibly could.

"What's going on?"

"I'm here."

"With a suitcase? For how long?"

"As long as you'll let me stay," I said.

His amazement changed quickly to a look of worry. "Er . . . I could get into trouble if you were here more than a night. You are underage, Roxy. You're not quite eighteen. You know I know the truth." He shook his head and put up his hands. "Look, I'm not ready or able to do something like this," he said. "What did you do, run away from home?"

"Sorta," I said.

He shook his head. "Go home, Roxy. This is a mistake that you'll regret."

"I guess it is," I said. "Too bad," I told him, and left him standing there in his doorway looking quite relieved.

I took the elevator down, walked through the small lobby, and stepped back into the street.

And that's how it all began.

1

I had learned about a neighborhood on the Lower West Side where runaways who still had a little money hung out. I had read about it in a newspaper article written by someone who was on the Pulitzer Prize short list for doing a series about "America's Forgotten Children." It intrigued me, and maybe, tucked way back in my brain in one of those secret places we all keep our fears and nightmares, I envisioned myself going there and checking into one of those roach nests because the cost was so minimal and no one who operated one cared who you were, how old you were, or if you lived or died that day. You could make up any name for yourself. The only identification you needed was a fifty-dollar bill.

It was late April, and despite the threat of rain, I suppose I could have survived sleeping in some discarded old car or under a bridge somewhere, but at least at this excuse for a hotel, I could have some sense of safety once I locked the door of the room.

Just as I had read, when I arrived at one of these places (they always had names beyond reality, like

Paradise Hotel), the man behind the small, battered dark-wood desk was uninterested in me and only brightened a bit when I produced a fifty-dollar bill. I had a feeling he wasn't as old as he looked, despite his very thin, cheaply dyed black hair and a face that looked like crinkled cellophane. He had a jaw I thought might have been squeezed with a pair of pliers while he was growing up. Deep lines rippled across his forehead. He coughed like someone suffering with emphysema, explained by an ashtray full of smoked-down thin cigars on the counter. He gave me a key to a room on the third floor and told me the only rule was no smoking in the room, which he said meant no smoking anything. Then he sat back again and closed his eyes as if I had interrupted an enjoyable dream he was having.

For a moment, I imagined I had been talking to Charon, the mythical ferryman of Hades, the Greek version of hell, who carried the souls of the dead across the rivers Styx and Acheron that divided the world of the living from the world of the dead, because coming to this hotel made me feel I had come to the land of the dead. I smiled to myself, imagining how proud of me Mr. Wheeler would be for remembering that lesson in mythology, but the truth was that despite the act I put on, I was very attentive in his English class.

The elevator was out of order, so I headed for the narrow stairway. The railing was loose and rattled, and the steps groaned even under my mere one hundred and twelve pounds. When I turned onto the third floor, I heard some loud music and laughter coming from the first room on the right. Fortunately, my room was four doors away, and I heard nothing from behind any of those doors at the moment. The entire hallway reeked of stale beer and cigarettes. There were no windows, no opportunity for any odor to escape or be diminished. It was as if every ugly scent was layered upon every other and now seeped through the walls.

Because the frame of my room's door was warped, I had to jerk it open after inserting the key, and for a few seconds, I stood in the doorway debating whether to just turn and run out or go in. I felt as if I were about to dive into a cesspool.

I swallowed hard and entered, searching for a light switch. The small ceiling light fixture had a bulb a size or two too small, probably placed there deliberately so that the room's new inhabitant couldn't see just how run-down the floors and walls were or how many roaches were building their own suburb. I felt my whole body cringe as if they were already crawling up and over my ankles, joyfully and excitedly making their way to get under my bra and into my heart. I saw that wallpaper was peeled off in spots as if someone suffering from agoraphobia had been scratching at it.

Being afraid to go outside in this neighborhood was understandable. The streets looked as if they last were cleaned around the time of the Civil War. When I had turned onto the block, I had the feeling that someone literally could die on the sidewalk and be unnoticed. What a contrast to our immaculate block on the Upper East Side.

The room, despite what the man at the desk forbade, reeked of cigarettes. The rug was worn down, revealing the wood beneath it in most places. I was afraid to look under the bed. Maybe the last person who stayed here had died under there. I had no doubt something had died under it. There was only a four-drawer dark brown dresser and a wooden folding chair beside it, both badly scratched, the dresser actually with a hole in one side. Of course, there was no television, radio, clock, heat, or air-conditioning.

The bed frame was plain, and the narrow mattress, in which some ugly, crawly thing was surely hatching, was covered by sheets that were gray and stained yellow. It looked as if there were some lipstick stains, too. At least, I hoped it was only lipstick. I peeled off the stringy blue wool blanket, the bottom of which was torn as if someone had slashed it with a sharp knife. Instead of the pillow, without a pillowcase, I decided to use my soft backpack. I knew that if I slept, I would have to sleep in my clothes. There were two small windows, one so stuck in place it was probably never closed, which on second thought was a good thing. At least there was some ventilation. The other window opened and closed. Neither had any curtains or blinds, so there was no way to keep out the morning light.

For a while, I just sat on the bed thinking. It was only natural for me to have some second thoughts and regrets, especially in a place like this, but every time I imagined myself running home to kowtow and plead for forgiveness, I felt sicker. No, I had to endure this, I told myself. I could just hear my father telling me that this was a five-star hotel compared with what soldiers had to endure in boot camp. "Soldier up!" was one of his favorite expressions whenever I complained about anything. Usually, that was just what I did. I soldiered up.

Nevertheless, it wasn't until nearly four in the morning that the sounds from the street below diminished and I was able to get some sleep. Until then, I could hear people screaming and cursing, car horns sounding, loud laughter, someone breaking bottles, and occasionally, someone crying just below my window.

What a contrast this was with my beautiful bedroom at home, with its king-size canopy bed and thick pink rug. Mama was a bit of a fanatic when it came to cleanliness and neatness. Papa had been brought up in military housing, so everything in its place with spit and polish was standard and expected operating procedure. I was confident that despite Papa's comparisons with a hard army life and meeting the challenge, neither Mama nor he would permit a stray dog to sleep in a place like this room. However, all I could imagine at the moment was Papa hoping that I would end up in just such a room.

"Let's see how tough she is now," he might mutter with a smile of smug satisfaction.

I think I managed to fall asleep for the rest of my first night merely out of spite. Whenever I began to feel sorry for myself, I forced myself to envision my father's red, enraged face and his confidence that I would return and plead for mercy and forgiveness, writing promises in blood. I was as strong and as stubborn as he was, however, and I was determined to have him cry "uncle" before I ever did.

During that first night and the days that passed afterward, I harbored the belief, perhaps more accurately called the hope, that somehow, someway, my mother would come looking for me, find me, and convince me that my father regretted throwing me out on the street. I actually looked for her on street corners, in nearby stores and restaurants, and in the hotel lobby, even though there was no way she could possibly know I was in this place or in this neighborhood. I tried to imagine her running around in a panic, asking strangers if they had seen me. I even envisioned her putting pictures of me on walls and utility poles, with desperate pleas for anyone who had seen me to call her. Maybe she would hock some of her best jewelry and put up a reward.

Whenever a policeman on the street looked at me, I stared back, expecting him to come rushing over, demanding to know if I was Roxy Wilcox. Perhaps by now, my picture had been given to all of the police in the city. But most of the time, the officer I saw would look right through me or just turn away, uninterested in the sight of just another runaway teenager, with so many more serious problems to face.

After the first few days, the reality hardened. I realized that Papa would resist reporting me to the police or permitting Mama to do so this soon. He would be too embarrassed at work if his colleagues found out, and if the police brought me home, he wouldn't feel victorious at all. He'd have to accept me without my surrendering, and he would have to assume most of the blame for an underage girl being thrown out onto the streets. I was still weeks away from being eighteen.

At first, I had no idea what I was going to do or how long I would remain where I was. I suppose anyone who has been thrown out of her home or has run away begins by thinking of other relatives to go to. Going to my father's family would probably be worse than going home. For all I knew, my grandfather would have me court-martialed and put in some military brig to scrub floors and wash dishes for years.

Rushing off to Mama's family in France loomed as a possibility, but I wasn't stupid. I knew I had to get more money together for such a trip. Perhaps more important, I knew how everyone there would react. They'd want me to go home immediately, and my uncles and aunts would force me onto the next flight back to the States. Relatives provided no hope, no option. I had no friends close enough to trust or concerned enough with my welfare to offer me any assistance here, either. Realizing that brought home the reality of who I was and how I had lived my life until now.

I would probably be the first to admit that I was too bitter, too selfish, and too distrusting to form any solid relationships with other girls. By now, most of them knew how their parents would feel about their being too friendly with me, even though I could see that so many wanted to be. They thought I could teach them things none of their other friends could, and there was the attraction to someone or something dangerous. However, I was the quintessential bad influence who, if I didn't get them to be as bad as I was, would do something wrong when they were with me that would get them into trouble, anyway. It was the old guilt-by-association thing. I might as well be carrying a fatal disease. Maybe I was. Even my teachers had begun to avoid contact with me recently, choosing to pretend I was invisible until I did something they couldn't ignore.

Only Mr. Wheeler made any real effort to save me. He said he could tell from the way I wrote that I was far brighter than my grades revealed.

"You could do something with your life," he said. "You could be proud of yourself, Roxy."

"Who says I'm not?" I fired back at him.

He smiled, his soft gray-blue eyes twinkling with that irony he could express and see in what others said or did. "You hate yourself, Roxy," he replied softly. "Others might fall for your act, but don't try to cover it up with that false bravado when you're talking to me. Remember your *Macbeth*. 'False face must hide what the false heart doth know.'"

I didn't spit something smart or nasty back at him. I could see how unhappy he was for me and how much he hated telling me that.

"Stop fighting everyone who wants to help you," he added. "Get that chip off your shoulder before it's too late."

I didn't want to continue the conversation. He was

the only one who could bring me to tears, and if there was one thing I never wanted to do, it was cry for myself or give anyone the satisfaction of seeing me do it, especially at school. My father had taught me that much. Good soldiers don't whine. They grin and bear it. What was I living as in my father's house if not a good soldier? I thought. *Soldier up!*

For the first few days at the roach hotel, I was comfortable deceiving and lying to myself, telling myself that I would be just fine on my own. I had enough money to get by eating at inexpensive restaurants for a while, and I had enough clothing. I walked around with this Pollyanna belief that somehow, someway, something would happen that would provide me with some sort of future in which I wouldn't be dependent on my parents ever again.

But as my money began to diminish and wandering about the city lost its novelty, I could feel myself beginning to despair and began to sense a growing desperation festering beneath my breasts. Sometimes I felt hot and flushed, and sometimes I just felt numb. Returning at night to my dingy room only reinforced this growing depression and melancholy. How low had I sunk? Where could I go from here? Had I lost my senses? Had my pride blinded me to reality? I didn't want to answer any of those questions.

Even so, I'd lie there at night, forbidding myself even to think of going home and begging for mercy, despite how many times I actually set out to do so, leaping off the rotten bed and charging toward the door. I never opened it. I stood staring at the doorknob and then retreated when I imagined the expression on Papa's face coming back at me in wave after wave, his angry smile rippling through my eyes and into my brain.

Even after hearing someone try to open my door at night, something that would surely terrify any other girl, I remained determined and stubborn. I was confident that I could deal with anything unpleasant. Where did I get the fortitude? Was it from my father? Should I be grateful to him for that, at least? Could I ever admit to being grateful to him for anything? Just thinking about it made me even more miserable. I was there because of him, and I could survive there because of him, but I didn't want either, not really.

To feel better about all this, I tried to call up images of my parents suffering. Surely they were both up all night thinking about me out on the cold, indifferent streets. Perhaps they feared that I had already been mugged, raped, or murdered. Now that time had passed, days had gone by, and I had not come home with my tail between my legs, my mother surely had become more frantic. She was crying, pleading every day, maybe even demanding that my father do something. Maybe they were at the stage where they weren't talking to each other, and every time Emmie asked about me, my mother would just break into hysterics, driving my father out of the house. He was suffering, I told myself. He had to be. He could put on his act, pretend to be strong and indifferent, but he was tossing and turning when he went to bed, maybe even taking sleeping pills, and all day, he was regretting his rage, regretting what he had done. I convinced myself that his bitterness was eating him up inside.

Convincing myself of all this did make me feel better for a short while, but the stench of the room, the ugly sounds from outside, the crying I heard frequently coming through the walls from other rooms, and the sight of other, far more lost young girls already down some path of drugs and prostitution, their complexions blotchy, their necks dirty, their eyes full of fear and dread, sickened me and filled me with new despair.

Was I looking at my immediate future? I couldn't get over the growing feeling that I was somehow dwindling and disappearing. I would soon lose my name, and one day, I would look into the smoky, cracked mirror in the rusty bathroom and be unable to recognize myself. The girl looking back at me wasn't the girl with stubborn pride anymore. She was a shadow of who she had been, a corpse on the prowl.

This really was a hotel for the dead, I thought. I had crossed over into Hades. The people living in it didn't realize who and what they had become. Soon I could be one of them, moving like people in a chain gang, drudging their way through the muck of their own making. They struggled to get up the stairs and to their rooms—or tombs, I should say. Some of them vomited, moaned, and sobbed along the way. Who else but the mythical Charon would want to own and operate such a graveyard?

Most of the time, there was that elderly, sick-looking man at the desk in the very small lobby, but occasionally, a young man with reddish-brown hair was there. He had a pockmarked face and slightly orange lips. Maybe he brushed some lipstick on them. As skinny as someone who had been near starvation for a week, he sat on a stool, with his small, feminine shoulders turned inward as he hovered over a checkerboard, apparently playing his right hand against his left like someone with a multiple-personality syndrome, both hands with the long, dirty fingernails of someone who had been scratching his way out of a grave. The first few times I saw him, he barely looked back at me, but one time, for some reason, he sat back and smiled, revealing two rows of nearly corn-yellow teeth.

"My grandfather told me to watch for you today," he said.

"Excuse me?"

"Pappy Morris. He owns the joint." He shrugged. "Someday it will be mine. My father ain't around no more. We don't know where he went. My mother left about ten years ago with a cable television salesman."

"Terrific," I said. "You gave me your biography in less than a minute."

I started to go up to my room.

"Hold up."

I paused and looked back. "What do you want? Is there some sort of discount for guests who endure more than two nights here or something?"

He smiled and shook his head. "You're different. Gramps is right."

"Really? How am I different?"

"You're clean, and so far, you've stayed clean."

"Excuse me?"

"What the hell are you doing here and still clean?"

"It isn't easy, considering the shower has water the color of a penny, and the warmest it gets is cold."

He shrugged, illustrating how low his concern for the residents of the hotel could go. "So why are you slumming?"

"Slumming?" I looked around, pretending to be shocked. "I thought this was the Plaza."

His laugh was more like someone gasping through clenched teeth and shuddering. "You know, if you need work or want to make more money, I know someone who'd put you at the top of his list. You just kick back ten percent to me. You know, like a manager or something."

"What sort of work?"

"You know. Work?" He smiled lecherously and turned his upper body like a flirtatious teenage girl. "The work the other girls who live here do."

"Oh. I see. Well, it's work to you," I said dryly, realizing what he meant. "To me, it sounds like digging in the garbage."

He lost his smile. "I'm just trying to be of some help."

"Yeah. That was exactly what the hangman used to say."

"Huh?"

"Thanks. I don't need work. I'm independently wealthy and here only to complete a major financial deal," I said, and headed for the rickety stairway again.

The elevator still had an out-of-order sign on it.

Actually, it looked as if it had been out of use for as long as the building had stood. Despite my sarcasm and defiance in the lobby, when I entered my hovel of a room, I felt myself sink into an even deeper sense of defeat and depression. The creep downstairs was right. Really, what was I doing there? The only thing that had happened was the creep downstairs offering to become my pimp.

Great accomplishment, Roxy, I told myself. *You showed them. You showed them all.*

How much longer could I do this? I had the money to stay for another couple of weeks, but where was it getting me?

This time, I had a great deal of trouble falling asleep. The sounds coming from other rooms began to resemble sounds I might hear in a jungle. Someone was obviously in great pain, someone sounded as if she was pleading for mercy, and someone else was coughing so much I was sure he would crack open his chest and drop his lungs on the floor. Later, someone again tried to open my door, and I had to shout, "Get away! I'm calling the police!"

I fell asleep again, but the nightmares were taking on more vividness. In one, I saw the inhabitants of the hotel coming up the stairs, but they were all just skeletons, their hair, no matter what the color had been, now a stringy ash-gray. The following morning, I rose very early and rushed out of the hotel, stopping only to get coffee in a takeout cup. Most of the time, I walked with my head down, bumping into people, crossing streets against the light, and hearing drivers

shout curses at me. I felt myself fleeing and didn't realize how far I had walked until I saw that I was turning
on a familiar street not far from my school. I got there
just when most of the students were arriving, but I
stepped back behind the corner of a newsstand so as
not to be seen.

I didn't know why I had walked up there, but I
stood watching the girls and the guys I knew. Just the
sight of them laughing and joking around disturbed
me. A few days ago, I either ignored or teased and
insulted many of them, but suddenly, I was watching them with envy. How nonchalant and carefree
they all seemed to me now. For some of the girls, not
catching the eye of a boy they had a crush on would
be the worst, most dreadful thing of the day. Others
would be jealous of another girl's clothes or jewelry.
What they would do on the weekend was their biggest
worry. Not one of them would be concerned about
how much money she had in her pockets and her
purse, and I couldn't imagine any of them worrying
about where they would sleep that night or if it would
be safe and clean.

Nevertheless, I wasn't prepared to tell myself how
good I'd had it just a week ago. I refused to admit that.
The truth was, I hated this longing and regret that had
come over me while watching them. I winced when
the bell rang for everyone to go inside to homeroom.
I always hated those bells, hated feeling like a trapped
mouse reacting to some stimulus, being in my assigned
seat, quiet and attentive. I was confident that most of
my teachers would look at my empty chair and be

relieved that I wasn't there. Only Mr. Wheeler would be sincerely upset. He would probably be the only one who would go to the dean to ask why I was absent so many days.

What would my parents tell the school? That I was sick? Would they claim that I had run off? Would anyone in the school bother to call them? *Why ruin a good thing?* they might think. Would the news of my continued absence trickle down to Emmie's class, or would one or two of the younger brothers or sisters of girls and guys in my class ask her about me? "What happened to your sister? Is she finally in jail or something?"

Poor Emmie, I thought. How confused and upset she must be. What sort of answers had Mama given her to use or to understand? Did Papa just grunt or say something like "Don't ask about her. Be happy she's not here"?

Somehow, I had thought it would be a no-brainer, easy to give it all up, even to give up my family, since we were at each other so much and so often. I had craved this independence. I had wanted this freedom.

Stop whining about it, I told myself. *You wanted to be out in the real world and on your own, with no one bossing you around. So now you are. You have what you wanted. So shut up. Soldier up!*

I stood there a while longer and then walked away quickly, hoping no one who knew me had seen me. How embarrassing that would be, I thought. Again, without consciously planning it, I walked in the direction of my house. When I arrived on our street, I stopped, like someone who had been picked up and dropped there, someone totally surprised at where she was and how she had gotten there. I stood looking at the front door and thinking, about Mama, mostly. Would she be coming out soon, perhaps to go grocery shopping or do some other errand? I wanted to see her. I waited and waited.

Finally, she did emerge, with Emmie. For some reason, she was either taking her to school late or taking her somewhere else. Emmie looked sad, as if she had been crying. Maybe she had asked about me so much that Papa had exploded at her. Secretly, I hoped that was it. I was tempted to step out and call to them. I might even let Mama talk me into coming back, I thought. But I couldn't do it, even though I knew Papa was at work and wouldn't know.

I defied the tears that were forming over my eyes and turned away quickly, now practically jogging down the street, through Central Park, and then into the subway station to go back downtown into the hell I had chosen for some sanctuary. Again and again, I asked myself what I was doing and what I had hoped to accomplish. I had to get hold of myself, get back securely on my feet. The way to do it, I thought, was to get a job and make enough money so I could either leave the city for some other place or at least get into a decent hotel.

So I decided to actively look for work, first in stores advertising for salespeople. I returned to the hotel and changed into my best pantsuit. It was a little wrinkled, but I had to make do. I had a bright red beret that I thought would be a nice added touch.

Then I went into the bathroom and did the best I could to make myself look put-together. After only several days in the rat hole, I had already begun to let myself go, not caring about my hair or what I wore and certainly not bothering with any makeup. I was starting to look like the others there. When you started to neglect how you looked, you began to diminish and slowly turn into a ghost, I thought. It put some panic in my chest.

With more determination, I worked on my face, brushed out my hair, put on a pair of earrings, and practiced my "older" look. Feeling confident again, I hurried out to go job hunting. The young man at the desk whistled at me and shook his limp hand.

"You're a looker," he said.

I didn't even pause.

"I can make you a lot of money," he called after me.

Despite my appearance, it took me three tries before I was able to meet with someone doing the hiring in a store. I was brought to a small office at the rear of a clothing store and met with the store manager, a man who looked about my father's age. He was surprised at my knowledge of some of the styles and designers, especially those doing clothes for younger women. I thought I was doing well and was on my way to getting the job, until I was asked for my identification.

What was I thinking? Why didn't I anticipate that would be a problem? The moment anyone learned my true age, eyes narrowed, and more detailed questioning started. Why wasn't I in school? Was this address on my ID my current address? They knew how up-scale the East Side neighborhood was. Why would someone from that world be looking for a full-time job? Using the dumpy hotel as an address wasn't going to work. How would I begin to explain why I was there?

One female manager, who was pretty dumpy and plain for someone running a boutique, in my opinion, actually stopped talking to me for a moment, narrowed her eyes suspiciously, and then simply said, "You're a runaway, aren't you? Well?"

I didn't respond. I just got up and left the office. Ironically, I did run away from her. I was afraid she would get on the phone and call the police or something. She looked like one of those do-gooders who poke their faces into other people's affairs because their own lives are so mundane and boring.

Maybe retail outlets weren't the best possibilities, I thought, and started to inquire at restaurants looking for waitresses and waiters. They might be less demanding. Surely my background wouldn't be as important. Didn't waiters and waitresses come and go all the time? I always thought I was an expert liar, but when it came to describing past experience at restaurants, I would readily admit myself that I sounded pathetic and dishonest. This wasn't going to work, either, I realized. My ID was too difficult a problem to solve, and by the end of the day, I was in a deep funk, discouraged and defeated. Whether I liked it or not, I was going to have to go back home and plead for mercy. What other choice did I have?

I stopped at a restaurant not far from where I was staying. It was the cleanest and nicest one I had eaten at since I had left home. I wasn't hungry, but I ordered a pasta salad and a mineral water just to have something to do while I sat there considering my desperate and now hopeless situation.

My stash of funds was looking pretty pathetic. I had rushed so much to leave the house after Papa ordered me out that I didn't take my best clothes or enough of anything, really. If I started buying myself new things, I'd soon be broke. I didn't even have enough makeup. I certainly didn't have the right shoes, and I was beginning to get blisters.

Face it, Lady Big Shot, I told myself, *your father knew what you would be up against. He probably told your mother they were giving you enough rope to hang yourself, something like that. He was confident you would return, plead for mercy, and get in line.* It was the way he was brought up, the way he was forced to compromise and obey until he was old enough to break free. Now that I was out there, I could appreciate what it took for him to be so independent, to defy his father and all that family tradition. He was too tough, too strong. I was a fool to think I could break him before he would break me.

No, I told myself, there was no sense in prolonging the pain. It was time to wave the white flag, surrender, and go crawling back.

I thought about calling Mama first so she could set up a smoke-the-peace-pipe meeting with my father. I rehearsed what I would say, the promises I would make, and the punishments I would accept. Every thought was like swallowing sour milk or being jolted by a surge of hot electricity on my spine. I was so down and depressed that I hated the image of myself I saw reflected in a nearby mirror, which was another reason I was so surprised by what happened next.

2

How anyone could look at me at this point and not be completely turned off by what he saw in my face amazed me. I was depressed, defeated, and soured by all that had happened, but when I raised my head and looked across the restaurant, I saw a man with a dark complexion, handsome and rather distinguished-looking in his dark gray suit and black tie, looking at me with interest and smiling. He had wavy light brown hair and looked to be in his late forties, early fifties. There was a confident, successful-movie-actor glow on his face, the look of someone who was untouched by the things that annoyed, irritated, and aged most people.

His smile wasn't licentious. I could sense that he wasn't flirting with me. Rather, he looked a little amused, but still expressed admiration, too. He was more like someone's nice uncle preparing to toss compliments at me. Of course, I thought, this could all be a façade, too. He might very well be a womanizer, someone who took advantage of young women, especially young women who wore a look of desperation.

Despite how much I wanted to think otherwise, I kept myself cautious. I didn't smile back at him or acknowledge him in any way, but that didn't appear to discourage him. In fact, I think my indifference only encouraged him.

He rose and crossed the restaurant to my table. I thought he had the most amazingly blue eyes, Caribbean Sea blue, with a softness that radiated kindness.

"*Pardonnez-moi,*" he said.

Every guy thinks he's cute imitating a Frenchman, I thought. And then I thought I'd fix him. "*Oui. Comment puis-je vous aider?*" I asked. I didn't know if he knew that meant "How can I help you?" but after I spoke, his smile widened.

"I had a suspicion you spoke French," he said. "That's why I said *pardonnez-moi.*"

"*Pourquoi?*"

"I don't know. Just your look. Anyway, I was sitting there watching you and thought to myself, what's a beautiful young woman like her doing here this time of the day by herself?"

"And what did you tell yourself?" I replied. "Or aren't you in the habit of answering your own questions?"

I thought I saw a slight nod of his head, confirming something he had suspected. Perhaps it was because I wasn't intimidated by someone his age approaching me. "I didn't have an answer for myself, but I thought I'd like to know the answer. Do you mind?" He nodded at the chair across from me.

I shrugged, and he sat.

"Are you a tourist?" he asked.

"Do I look like a tourist?"

"Not exactly," he said. The waitress approached. "Would you like something else? A coffee?"

"A cappuccino with low-fat milk," I ordered.

"Make that two, Paula," the gentleman said. The waitress nodded and walked off. "You work around here?"

"Why all this interest in me?" I asked. "Do I remind you of someone?"

"Not exactly that, but I'd have to be a pretty dull boy not to be interested in someone who looked like you."

"Oh, I see," I said with a tight smirk.

"No, no. You misunderstand. I guess you can say I'm kind of an agent always on the lookout for new talent."

I pushed my pasta salad aside and clasped my hands with my elbows on the table, leaning toward him a little. It was what my father would do when he wanted to indicate he'd had it with silly talk and wanted clear, truthful answers. It didn't surprise me that I had taken on some of his gestures. He never successfully intimidated me, but when I wanted to intimidate any of the guys or girls at my school, I would take on my father's persona.

"Kind of?" I said. "What's that supposed to mean. You can make me a movie star or get me on television, Mr. . . . ?"

"Everyone who knows me calls me Mr. Bob."

"I don't know you," I said.

"I'm hoping you will get to know me."

"Why?"

"Are you in college in the city?"

"No."

"Do you live in the city?"

"Yes."

"In this neighborhood?" he followed, showing skepticism.

"Maybe, why?"

"You don't look like you belong in this neighborhood."

"Where do I look like I belong?"

"Somewhere better."

"Really," I said dryly. "Well, if this area is so bad, what are you doing here?"

"Scouting," he said. "You know, like those guys who go around the country looking for great baseball or basketball prospects."

"I'm not into sports."

"What are you into, then?"

"Before I answer any more questions, I want to see a lawyer," I said, sitting back, and he laughed.

"Something told me you weren't going to be dull."

"You're right there. I've been accused of lots of things but never of being dull."

The waitress brought our cappuccinos.

"Thank you, Paula. So who are you?" he asked.

I sipped my cappuccino and looked at him. "Why is it so important for you to know?"

"I told you. I'm in the business of making discoveries."

"Discoveries? Of what? Not baseball or basketball players. I have a terrible swing, don't like all the spitting, and hate running up and down any court."

He laughed and turned to look at the closest other customer to see if he was listening to our conversation. The other man turned away quickly.

"No, I'm not after sports possibilities. I look for beautiful young women who have a certain *je ne sais quoi*, a mysterious quality about them that makes them extra special. There are many beautiful young women in New York, but not all have that *je ne sais quoi*. Know what I mean?"

"Maybe. I certainly understand the expression and can understand why you might say that." I knew that answer surprised him, but I wasn't down on myself enough to believe that I wasn't special. Besides, modesty always struck me as a weakness in this world.

He sipped his cappuccino and continued to study me.

"Okay, I'll bite," I said when he remained silent. "What is it you see in me—besides my French heritage, that is?"

"There's a wisdom about you that one wouldn't expect of someone your age, yet you don't look that street-smart, either. In short, you have me intrigued."

He continued to sip his cappuccino, and I sipped mine, neither of us shifting our eyes from the other. All sorts of suspicions, like sleeping snakes, began to raise their heads in my mind.

"You're not going to show me some kind of badge any minute, are you?"

That brought real laughter from him. "Hardly,"

he said, "although I have a badge to flash if I'm ever in trouble. It was a gift from a high-level government employee. You have nothing to fear about me on that score. In fact, you have nothing whatsoever to fear about talking to me."

"Right. It's very common for a man your age, dressed like you, to start a conversation with someone my age because she has a certain *je ne sais quoi*. I see it happening all over the city every day."

He held his smile. It seemed that neither my sarcasm nor my indifference could discourage him. I noticed the expensive-looking diamond pinkie ring on his left hand, but I saw no wedding ring. I knew what a Rolex was, and what he was wearing did not look like a cheap imitation. Mama always told me to look at a man's shoes first when assessing if he was authentic. Well-to-do men always had expensive shoes, and those shoes were always maintained well. His shoes didn't exactly have the military shine, but they looked well cared for. He was exactly the sort of man I could imagine sitting in the shoe shiner's chair in some subway station reading the *Wall Street Journal*.

"You are something else," he said. "I knew it. Please, tell me about yourself."

I finished my cappuccino but held the cup as I pondered whether I should stay or simply get up and leave without another word.

"I'm not a tourist. I'm not in college. I don't work anywhere in the city. This isn't really my neighborhood, okay? Satisfied? Did I earn my cappuccino?"

"Hardly satisfied," he said. He tilted his head a

bit as he took another long look at me. "Don't tell me you're in high school?"

"Okay, I won't tell you."

His eyes brightened and his lips softened. "You are, aren't you?"

"Not at the moment and not in the immediate future."

"Now I am intrigued. You either cut school or quit, right? Are you on your own?"

"Aren't we all?"

"We don't have to be," he said.

"Oh." I put my cup down. I thought I knew what that line meant, what he was leading up to. He had just taken a more circuitous route to get there. "Now I understand. I think it's time for me to go."

"No, no, you're misunderstanding me. I'm not here to pick you up or anything like that."

"No? You're just here to buy me a cappuccino because I have an intriguing face and speak French?"

"Maybe. Maybe all I will do is buy you a cappuccino. It's up to you."

I was locked in my motion to get up and leave, but I hesitated. What did he mean? What could be up to me? What was he offering?

"So what's your story?" he asked when I relaxed in my chair again.

I thought a moment and decided to test him with the truth. "My father threw me out of our house the other day. I've been excommunicated from my family for committing a series of somewhat unforgivable sins. My father was brought up in a military family, so after just so much KP duty, there was nothing left to do but give me a dishonorable discharge."

He didn't laugh or smile. "How serious were the sins?"

"A little pilfering here and there, insubordination in school, unmotivated in my schoolwork, failing some classes, caught smoking some weed in the girls' room, violating curfews. Things like that. I was working up to first-degree murder when I was kicked off the base."

He smiled again. "You don't look like the average dropout," he said, "and your French is perfect. I spent quite a long time in Paris and return often. And I have visited most of the Riviera. Places like Cannes, Monaco, Èze. Have you been?"

"My mother is French. Her family is there. We've visited them in and outside of Paris but not for some time. No, I've never been to the Riviera."

"How is she taking this excommunication?"

"She's my father's wife."

"So?"

"My mother is old-fashioned. She's the obedient sort," I said. "I don't think she's happy about what's happened, but I don't think she's going to do anything dramatic about it, either."

"Do you plan on going home soon?"

I looked away and then turned back to him. "I don't want to, but I don't seem to have much of a choice in the matter."

"Maybe you do."

"What are we back to, an invitation to come home with you?"

"No. Not that I wouldn't like that. It's just not what I do."

"So what do you do, Mr. Bob? I think I've been honest with you. How about a little quid pro quo?"

He raised his eyebrows. "'Quid pro quo'? You're a bad student?"

"I didn't say bad. I said unmotivated, but I read."

He nodded. "You might be just the perfect candidate."

"Candidate? For what? Congress?"

"No," he said, laughing. Then he leaned over the table to whisper. "How would you like to be really independent? Live in a beautiful place, be able to buy the most expensive clothes . . ."

"And marry a prince?"

"Seriously?"

I tilted my head, looking at him askance. "I try to keep up with the newest approaches. Older men have hit on me, but this is definitely a first for me."

"I told you. I'm not making a pass at you," he said, now with his first note of annoyance.

"Then what are you doing?"

"I'm simply asking you if you want to get into something that will make you not only independent but also very well off. As I said, I'm just a scout."

"You're not a Boy Scout. That's for sure."

He smirked. I thought he was finally going to get up and walk away, but he just stared at me.

"All right. I'll bite again," I said. "How do I do all this?"

He leaned forward and spoke again in a voice just

above a whisper. "You meet someone first, someone who will be much more scrutinizing than I am. She might even bring you to tears before throwing you out, but I haven't been wrong that often, and I've never felt as confident about someone as I do about you. I have good instincts."

"Meet who?"

"Whom."

"Yeah, I forgot the difference between objective and subjective. I can see that disturbs you."

"Not me, but this person I want you to meet, maybe. She looks for very special candidates."

"Really. So when do I meet this person and where?"

"Tonight. You come with me. It's on Long Island."

I smirked. "Don't you know my mother told me never to talk to strangers, much less go for a ride with one?"

"Tell you what," he said, and reached into his inside jacket pocket to produce his wallet. He opened it and took out his driver's license. "Here's my driver's license. See?" He turned it toward me. "My picture is on it and my name. Robert Diamant. Leave it with anyone you trust, and tell them this is the man you are going to take a ride with. Tell them to call the police if you're not back by eleven. Anything happens to you, I'm toast. Go on, keep my license," he insisted.

I looked at it. How could I tell him I knew no one I could trust now? I took it from him and studied it. It could be a phony license with a phony name, I thought, but it wasn't a phony picture. It was clearly Mr. Bob.

"And if I do this?"

"We go for the ride, visit with this person. She'll decide about you, and then we'll return to wherever you're staying. Safely back, you return my license. Okay?"

I stared at it. For one thing, I was too embarrassed to tell him where I was staying. He would think I was a complete loser, and I didn't want that, even though I still didn't know what he was offering.

"I don't know," I said, putting the license down on the table.

"Listen, you have to take some risks to get anywhere or do anything. I think you've already learned that. You just haven't gotten anywhere yet."

"Maybe I'm just starting out."

"Oh, no question that you are, but that's why I wanted to approach you, to get to you before you were spoiled."

"Spoiled?"

"Life on your own, especially in a city like New York, is very hard on anyone, let alone a young, beautiful girl like yourself. No matter how smart you think you are, someone will get to you and drag you down in the gutter. A year from now, your parents won't recognize you, anyway."

"Thanks for the encouragement."

"But none of that will matter once you come with me. I'm confident," he added.

I looked at his license again. I guessed I would take

it. How would he know I had no one to trust? "When exactly do I meet with this person?"

He looked at his watch. "I'll pick you up in two hours. Are those the best clothes you have to wear right now?"

"Yes."

He looked at his watch again. "Would you mind if I bought you something to wear? It's important."

I didn't know whether to laugh or make for the door. "You want to buy me something to wear?"

"There's a boutique just two blocks east, Ooh La La. They have what you need. We'll go right now. It's a five-minute walk." He waved to the waitress. "Add all this to my monthly bill, Paula," he said, "and add a twenty-percent tip."

She smiled and nodded.

"You have a bill here?"

"I have a running account at a few of my favorite places," he said, standing. "Shall we go?"

I got up. He nodded toward the table. I had forgotten to take his license. I picked it up and put it into my purse and then followed him out. All the while, I was thinking, *This is insane. He's going to turn out to be some sort of nutcase for sure, but then why would the restaurant trust him?* I looked back at the waitress as we left. She smiled at me and gave me a thumbs-up.

Huh? What did she know?

"So, tell me more about yourself," he said as we started toward the corner of the street. "Where exactly does your family live?"

"The East Side," I said. I didn't want to give him the exact address.

"Any brothers or sisters?"

"A much younger sister. My mother wasn't supposed to have either of us."

"Oh. My mother always used to tell me that," he said. "I was brought up in Philadelphia. My father was a very successful dentist. I have an older sister. She lives in California. So what subject did you like the best at school?"

"English, I guess."

"Yes, that's right. You read. Any boyfriends you've left behind?"

"All of them," I told him, and he laughed. "I wasn't ever attached to anyone too long."

"I bet they regretted it," he said.

"Yes, but I didn't."

He laughed harder, and we crossed a street, turned, and stopped halfway down the block at the store he had described. He opened the door for me, and as soon as we stepped in, the young woman attending a customer turned and immediately smiled. She said something to her customer and approached us quickly.

"Mr. Bob, how are you?"

"I'm a hundred and five percent, Clea. This is . . ." He suddenly realized he didn't know my name, and that made him blush. For a moment, I thought I would let him dangle and look foolish, but then I smiled and came to his rescue.

"Roxy," I told the salesgirl.

"Yes, Roxy. We need an elegant black cocktail

dress, and I know you have the right shoes and purse to go with it," he added.

Clea looked me over. "I have the exact dress for her, Mr. Bob. Please, follow me." She led me to the changing room in the rear.

I was anticipating that she would ask me questions to find out who I was and why I was with Mr. Bob, but she said nothing. She opened the changing room and went to get the dress she was proposing. She returned quickly, as if she did know exactly what I should wear. She held it up, and the label dangled. It read "Emilio Pucci," and the price was $1,500. I looked at her as if she was crazy.

"Believe me, this is your dress," she said. It was a figure-fitting, lightweight jersey knit with a bold butterfly print in a modern one-shoulder design. I took it from her slowly. She smiled and closed the door. For a moment, I just gazed at myself in the mirror. *Is this nuts?* I asked my image. I took off my clothes and put on the dress. It fit me as if it had been custom-made for me. The beauty of the dress and the way I looked seemed to wash away the sadness and defeats of the day. I saw the flush flow through my neck and into my face.

Many times I had looked at myself and thought, *I'm not bad,* but at this moment, I suddenly realized I was far more than that. I really was very beautiful. I didn't have to convince myself of it. I had spent so much time being angry and resentful that I hadn't permitted what could flower and blossom in me to do so. Right now, it was doing just that. I heard a knock on the door. The salesgirl smiled when she saw me and then handed me a pair of platform pumps in shiny pink patent leather. These, too, had been made in Italy. The price tag read "$700." I slipped them on. They were also a perfect fit. The four-inch heels made me statuesque. I stood staring at myself in the mirror.

"How are we doing?" I heard Mr. Bob ask.

"I think *magnifique*," the salesgirl said.

I stepped out slowly, and Mr. Bob's smile widened, his eyes brightening. "How can I be so right all the time?" he asked the salesgirl.

"Some people have an eye for beautiful jewelry, beautiful art. You have an eye for beautiful women," she replied.

"How do you like it?" he asked me.

"Do you know how much all this costs?"

"A safe investment, in my mind. And the purse?" he asked the salesgirl.

"Ah, *oui*." She went out and brought one back. Its price was $500.

"Perfect," Mr. Bob said.

I looked at the salesgirl and then at the other customer, who had stopped buying anything for herself and was now more fascinated by what was going on with us. What was I getting myself into? How come the restaurant and this salesgirl knew him so well? I tried to imagine what my father would say if he knew where I was and what I was doing. Mama would probably start crying.

Mr. Bob looked at his watch. "You might want to

freshen up or something before we start out," he suggested.

This was my time to back out. I could just go into that changing room, get back into my own clothes, hand the beautiful dress and shoes to the salesgirl, and walk away. But I didn't.

I returned to the changing room and got back into my clothes. The salesgirl took the dress, shoes, and purse and packaged it all in a pretty bag with the store's name. Once again, I heard Mr. Bob say, "Put it on my bill, *s'il vous plaît*."

"*Très bien*," she replied. Another customer entered, but the first had remained and was still watching us as we left the store.

"Okay, that's done," Mr. Bob said. "So where do I pick you up in"—he looked at his watch—"about an hour?"

"I'll meet you in front of the restaurant we were at," I said.

"Really?" He studied my face for a moment. He understood and nodded. "Fine. An hour."

We parted at the corner, and I hurried away. My mind was spinning with the possibilities. He really was an agent, probably an agent for a modeling firm. He was taking me to meet the owner of the firm. Other girls dreamed of becoming international models making tons of money. The idea had flashed through my mind from time to time, but I never really dwelled on it or on the thought of becoming a movie or television star. I had a nice voice, but I couldn't imagine myself going on some television show and winning. The truth was, I never had high ambitions for myself. Miss Gene loved to point that out whenever I was brought into the guidance office for a session.

It was something else I could easily blame on my father, I thought. He criticized and chastised me so much it was impossible for me to have a good image of myself, or at least one good enough to build some ambition on it. And my mother didn't imagine great things for me, either. Yes, she wanted me to do well in school, but she never pushed me to do anything. It was as if I would magically fall into something that would clarify my future and save us all from the deep, disastrous pit lying in wait for me.

What else could this be but a modeling job? I was determined to do my best to get it, because I knew I would make enough money to do just what Mr. Bob suggested and be independent. It was all a great stroke of luck. If I hadn't been in that restaurant when he was, none of this would be happening. I should be grateful now that no one had even thought of hiring me for one of those low-paying jobs.

I sped up. I wanted to work harder on my hair and do the best job on my makeup that I could with what little I had before returning to meet Mr. Bob. I felt strong and confident again. When I entered the fleabag hotel, the old man was behind the counter. He widened his eyes and looked surprised at the smile I had for him.

"You staying another day?" he asked.

"Maybe," I said. "Maybe not."

I laughed and hurried up to my room. I laid the

dress, shoes, and purse on the bed and stared at it all. With taxes, this man had just spent almost three thousand dollars on me. How did he even know I would show up and he would ever see me again? Surely he saw something in me that gave him so much confidence.

It was only when I looked into the smoky, cracked mirror that I thought to myself, *If this turns out to be nothing or something disappointing, Papa will have won.*

And it would be a long time before I smiled with the arrogance and confidence with which I had smiled at the old man downstairs again.

3

I was in front of the restaurant early. As I stood there, I thought that maybe being early was a mistake. It showed too much eagerness, and in my experience, when you showed too much eagerness for anything someone else could do for you or give you, you were at a big disadvantage. All my life, I believed it was the nature of people to enjoy the feeling of superiority that your being in debt to them brought them. Papa and his military family taught me that with their ranks and officers and the way underlings were often treated. All that bullying was supposed to make the victim tougher and build character, but to me, it was simply a way for those in charge to feel more important. Maybe that was why I was so defiant most of the time.

Watching the buses and cars go by, I wondered if Mr. Bob had expected me to have a proper shawl or jacket to go along with my new dress. I glanced at my image in the window. I was wearing a beautiful dress with beautiful shoes, but I couldn't help feeling awkward and out of place. I was certainly too formally dressed to be standing on a sidewalk in this neighborhood. The longer I waited, the more ridiculous I began to feel, despite the admiring looks and comments I was getting from men of all ages who were passing by or going in and out of the restaurant.

I had almost turned to flee when a black stretch limousine suddenly pulled up to the curb. The driver, in full chauffeur uniform, stepped out quickly and opened the rear door. He turned to me and nodded. I was a bit dumbfounded, but when I looked into the automobile, I saw Mr. Bob smiling.

"You look great," he said.

I got in, and the driver closed the door.

"I like what you did with your hair, but you really do need some professional help with it and with your makeup. You'd be surprised at the difference it will make when a professional gets to work on you. I'm sure Mrs. Brittany will have something to say about all that. If anyone can turn a swan into a princess, it's Mrs. Brittany."

"Mrs. Brittany? That's whom we're going to see?" I stressed "whom."

"Yes. She has a title, but she never uses it. She's actually a Belgian countess. She was born in France but married a man who was a descendant of Robert of Flanders, Count James Brittany. Don't smirk. These aristocratic Europeans have real evidence of their ancestry. They all have books detailing their lineage, with pictures of their ancestors, their houses, and their art. It's all quite impressive, but as Mrs. Brittany will tell you, many of the blue bloods have little to show for it. The truth is, when her husband died, he left her little more than the nice apartment they had bought in Paris and some expensive jewelry and art. However, she was always a very enterprising woman and turned her inheritance into a multimillion-dollar venture. She had married very young. Her husband was nearly twenty years older."

"Twenty years?"

"It's not that uncommon. You might say it was something of an arranged affair."

"Did she remarry?"

"No, although she's been proposed to by some of the wealthiest men in the world. If you want to know and understand what it means to be an independent woman, you'll learn quickly when you get to know her. *If* you get to know her," he added. "Don't misunderstand me. I'm feeling very confident about you, but I don't want to give you the impression that this is a done deal. Although she has rarely rejected a prospect I've brought her, she has on occasion."

He leaned toward me and patted my hand.

"Just be yourself," he advised. "You'll do fine. Anyway, Mrs. Brittany is a very accomplished woman. She speaks four languages, including Japanese. She's about as traveled a person as I have ever met, and she is on a friendly basis with some of the most powerful and influential people in the world, besides being an elegant beauty herself."

"Rich, powerful, beautiful, intelligent, royal," I catalogued. "She doesn't sound real."

"Oh, she's real enough. You'll see that. She's just not someone who suffers fools gladly, if you know what I mean. When she makes a decision, it's final, but if she likes what she sees, she's completely invested. I'm confident that she's going to like what she sees when she meets you. In fact, I'm so confident, I thought we'd begin with a little toast, anticipating both your success and mine."

He reached forward to pluck an opened bottle of champagne from the ice bucket and handed me a glass that had a strawberry in it.

"You like champagne?" he asked.

"I like real champagne," I said.

His eyes widened. "Real champagne?"

"My mother is from France," I reminded him. "I know the difference between ordinary sparkling wine and champagne. Only the sparkling wine grown and produced in the region of Champagne in France can be truly called champagne."

"*Très bien*," he said. He turned the bottle around to show me the label, Moët & Chandon, and then spun it again to show me where it had been produced and bottled. "Satisfied?"

I nodded, and he poured me half a glass. "So," I said after taking a sip, "when are you going to tell me what it is I'm trying out for? Modeling, I imagine?"

"Oh, absolutely. In a way."

"In a way? What does that mean?"

"You'll learn everything a successful runway model knows, and you'll be treated just as well, if not better."

"But I won't be one?"

"Not exactly." He smiled and raised his eyebrows.

"You won't be on display for just anyone. No runways, no pictures in newspapers and magazines, nothing like that."

I sipped some more champagne and sat back. "Please continue," I said. "I'd like to know what I'm getting myself into."

He laughed. "When you glare at me like that, you actually remind me of Mrs. Brittany. It's futile to lie to someone like her."

"So don't try," I said. "Well?" I added when he didn't speak.

"Mrs. Brittany likes to do the explaining."

"You mean you want to wait until I'm more or less a captive audience?"

"No, no, nothing like that. I'm just afraid I won't do the description justice."

"Take a chance," I said. "Risk it."

He looked at me, smiled, and shook his head. "You *are* different. Okay. I'll get more into it."

He sat up straighter and took on a more serious demeanor, as if he were on the witness stand in a courtroom or something.

"Very wealthy and very successful men are often too busy to look after their social lives, especially when they are out of town, and for many of these men, New York City is out of town. They fly in for very important meetings and conferences, often on their private jets. Some own them, and some fly their companies' planes. They're generally very goal-oriented, hardworking executives, who, when they do get a chance to relax, like to relax with women who meet their expectations."

"What expectations?"

"Intellect, grace, style, beauty, humor—in short, high-class escorts. When I looked at you, and especially after I spoke with you, I sensed that you could be a star in this organization. I like to take pride in my ability to spot someone like you, someone who already has some of what is required in her and just needs to be placed in Mrs. Brittany's capable hands to develop and nurture the rest."

"You sound like you're casting me in a movie."

"In a sense, I am. I really was an entertainment agent once," he quickly continued. "That's a cutthroat business. I was at it night and day. Besides finding work for my clients, I had to babysit many of them. It got so I didn't have a personal life anymore, and then I met Mrs. Brittany through a mutual friend, the head of a movie studio.

"At the time, her enterprise was already quite successful, but she is always on the lookout for new employees. She is a very careful woman when it comes to her associates. Believe me, I went through a far more thorough and tougher vetting than you will. I'm proud to say I've been with her for nearly ten years."

He finished his champagne and looked at me. I finished mine and handed him the glass before I sat back again.

"Let me understand this," I said. "You're basically an agent for a high-class pimp?"

Even in the low light of the limousine's interior, I could see him become pale and then flush red. "Absolutely not! Don't you even think such a thing."

"You said Mrs. Brittany provides escorts for rich and powerful men, and you find her women to be these escorts."

"Yes, but not as prostitutes. I told you that she'll explain it to you better than I can, if she wants to go that far with you," he replied, still a bit peeved. "Look, you're going to her home to interview and judge her and what she has to offer, as much as she will judge you before she makes any offer. There's no obligation."

"Despite all you have spent on me?"

"I told you. It was an investment."

"Now that I hear more about it, it sounds more like a long-shot gamble."

"That's what any investment is, once you take off the gift wrapping."

I glanced out the window as the limousine picked up speed. Darkness was invading the streets. I never really thought about living in New York, the anonymity of it. There were so many people on our block, but less than a handful who knew us. I saw how people walking the sidewalks, crossing streets, and coming out of buildings and stores barely looked at anyone. The blur of the lights, the empty faces, and the endless traffic suddenly made me feel very sad, very alone, and very vulnerable. What was happening to my arrogance and self-confidence? Was I right to think I had the strength and determination to live without the safety net of my family, or was I just fooling myself?

I turned back to him. What were he and Mrs.

Brittany really offering me? If I wasn't intended to be some high-priced hooker booked out to wealthy businessmen, what was I to be? Was Mr. Bob denying it just to get me to play along, hoping this woman, who was probably nowhere near the woman he claimed she was, could talk me into it?

I anticipated meeting some over-the-hill, overly made-up prostitute who had enough knowledge of the business, if I could call it that, to provide young women to wealthy men. What had I gotten myself into now? It was just a few steps up from that goofy, ugly grandson of the hotel owner, who was at least upfront about what he wanted from me.

"I still don't understand what you're describing. You say this is not an organization for high-priced prostitutes. What exactly do these women do with these rich and powerful men? Play video games?"

"Mrs. Brittany likes to say they complete them, make them more presentable. They wear them on their arms the way they wear their expensive clothes or jeweled watches on their wrists when they go to exclusive restaurants or social events. But the most successful of her escorts provide much more than just helping them to look good and feel good about themselves. They entertain them."

"Entertain them?" I started to laugh. "Without having sex? What, are they all gay men or eunuchs?"

"I'm serious. You shouldn't ridicule this. You'll be sorry."

"Well, I don't get it. You're not telling me enough for me to understand."

The frustration practically foamed over his lips. He stiffened and looked more determined. "You know what geishas are in Japan?"

"I think so. Aren't they prostitutes?"

"Not really. Not the high-class, authentic ones. There's a long history of their existence. The first geishas were actually men. The main purpose was always to entertain with their beauty and their talent. Authentic geisha girls today are not sold into indentured service, nor are they forced into sexual relations. A geisha's sex life is her private affair."

"So?"

"Well, it was Mrs. Brittany's idea to create a Western form of geisha. There really is no equivalent to them in our society. They are truly a form of Japanese art."

"I still don't fully understand what Mrs. Brittany is looking for or what she does with her girls. She turns them into geishas? They wear those costumes and that makeup? Don't they do something weird with their feet?"

"You misunderstand. It's not exactly that. It's different. It's . . ."

I shook my head. "You're not making any sense."

He sighed with frustration. "I'm sure she'll do a far better job of explaining it. The point is that if she thinks you qualify, she will spend a lot of money developing you, providing everything you need, from clothes to hairstylists and makeup artists to full medical care. When you're ready, she'll turn over a beautiful New York apartment to you, fully furnished and equipped. Of course, her own business manager will handle all your expenses and invest all your money for you. In short, you'll lack nothing."

"Except a family," I muttered, mostly to myself, but he had heard it.

"No. Mrs. Brittany and everyone associated with you will become your family."

"And who will you be in this new family, my uncle Bob?"

He finally smiled. "Just Bob, I hope."

We were leaving the city and heading for Long Island. I sat back, mulling over some of what he had told me.

Then I sat forward. "What kind of money are we talking about?" I asked him.

"Different girls earn different amounts, but Mrs. Brittany's top girls make a quarter of a million, some maybe more." He leaned forward to add, "Tax-free."

I stared at him. A quarter of a million? Tax-free? Did my father make that much?

"You'll vacation anywhere you want to in the world, often on a private jet taking you to stay at the most expensive resorts. You'll meet the most interesting people. Believe me, you'll feel like a princess. I often wish I was a girl your age with your looks," he said, smiling.

"Oh, you do, do you? You're quite a salesman, Mr. Bob. You ought to sell cars," I said dryly.

I think my skepticism and cynicism were beginning to get to him, even to worry him. I had the feeling that his reputation and perhaps his income depended entirely on his success when he brought someone new to this Mrs. Brittany. Maybe he was having second thoughts about me. I certainly had second, even third, thoughts about him and this whole idea.

I didn't pay attention to the route we took once we left the Long Island Expressway, but before long, we were turning up less populated streets with much bigger houses on much larger tracts of land.

"Almost there," Mr. Bob said when we made another turn and then another.

Moments later, I could see an enormous mansion with a two-story portico entrance. It seemed to have acres and acres of land around it. The driveway looked as long as an airport runway, and when I looked to the right, I did see a helicopter. The trees that lined the driveway and the landscaping looked picture-perfect. It was as if I had opened some fairy-tale picture book and somehow stepped into it.

"This is her house?"

"Exactly."

"One woman lives here?" I asked.

"There are often two or three of her girls either training here or visiting, among other guests from time to time, and the servants, of course. Her personal secretary is Ruth Pratt. She's been with her since Mrs. Brittany left Europe. Of course, Mrs. Brittany has a villa in Beaulieu-sur-Mer and apartments in many other cities, like London, Paris, Madrid, and even Moscow."

"You said girls were here training?"

"Absolutely. In a real sense, this is a college, a

charm school like you've never seen or probably could ever imagine."

My eyes went everywhere as we approached the house. I saw tennis courts, fountains, and lots of statues that looked as if they had been imported from Greece or Rome. Perhaps he was telling me the truth about this woman.

"This is an original Georgian mansion," he continued. "The pastoral surroundings were planned as an integral part of it. Around the turn of the twentieth century, many very wealthy Americans fleeing urban industrial life built these estates. Mrs. Brittany's was originally owned by John Temple Morris. He was very big in shipping," Mr. Bob added. "Of course, Mrs. Brittany has modernized much of the inside. There's an indoor pool, a sauna, a salon with a cosmetician and a hairdresser on call, a dining room that can seat thirty if necessary, and a full gym, among other things you'd expect to find only in hotels."

"It looks big enough to be a hotel."

"There are estates like this that have been turned into exclusive hotels."

The limousine stopped at the front of the mansion. Mr. Bob waited for the chauffeur to get out and open the doors for both of us. When he got out, he waited for me to come around and then held out his arm.

"M'lady," he said, and I took his arm. He put his left hand over mine. "Good luck," he said as we started up the stairs to the front entrance.

The tall dark oak door opened as if by magic, and a tall, lean dark-haired man in a butler's tuxedo stood

there to greet us. He had long, spidery fingers and a
narrow neck with a prominent Adam's apple.

"Hello, Jeffries," Mr. Bob said.

"Good evening, sir."

"This is Roxy Wilcox," Mr. Bob told him.

"Welcome, Miss Wilcox," Jeffries replied without
so much as relaxing his lips, much less smiling, and he
stepped to the side.

I felt as if I really were entering a palace. Directly
ahead of us was an elegant baronial double staircase.
There were large oil paintings on every wall. They
looked like paintings you would see only in a museum. The large entryway's floor was covered with
a crimson rug interwoven with black stars. My eyes
went everywhere because there was so much to see, so
many things that looked like antiques.

"Is this the way the house came?"

"There is much that is vintage in it," Mr. Bob said,
"but Mrs. Brittany is something of a collector, too. She
has brought paintings, furnishings, accessories from
Europe, much of it authentic but refurbished. There
are twenty-five rooms in this house, seven of which
are bedroom suites."

"Mrs. Brittany is expecting you. Everyone is in the
sitting room, Mr. Bob," Jeffries said, as if he was worried we were taking too long. He led the way down
the hall and paused in a doorway.

"Take a deep breath," Mr. Bob said. "You're about
to go underwater."

He escorted me to the sitting-room entrance. The
woman who was obviously Mrs. Brittany didn't look

older than in her mid to possibly late forties, but she sat regally in an oversize armchair across from two very beautiful young women, one with absolutely gorgeous layered, shoulder-length, soft ebony hair and the other with short styled amber hair. They sat on a settee and turned to look at us. The one with amber hair had eyes a unique shade of green, and the other had hazel eyes. Although neither was what I would call heavily made-up, they looked as if they had faces painted on a canvas, their complexions smooth, everything about their petite features perfectly balanced.

"Well, bring her in, Bob," Mrs. Brittany said. "You're standing there as if you expect to be announced."

He laughed and guided me farther into the room.

Mrs. Brittany's hair wasn't as soft-looking. Actually, I thought she was a bit old-fashioned, wearing her light brown hair in a teased style. She was in a low-cut emerald-green dress with a string of small pearls around her neck and matching pearl earrings.

"You can let her go now," she told Mr. Bob. "I expect she can stand on her own."

He laughed and unhooked his arm from mine.

I looked from Mrs. Brittany to the two young women and then back at her.

She nodded. "Nearly good posture," she said, and looked at the two young women, who nodded.

Nearly? I thought. Not even my father complained about my posture.

She stood up and approached me. I thought she was at least five feet eleven and probably five or six pounds overweight, but she was very attractive with her cerulean-blue eyes, full lips, and high cheekbones. She circled me and then nodded approval at Mr. Bob.

"Very nice," she said.

I didn't like the way she said it, even though I saw his face brighten. It made me feel as if I was at a slave auction or something. Next, she would ask to see my teeth, I imagined.

"Girls?"

"Yes, I agree, Mrs. Brittany," the one with amber hair said in a very clear, clipped British accent.

"Absolutely, I agree, Mrs. Brittany," the other followed. She sounded more like a New Yorker.

Mrs. Brittany stood directly in front of me. "Introduce yourself," she ordered.

"Excuse me?"

"Pretend you came into the room by yourself."

I glanced at Mr. Bob. He nodded slightly.

"I'm Roxy Wilcox," I said. I thought for a moment and then extended my hand. She just looked at it.

"Tell me again," she said. "Only this time, let me know what you think of yourself."

I started to frown but stopped and looked at the two young women. It was as if they were watching a life-or-death event.

"I'm Roxy Wilcox," I said with what my father would call timbre in my voice. "And you are?" I asked with full expectation.

Mrs. Brittany smiled. She looked at the two young women, who also smiled.

"This is Camelia," she said, nodding at the girl

with amber hair, "and this is Portia. They're leaving now to tend to some other matters."

The moment she said that, they both stood up. She nodded at them, and they started out, both flashing smiles at me.

Mrs. Brittany returned to her chair. "You may sit," she said, nodding toward the settee.

I glanced at Mr. Bob. I had the sense that every move I made, every sound I uttered, was being scrutinized. Although it made me self-conscious, I didn't act timid. I sat as gracefully as I could and looked at her.

"Perfect dress for her, Bob."

"Thank you," he said.

"Where did you get your hair done?"

"I didn't. I did it myself."

"Looks it," she said. "So," she continued, her arms resting on the arms of the oversize chair, "from what Bob tells me, you're a reluctant runaway. You were thrown out and didn't leave home of your own accord. How do I know you won't tuck your tail between your legs and run home to Mommy and Daddy, begging for forgiveness and another chance?"

"I don't know why it's any of your business, but I have no intention of going home," I replied, even though I had been on the brink of making just that choice. "I'd rather beg in the streets."

Mrs. Brittany smiled and nodded. "Good." She looked at Mr. Bob. "She's got fire in her."

"I told you."

"Don't congratulate yourself just yet, Bob." He lost his smile. She turned back to me. "Why are you so certain that your father won't have the police looking for you?"

"When my father makes a decision the way he made this one, he usually doesn't back down, and he knows that even if I were forcibly brought back, I'd surely run away again. We have an understanding. He orders and threatens, and I ignore him. It's a game we've played all my life. He got tired of playing it. Besides, I'm going to be eighteen in a few weeks."

She widened her smile. "That's good, but what about the rest of your family, uncles, aunts? Why didn't you run to them?"

"I have little or nothing to do with anyone on my father's side. They're military people, and my mother's family is in France."

She continued to smile, as if I had given her the answers she had hoped to hear. "Yes, I understand you speak French fluently."

"*Tout à fait.*"

She nodded. "So you're on your own?"

"Yes."

"What do you fear the most right now?" she asked.

"You mean while I'm here?"

"No, of course not. I mean in general. What's your biggest fear?"

I didn't have to think too hard about it. "Being dependent on other people," I replied.

She held her gaze on me, but I saw the way her eyes brightened. "Why don't you go get yourself a drink in the bar, Bob? Roxy and I have a lot to discuss, and your standing there looking like an expectant father is disconcerting."

Mr. Bob laughed. "If there is one thing I don't want to be, it's an expectant father."

He winked at me and left. She waited until he was completely gone and then turned back to me.

"If you join my organization, you'll be dependent on only one person," she said.

I tightened my lips and nodded. "I guess that's you," I said.

"No, my dear. You'll be dependent only on yourself."

4

"I don't understand what that means," I said. "If I'm working for you, how am I only dependent on myself?"

She smiled. "If I think you're right for us, I'll do my best to get you where you should be to be a success, Roxy, but whether you are or not is up to you. You have to have the ambition, the attitude, and the determination, not me. I'm already a success. What's the matter?" she asked when I didn't respond. "Do I sound too much like your teachers?"

"Yes, you do."

"Let me clue you in. They're not speaking in platitudes, telling you what they are told to tell you. They're not giving you advice that's not useful. What you do with it is your choice. Apparently, you've decided to ignore it. No one gets along well in this world without something of value to offer other people—a talent, an education, some skill. What did you expect to find when you left your home? Some sugar daddy to replace your father?"

"No, and he was far from a sugar daddy."

"You don't have much of a formal education, apparently, and it remains to be seen if you have any talent. Your looks can get you just so far on their own, and there are many girls your age who are just as attractive, if not more so. You probably have fifty cents in your pocket, no friends or, according to you, close relatives to turn to for some sort of assistance. You're as close to being a homeless creature as can be. Have I summed you up correctly? Well? What do you say about all this?"

No one, not even my father, could bring tears into my eyes this quickly, but when I thought about what was outside her door for me and how right she was, I did feel sorry for myself.

"I don't know what to say," I said. "You seem to have said it all."

"Well, I do know what you should say," she said, her nostrils flaring. "I've seen girls like you all my life, and I know what happens to you. You'll either go home or become a street prostitute and eventually a drug addict and die in some alley like the butterfly who died on the water and thought he had died on the moon."

"What?"

"Can't you imagine why he thought he had died on the moon?" she asked, smiling. It had the ring of a teacher testing to see if a student had read her homework assignment.

"Yes, I know why he would think that. He died on the reflection on the water."

"Exactly. Not real, an illusion. Here we deal only

in reality. I want to know more about you," she said, folding her hands over each other on her lap and changing her tone to a more officious-sounding one. "I want to know about your family, what sort of things you have been doing, what you like and don't like. But before I waste my time learning about you, I want to see if you can fit in here. My time is very valuable to me and to those who depend on me."

"I still don't really understand what being here means. Mr. Bob told me you train girls to be escorts. He said it's something like geisha girls."

"Geishas are probably more artistic, more talented, and more intelligent," she said dryly, "but we're something like that."

"What about sex?" I said, convinced that Mr. Bob hadn't told me the whole truth.

She bristled. "My girls are not prostitutes. You'll never see any one of my girls on the street, and no one, and I mean no one, gets to any of my girls without first going through me and a highly selective process. In all the years I've been in business, I'm proud to say I have never had a single one of my girls harmed. They know how to handle themselves in just about every situation they might confront. More important, however, is the fact that the men they escort respect them, know they are bright and resourceful women. We have no bimbos here. My girls are refined, educated, and full of poise and self-confidence. You're full of defiance. There's a difference."

"If you see so much wrong with me, why don't

you just ask Mr. Bob to bring me back to the city?" I shot back at her. I was tired of hearing how dreadful I was and how helpless.

She shrugged, undisturbed by the sharpness in my voice or the fury in my eyes. "Well, I haven't seen enough of you yet, nor have my people, who will give you an honest assessment. Besides, Bob raved about you, and when Bob raves about a girl, I listen. Don't tell him I said so. I don't want his head to swell up, but he has an eye for just the sort of young woman who can be a success in my company."

"Company?"

"Business. Don't act thick," she shot back, her eyes now taking on a blazing fury. I remembered what Bob had told me about her not suffering fools gladly. "This isn't some hobby of mine. I'd think even someone like you, in your state of mind and with your background, could realize it."

"I resent being anyone's punching bag. Maybe I should leave," I said.

"Maybe you should. I can see why you couldn't stand being told what to do, whether it was your father or your teachers. Believe me, Roxy, as good as it might make you feel, being headstrong is not an advantage. Nine times out of ten, you'll just hit a wall and land on your derrière. Here, obedience and following orders are not a disadvantage."

"I didn't check out of my father's house just to enlist in another army," I replied.

She held her gaze and then surprised me with a smile. "Army. I don't think we'd fit any definition of that, but we have rules, discipline, and, most of all, expectations."

She fixed her eyes on me and tightened the corners of her mouth. I could see her patience was wearing thin.

"Do you want to know more about all this, or don't you?" she demanded.

I stared at her a few moments and thought. Nowhere in Mama's or Papa's imagination could either envision me sitting here in this mansion talking to this obviously very successful woman about becoming a high-class escort. How confident Papa must have been that first night and even days afterward that I would come running back, desperately pleading for his forgiveness. I was tempted to do this just to spite him, but even more so now, I was intrigued. Were those two beautiful young women in here when I arrived once just like me? How could I look at all this and not want to be part of it, especially with all that was promised to me?

"Yes," I said. "I would."

She nodded, and then a woman appeared, as if she had been waiting and listening to our conversation just outside the door. She was older than Mrs. Brittany, probably in her sixties, about my height, with beautiful gray hair pulled into a basic chignon. Mama often wore her hair that way. She told me "chignon" came from the French phrase *chignon du cou*, which means "nape of the neck," but this woman looked more English than French. She stood so perfectly straight that I thought she must have a steel rod for a spine.

"Ah, Mrs. Pratt, just in time," Mrs. Brittany said. "I'd like you to give our guest a little tour of the house and then bring her to my office when you're finished."

"Very good, madam," Mrs. Pratt said. She had a very educated-sounding accent, reminding me of Mrs. Roster, who made her consonants so sharp she could cut your earlobes. This woman had a narrow face with thin lips and grayish-brown eyes beneath a pair of very stylish eyeglasses. I was up enough on women's fashion to recognize a St. John dress. She was wearing one. Mama had two.

Mrs. Pratt nodded at me.

I looked at Mrs. Brittany. Either she wasn't going to give this woman any more information about me or she already had told her what she knew thanks to Mr. Bob.

"Well, go on," she said. "You don't need my permission to breathe." She laughed and then said, "At least, not yet."

I rose quickly and followed Mrs. Pratt out of the sitting room and down the long, wide hallway.

"I hope it's cooler out here," I muttered. She looked at me but didn't react to that.

"You can't tell from the front of the house," Mrs. Pratt began instead, speaking like a guide in a museum, "but Mrs. Brittany has added considerably to the original structure, which was considerable at the start."

She looked at me in anticipation of some response. All I could think to say was, "Yes, considerable."

We turned to the right and paused. She opened a door and flipped the light switch to reveal a fitness center as complete as any I had seen.

"Lance Martin is the fitness trainer," she said. "He was on an Olympic swimming team. Mrs. Brittany insists that all her women be in the best possible shape. If you become part of the organization, you will undergo fitness training immediately and be put on dietary supplements. Mrs. Brittany's chef, Gordon Leceister, is a registered dietitian, so you will be eating right most of the time.

"Now, if you look off to the right," she added, nodding toward the fitness room, "you will see the tanning salon and spa. Olga Swensen is our masseuse. At one time, she had her own very famous spa in Stockholm."

When I didn't react, she added, "You know that Stockholm is in Sweden?"

"Of course," I said.

"While the Swedes didn't invent massage, their techniques are highly regarded. You will have a massage daily in the beginning and then eventually weekly."

"Weekly?" I asked. How long was I going to be there? She ignored me and flipped off the light. Across the hall were double doors that opened onto an indoor pool. It was lit, and I saw Camelia and Portia swimming with a good-looking young man who looked as if he didn't have an inch of fat on his body.

"That's Lance Martin," Mrs. Pratt said.

Camelia and Portia, both in abbreviated bikinis, waved. I nodded. Mrs. Pratt saw the way I was staring at the three of them.

"Any relationships between Mrs. Brittany's women

and the staff are strictly forbidden," she said. "That goes for relationships with men or women."

I looked at her as if she was nuts, but she just turned and led me farther down the hallway. She opened a door on the left and again turned on the lights, this time to reveal a full beauty salon.

"Mrs. Brittany likes to rotate her beauticians and stylists periodically. This month, we have Claudine Laffette from Paris. She's an expert at both cosmetics and hairstyling."

"Does everyone come here to be made up and stuff?"

"Stuff?" she replied.

"I mean get their hair and makeup done."

"This is a training facility. Our girls are first re-made here, and then they return periodically, but those who are out in the field have their own fitness centers, salons, and favorite boutiques."

"How long is the training?" I asked, this time more firmly.

She looked me up and down. "That depends on the candidate, of course. Suffice it to say, no one is brought here who doesn't already have a great deal to recommend her. You have a beautiful figure, but you're young. If you are not taught how to maintain it, it won't service you for long."

"Service me?"

"Everything we have, everything we do, is meant to service us, my dear. That's something you have to realize as soon as possible. Unfortunately, most realize it too late," she added.

I had often heard that people get to look like their pets, especially their dogs. Mrs. Pratt was not nearly as attractive as Mrs. Brittany, but she certainly took after her with her tone and attitude, especially toward me. Maybe mirroring Mrs. Brittany was the only way anyone could last working for her.

Just a few feet farther, she opened another door on the right and revealed a beautiful dining room. There were two dark maple tables, one that sat four and one that sat ten. The room looked about six feet larger than our dining room, with rich paneling and a hardwood floor. There were beautiful paintings of country scenes and lakes on the wall at my left and a full wall mirror at my right

"This is the main dining room?" I asked.

She laughed. "Hardly," she said. "This is a class-room. Nigel Whitehouse, a famous restaurateur from London, conducts lessons in dining etiquette, appreciation of wines, and knowledge of some of the world's most famous restaurants and recipes. When a girl leaves this room, any man she meets would think she was brought up in one of the finest royal families in Europe. The girls return periodically for updates and, shall we say, recertification."

"My parents taught me dinner etiquette," I said. "And I probably know as much about good wine as he does."

She smiled. "I love it when a girl your age has such arrogance. It's like watching a bullfight. Have you ever?"

"No."

"You'll learn about them. When a girl like you comes here with your attitude, it truly is like watching a bullfight. The bull is so strong and confident at the start. Slowly, the matador frustrates and frustrates it, forcing it to realize its failure and inadequacies until it practically falls on his sword."

"That's the first time I've been compared to a bull."

"Really? No one's called you bull-headed?"

I had to laugh. Papa had done that often. "I'm afraid someone has."

"I understand you speak French?"

"*Oui. J'ai parlé français toute ma vie. Parlez-vous français?*"

"*Bien sûr*. That's a big plus for you. Learning another language is always the most difficult thing for a trainee to accomplish, but Mrs. Brittany won't put a girl into the field who doesn't demonstrate sufficient proficiency with at least one other language. Many of our clients come from Europe, and they love it when an escort can speak their language."

I looked at the dining room, thought about what I had been shown, and shook my head. "Learning another language?"

"Enough to fake it," she replied, "but they continue to get lessons in the field. In a day or so," she continued, "you'll be shown the stables."

"Stables?"

"Mrs. Brittany has three of the finest Arabian riding horses. Do you ride?"

"A horse?" I started to smile.

"Equestrianism is the art of horse riding. It teaches

you grace and is excellent physical exercise. Many of Mrs. Brittany's clients have private stables, and if you should be lucky enough to attract one of them, he could invite you to ride."

"But I never . . ."

"Brendon Walsh is in charge of the stables and trains our girls. He was part of the Irish champion equestrian team."

"Champion team, Olympic team, famous masseuse. Is anyone here just anybody?"

She laughed. "No, my dear. Everyone here is somebody. Let's continue," she said, and led me farther down the hall to another room, a beautiful library with what looked like hundreds of books if not more than a thousand, two computers, printers, and a rack of newspapers. A tall, thin man in a dark brown sports coat and brown slacks came out of an inner office. He had four books in his hands. He wore a pair of glasses in round frames and had his charcoal-gray hair pulled back and tied in a short ponytail.

"Ah, Professor Marx," Mrs. Pratt said. "Roxy Wilcox might be your new student."

"Excellent," Professor Marx said, barely giving me a glance. He turned and began to place the books he carried in the bookcase on his right.

"I didn't mean to create such excitement," I muttered when we stepped out of the library.

Mrs. Pratt nearly laughed. She stopped with an extended smile. "Professor Marx is our resident intellectual. He was a college professor at one of the nation's most prestigious universities."

"What would I do in there?"

"You would be schooled in current events and historical background, along with the arts, literature, classical music, even pop and jazz. Of course, you need to have a good working knowledge of business and some math."

"Math, too?" I groaned.

"Just to make it seem as though you know what the Pythagorean theorem means," she said. "I'm kidding. You'll get a smattering of the subject."

"What about business?"

"Very important. Most of Mrs. Brittany's clients are involved in high finance. You know the difference between a put and a call, shorting a stock, capital gains, things like that?"

"I know a great deal about that, actually," I said. "My father is in finance."

"Oh, that's good. You'll learn more about it, of course, have a deeper understanding. It's all just information that will help you conduct an intelligent conversation. Don't worry. It's not that intense. Professor Marx is an expert in giving our girls just enough to convince any man that they're not airheads."

"I was lousy in school, but I'm not stupid, even though I'm sure I won't know most of what he expects me to know," I insisted.

"I wouldn't be showing you around here if Mrs. Brittany thought you were stupid, Roxy. I assure you of that," she replied. "You will also go to the library to meet with Professor Brenner, a retired speech and drama professor, who will give you speaking lessons."

"Speaking lessons?"

"Improve your speaking, I should say. Make you more conscious of how you pronounce words, avoid slurring. You want to sound like someone who deserves to be making the sort of money you'll be making, don't you? It's all about impressing people, Roxy. Making good first impressions."

I looked into the classroom dining room as we passed by it again and digested all she had told me so far, all that I had to learn and achieve.

"Professor Marx knows about all those subjects you listed?"

"As I said, he'll make sure you know enough for your needs," she replied.

"Really, Mrs. Pratt, I'd like to know, how long does this all take?"

"I told you it depends on the trainee, obviously. Some can't hack it and are given a kill fee and sent on their way."

"Kill fee?"

"Some money to leave with," she said dryly. She looked at her watch.

"Is there anything else?" I asked.

"Training-wise?"

"Yes."

"Mrs. Brittany herself will evaluate how you walk and move, whether you have proper poise, and she will instruct you in that regard."

"You mean I don't walk right or sit right?"

She looked at me and nodded. "You have a bit of a slouch. That must go, and when you walk, you tend

to keep your head down, which makes you look insecure. But don't worry. If she thinks you're worth it,
she'll get you up to snuff. Let's proceed to Mrs. Brittany's office."

She led me back into the main house, and we
crossed in front of the stairway and went down another corridor. I couldn't imagine how many maids
were used to keep the place in shape. Jeffries stepped
out of a room, nodded at us, and continued toward the
front of the mansion. We paused at two beautiful tall
light oak doors embossed with Greek nymphs in trees.
Mrs. Pratt knocked on the door.

"Yes?" Mrs. Brittany said, and we entered. Mr.
Bob was sitting off to the right on a beautiful black
leather sofa. He had a brandy snifter in his hand.

Mrs. Brittany's office was as large as, if not larger
than, most living rooms, I thought. It was richly
paneled, and behind her were large double windows. It was too dark by now to see what her view
was. She sat behind an oversize dark oak desk with
everything on it very neatly organized. There were
framed pictures all over the wall on the left, many
with politicians I recognized, and an oil portrait of
her hung on the wall behind Mr. Bob. In it, she was
probably twenty years younger, wearing a beautiful
pearl-colored gown and a diamond tiara. There was
no doubt that she had been a remarkably beautiful
young woman.

"Thank you, Mrs. Pratt," Mrs. Brittany said, obviously dismissing her.

Mrs. Pratt left, closing the door behind her.

"You may sit," Mrs. Brittany told me, nodding toward the sofa on which Mr. Bob sat.

He smiled and nodded. "Quite a place, isn't it?" he asked me.

"Yes," I said.

"Do you have any questions now?" Mrs. Brittany asked.

"How many women do you employ?"

"That's not your concern. Ask me things that concern only you."

"I guess I would live here while doing what you call training?"

"What do you call it? It's an education, a refinement, a preparation. You're bright enough to understand that much."

I was silent.

"Yes, of course, you would live here. And you would be evaluated every moment you were here."

"And then what?"

"Well, if you meet the test, are ready to go out into the field, I'd place you in your own apartment. In the beginning I would line up your assignments, but I would hope that in time, you would become a request. We'd give you your name."

"My name?"

"How you would be known when gentlemen called our service. I won't give you that until I'm convinced that you're ready."

"How long does that usually take? I know it depends on the candidate. By the way, is that a good word for girls like me?" I asked. "'Candidate?'"

She smiled. "Yes, *très bien*. Since you speak French, if you were still in question after six months, I would reconsider."

"Yes, and give me a kill fee. I was told."

"Good. What else?"

"I don't have to have sex with these men?"

She closed her eyes and sighed before opening them again. "No, no, I already explained that. All of my clients understand that having sexual relations is a decision our girls make themselves." She sat forward. "However, I'd be lying if I didn't tell you that some of my girls hold on to very high-paying clients by granting sexual pleasure, but that is not a requirement or a service we advertise. Furthermore, if one of my girls got pregnant, that would be the end of her association with my organization. I won't tolerate any such stupidity."

"I don't blame you for that," I said. "Nevertheless," I insisted, "if one of your girls is doing it for money, then she's a prostitute."

She tightened her lips and looked at me with laserlike intensity. "Even a geisha, a member of a long-standing traditional and cultural phenomenon in Japan, has sexual relations if she so desires, and no one would call her a prostitute, but I stress, and obviously have to repeat, it's not part of the job description."

I shrugged. "I'm not saying I have a holier-than-thou attitude. I just wouldn't like to think of myself that way."

"Nor should you." She leaned forward again, her eyes narrow, intense. "Let me make something perfectly clear. None of my successful girls thinks ill of herself. On the contrary, they enjoy their lives, their pleasures, and their rewards and have a great deal of pride. They have great self-respect. If you should be lucky enough to reach that level, you'll understand."

I could feel Mr. Bob watching my reactions. Mrs. Brittany sat back, her mouth twisting. My silence seemed to annoy her. I wasn't pleading enough for her to keep me.

"You can get up and walk out of here without any problem," she said. "We'll deliver you to whatever hole in the wall you've found, no questions asked. You can even keep that dress and those shoes, right, Bob?"

"Oh, absolutely."

"I'm just asking questions. You told me to ask them. I'm not saying I don't want to do this," I said.

"I'd like to hear you say 'I do,'" she replied. "With a convincing tone."

"Sounds like I'm getting married," I quipped, looking at Bob for a smile, but he didn't even blink. I took a deep breath. "Okay," I said, with all the firmness I could muster. "I do."

"Good. Now we have only one question to answer," she said.

"Which is?"

"Will you do?"

5

Mrs. Brittany stared at me a moment. Then she smiled, nodded, and opened a desk drawer to produce a printed document.

"I want you to read this and sign it. I ask everyone we're considering to do so. The document is not legally binding in any court except the court I hold here, but I like certain things made very clear in black and white so that there are no misunderstandings."

She pushed the papers across her desk. I rose, picked them up, and began to read them. It certainly was written like a legal document. In return for the privilege of being trained to become a member of Mrs. Brittany's enterprise, I had to agree to a number of rules and conditions. Nothing guaranteed that I would become a member. That was clearly stated, as were the conditions.

I was never to smoke unless the man I was with smoked, and then only if he approved. If I was already a smoker, I was to stop immediately.

I was never to do any drugs or ever drink too much or do anything to embarrass myself in public.

I was to keep in mind that I always represented Mrs. Brittany.

Except to Mrs. Brittany or someone she had approved, I was never to talk about anyone I had been with or what they did or what we did together.

I was never to discuss Mrs. Brittany or the organization or speak about Mrs. Brittany's residence and my training, and if I should be approved, never without her prior permission was I to reveal to anyone that I was an employee of her company.

Pregnancy, even if I could have an abortion, was grounds for immediate dismissal.

I was never to leave the country without permission or be unavailable for an assignment unless Mrs. Brittany had sufficient warning.

I couldn't change my hairstyle, my makeup, or the style of clothes I wore without first getting her approval, and I could go only to salons that she approved.

I paused in my reading.

"This sounds more like a form of slavery," I said. She smiled at Mr. Bob, who also smiled. "I had more freedom living under my father's iron hand."

"And you have the freedom to return to it," Mrs. Brittany said.

I glared back at her a moment and then returned to the document. Something occurred to me, and I looked up again. "I understand you want everything I do kept secret, but what if my picture is taken with one of these men and it appears in a magazine or a newspaper?"

"Not likely," Mrs. Brittany said. "Many of them will be married or engaged or men who do not want to be compromised in any way. If that should happen, you would always be listed as an unknown escort, anyway. You might see celebrities, but they will avoid being seen with you in public. It's a requirement that they accept and cherish. We take great pains to protect our clients. You'll see, if you get there. I especially don't want my girls pursued by the paparazzi. Something like that could ruin them, and I have too much of an investment in every one of my girls to risk that. Understand?"

I nodded and read on.

The second page went into the training. The first thing mentioned was what Mrs. Pratt had told me: I was forbidden to have any sexual relationship with any member of Mrs. Brittany's staff.

I had to follow all instructions regarding my exercise and diet. Any resistance or insubordination would result in immediate termination. I was not to have any communication with anyone on the outside while I was here.

There was also, as Mrs. Pratt had mentioned, a kill or termination fee. It was five thousand dollars.

I looked up sharply when I read that. I could start and quit and get five thousand dollars?

Mrs. Brittany smiled. It was as though she could read my mind.

"The reason the termination fee is so high is, first, to ensure your discretion and, second, to give you a concept of how much more you will make should you complete your training and get placed in the field.

"However," she continued, "if you took that kill fee and then betrayed my confidences, there would be other consequences. I have many friends in high places. Fortunately or unfortunately, depending on your viewpoint, we live in a world where it isn't what you know so much as whom you know. Do you understand?"

I looked at Mr. Bob. He was watching to see my reaction to that. It rang like a Mafia threat in my ears, but I just shrugged and said, "Of course," and continued reading the dos and don'ts.

One paragraph stated that in the event there were any legal issues involving me, the organization would provide an attorney. It would be decided afterward whether the costs were incurred because of something that was my fault. If so, the cost would come out of my commission, which was simply stated as fifteen percent the first year, rising five percent every subsequent year until I had reached fifty percent.

"What's the amount I get a percentage of?"

She smiled. "Now, that's your first good question, as far as I'm concerned. The amount will be based on how much in demand you become. I'll decide the initial fee, depending on how I evaluate you at the start. It could be anywhere from two thousand to ten thousand."

"Each time?"

"No, each hour."

I didn't want to gasp or look astonished, but how could I not? There were men who would pay as much as ten thousand dollars an hour to be escorted by one of Mrs. Brittany's women? The full meaning of all this was settling into my brain like a stone in quicksand. *An hour?* The cash register in my imagination began to purr.

"How often would I work?"

"Again, that will be up to how much in demand you become, but at the start, my girls usually work five or so times a month."

I quickly did the math. My brain spun with the possibilities. I could become a wealthy woman in a relatively short span of time.

"There's one other thing that's not written there," Mrs. Brittany said, nodding toward the papers.

"And what's that? I donate a pint of blood a week or something?"

She smiled. Mr. Bob chuckled.

"Not quite. We take nothing from your body. Only your soul," she said, seemingly half in jest. "On occasion," she continued, "I get requests from very important female CEOs and the like, especially celebrities. They like being accompanied by an attractive female or merely sharing her company privately. Is that something you absolutely cannot see yourself doing?"

I glanced again at Mr. Bob. The expression on his face told me it was important not to refuse.

I shrugged. "I've always liked boys better, but whatever," I said.

She didn't laugh or smile. "Don't make the mistake of treating any of this too casually, Roxy. Indifference usually leads to self-destruction," she warned.

"I'm not indifferent. Nothing here intimidates me. That's all."

"Good."

"Anything else you want to add?" I asked.

"Nothing else for now."

There was a place for me to sign at the bottom of the second sheet. Mrs. Brittany's signature was already there. I nodded to myself. It did feel as if I was making a deal with the devil, but just like anyone who did, I felt I had been tempted into it by the devil's knowing where and what my weaknesses were. I put the papers down, reached for the pen on her desk, and signed. She took it and dated it.

"Very good," she said. "I hope the next time we do something this formal will be when I welcome you into the company."

"What will that be, an initiation ceremony with animals sacrificed or something?"

She shook her head and looked at Mr. Bob. "She'll either rise quickly to the top or sink quickly to the bottom," she told him.

He nodded and smiled at me. "I think she'll rise to the top."

"Um," Mrs. Brittany said through tight lips.

She picked up her phone to call Mrs. Pratt, who again seemed to have been waiting just outside the door.

"Please show our new"—she looked up at me and smiled—"candidate to her suite."

"I'm staying here now, tonight?"

"Is there any reason for you to go back to your whatever tonight? If there's anything of value there, tell Bob, and he'll see after it."

"No, there's nothing of value," I said, "but these are the only clothes I have, and . . ."

"Please," she said, holding up her hand, palm toward me. "Don't insult me. You will have all that you need for tonight and for your time here. Periodically, I will take you on shopping trips, and we'll begin your wardrobe as I become more confident that you will, shall we say, graduate. Everything else you need will be in your suite. I think it's important that you get a good night's rest. I believe in getting a new girl right into things. Time, as they say, is money, and for us, that's really true, isn't it, Bob?"

"Absolutely," Mr. Bob said. He was beaming. I guessed whatever finder's fee he expected, he would get, but then I wondered if he had to give it back if I failed or if he would get more if I succeeded.

"Give her the scarlet suite, Mrs. Pratt. It has the best view. I think our new candidate needs to improve her view of everything."

"Yes, madam," Mrs. Pratt said. She stood waiting for me.

I turned to leave.

"Hold up," Mr. Bob said, gently seizing my right arm. "You have something of mine left with someone. I should know who that is so that I can retrieve it. You'll have to call to let them know." He looked at Mrs. Brittany when she groaned.

"You didn't do that silly thing again with your license, did you?" she asked him.

He shrugged. "I thought it was necessary. She had her skepticism, and I thought she was worth it."

"Nothing to worry about," I told him, and took his license out of my purse. "I had no one to trust with it and thought you were worth taking a chance on."

"Well, there. You see?" Mrs. Brittany said. "You do have a trusting way about you, after all, Bob."

He smiled and put his license back into his wallet. "I like this girl," he said. "She's got guts."

"We'll see," Mrs. Brittany said. "It takes more than just guts." She nodded at me, and I followed Mrs. Pratt out of the office.

"This way," Mrs. Pratt told me in the hallway. We returned to the foyer and started up the magnificent stairway. "You'll be woken at six-thirty for breakfast," she began as we walked. "I'll lay out what you are to wear tomorrow. Everything is in your closet."

"Six-thirty?"

She paused and looked back at me. "There's not enough time in the day to do all you have to do as it is."

"Well, it's no good if I'm not awake."

"Oh, you'll be awake," she assured me.

The second floor was just as elaborate as the floor below. Again, there were paintings on every wall, beautiful lamps and statuary in niches, and chandeliers hanging from the ceiling.

"These are the guest suites," she continued, nodding at closed doors. "Currently, only Camelia and Portia are in residence." She paused at the third door on the right. "Mrs. Brittany frowns on our girls partying in any of the suites. You can fraternize if you're taking a lesson together with someone, but it's better when you retire for the evening that you get your rest."

"This sounds more like boot camp every minute," I muttered.

She smiled. "Yes, but the boots you wear here are Gucci."

Finally, I had something to laugh about. Maybe she wasn't as hard and cold as I first thought. She opened the door, and I nearly gasped with surprise and delight.

The suite was easily three times the size of Mama and Papa's bedroom. There was a king-size bed with a scarlet canopy and oversize pillows, all the bedding a lighter shade of scarlet. The bed was so high that there was a footstool beside it. The walls were also a lighter shade of scarlet, as were the curtains. All the furniture—the bed frame, the dressers, the night tables and vanity table—was made from a cherry wood whose rich color I had never seen. And there was a fluffy white area rug. The rest of the floor was a continuation of the hardwood floor in the hallway.

Two large windows were evenly spaced, each on one side of the headboard. The curtains were drawn closed at the moment. Mrs. Pratt entered and put the light on in the en suite bathroom. I walked in and looked at it. The bathroom was easily as big as my bedroom at home. It had a double-size shower stall, a Jacuzzi tub, two sinks, a bidet in addition to a toilet, cabinets, and wall mirrors everywhere. A professional scale stood beside the sink on the right. The bathroom was done in a swirling pink tile. There was a wall telephone and even a small television on the wall so that someone soaking in a bath could watch something.

Mrs. Pratt turned without comment and crossed the bedroom to the walk-in closet. She flipped another light switch. I saw clothes on the racks.

"What's all that?"

"For now, you have what we call the basics, some blouses and slacks and a proper dress for an informal dinner."

"What about size?"

"There's a variety in here, but you'll surely find something that fits well. We had a little warning about you."

"What warning? You mean since the time Mr. Bob bought me this dress, shoes, and purse, these things were bought?"

"Something like that," she said, smiling. "You needn't be concerned with how fast Mrs. Brittany can get things done. She gets them done fast enough to satisfy her requirements. There are running shoes and some flats here that should also fit you. In these drawers," she said, opening one of the drawers in the built-in dresser, "you'll find panties, three styles of bras, and a sports bra, plus socks, belts, and handkerchiefs. All silk, of course. Lance Martin will have your bathing suit for you."

She closed the drawer and opened another to take out a brand-new pink sweatsuit. She placed it on top of the dresser.

"This is for tomorrow morning," she said. We

walked out of the closet, and she nodded at the vanity table.

"For now, you have only a hairbrush. The table is not yet stocked. This will occur after you meet with Claudine Laffette and she decides on what would bring out the best qualities in your face, primarily your eyes and mouth. You'll find sleepwear in your dresser here. There are slippers and a robe in the bathroom. I would recommend that you take a warm bath and go to bed. You're about to begin quite a demanding period of development." She started for the door.

"Oh," she said, pausing. She returned to open a small cabinet beside the dresser. "This is a small built-in refrigerator. There are bottles of mineral water in here. If you need anything else now or during the night, just press zero on your phone. There's someone available around the clock. Are there any questions? I'm sorry to be so abrupt, but I have to go over some economic matters with Mrs. Brittany. She has an important meeting tomorrow."

"No," I said. What was left to ask? What they served for breakfast?

She flashed a smile, nodded, and left, closing the door behind her.

For a moment, I just stood there staring at the door. Then I looked around. I didn't know whether to feel like Cinderella or the Prisoner of Zenda. I knew all this should make me feel very happy, but it also filled me with new fears, and I wasn't one to care or worry too much about fears. As a child, I rarely called out after a nightmare. I didn't want to see my father's

disapproving face as he stood behind my mother,
clearly revealing his displeasure in my having woken
them. I learned how to swallow back my childhood
demons the way we swallow down something that
wants to come up out of our stomachs. Grin and bear
it, or as Papa would say to me even when I was four,
"Soldier up."

It didn't take much soldiering up to tolerate this, I
thought. The bed felt like a large marshmallow when I
sat on it and then tested it lying down. My head sank
softly and slowly into the oversize pillow. It was like
sinking into a cloud. I hadn't noticed it before, but
there was a perfume aroma in the room. It smelled
like lavender. I rose and went into the bathroom.
That beautiful bathtub did look inviting, and I always
enjoyed bubbling jets. I saw bath oils and powders,
perfumed soaps, and soft washcloths and towels. First,
I found the nightgown I'd wear, and then I started the
water to fill the tub.

After I got undressed and was soaking in ecstasy, I
thought about the hovel of a room in the hotel I had
found when Papa had kicked me out of the house,
where I would be right now if Mr. Bob hadn't been in
that restaurant. I tried to convince myself that from
the way he and Mrs. Brittany had described what escorts do, I wasn't really selling my soul to the devil. It
was more like acting. I would learn a great deal here,
and then I would go out on a stage, not into the field,
as she had said. On this stage, I would pretend to care
for and appreciate whomever I was with. I would be
so charming and beautiful that my date—could I use

that word?—would ask for me repeatedly, and I'd make a fortune.

Maybe there would be a handsome, exciting young businessman or a movie star with whom I would want to have sex. So what? I had made love with boys for relatively nothing. As long as I was careful and made sure I didn't get pregnant, I'd be fine. Why wouldn't I do it if I wasn't unhappy about it and I could make a lot of money?

I glanced at myself in the mirror as I thought these thoughts and asked that question of myself again. Mama would be devastated if she had any idea, not only of what I might do here but of what I had done. Papa would be so self-satisfied. If he learned where I was and what I was going to do, he would feel justified for the way he had thrown me out of the house. I could hear him now: "I knew we had to get rid of her. Imagine the sort of influence she would have been when Emmie was older."

Mama would cry, but she would cry mostly when she was alone. If she shed any tears in front of him, it would just elevate his rage and make him blame me more, blame me for the pain and suffering my mother endured. I had caused it at birth and would forever.

What could I do about it? Just as he could never change me, I could never change him. Can you ever truly love someone who disappoints you? What was more painful, not loving my father because he didn't love me or not loving myself because I couldn't get him to love me?

I closed my eyes and lay back in the water. Then

I pressed the buttons and started the jets. Squealing with delight, I looked at myself in the mirror. *Shut down any second thoughts, Roxy Wilcox,* I told myself. *You're on your way to better things and places you never pictured even in your dreams.*

The bath turned out to be just what I had needed. Mrs. Pratt was right to suggest it. I had no idea how much tension I had been under and how tight every muscle in my body had become. Wasn't it wonderful to have all this now, to be hedonistic and soak up all the pleasure I could? I always wanted to be spoiled, and Papa was always accusing me of that because Mama did so much for me and I was terrible about fulfilling my responsibilities and chores at home. She would always cover up for me, but he always seemed to know that and bawl her out for it.

Yes, I felt guilty about it, but I didn't improve very much. I wasn't going to deny it. I hated kitchen chores and housework. I wasn't even very good about keeping my own room in order, which was something I knew irritated my father a great deal. He was practically brought up in a barracks. His room had to be neat and organized at all times, and he had to make his own bed, he claimed, when he was only five, "and make it perfectly." He said his father actually used a bouncing coin to check how tightly made his and his brother's beds were. He knew his coins might disappear if he tried that on my bed. If Mama didn't get into my room quickly enough and he saw it, he would go on and on about it, first attempting to take away things that were out of place. When that didn't bother me, he stopped, but he still complained.

Emmie was already taking good care of her room. I used to look at her and wonder how we could be born of the same parents. I looked enough like both of them never to doubt that my father was my father, but the resemblances felt more like a shell in my mind. I was so unlike Emmie when I was her age, and I couldn't imagine her becoming more like me as she grew older. Maybe if I had paid more attention in biology class, I would understand how sisters could be so different. I thought she loved me, even looked up to me in certain ways. But she couldn't have been oblivious to all of Papa's criticism of me, and I felt certain that when I wasn't around, he told her to be wary of me, not to emulate me, and in fact, to think of me as someone not to be and the things I did as things not to do. I was a good teaching tool for him, so good that he probably shouldn't have thrown me out. I was a living, breathing example of all that was wrong. All he had to do was point his finger or nod in my direction and look at her, maybe adding, "See? That is exactly what you don't want to do or be when you're your sister's age."

I suppose I was simply a mystery to her. How could the same parents who loved and cherished her so much be so critical of me? How did I get this way in the same house, hearing the same things, eating the same food, and participating in family events, holidays, and trips? Sometimes I would catch her staring at me across a room, or I would feel her standing behind me, watching me. I knew she was struggling to understand me. Maybe my being gone wasn't a surprise for her at all. Maybe she didn't even look in my room anymore or glance at my empty seat at the dinner table. Perhaps my sudden disappearance was as inevitable as death itself. You knew it was waiting to happen. You just didn't want to talk about it or think about it or even prepare for it.

I knew that after I had crawled into the luxurious bed in the magnificent suite, I should have been filled with renewed hope and happiness. Papa wasn't going to win, after all, and there was a very good chance I would enjoy things and see things I would never have, even if he had tolerated me forever. I was surrounded by beauty and opulence, all of it soon to be at my beck and call.

Maybe my high school English teacher, Mr. Wheeler, was right on target when he said I hated myself, but you didn't wake up one morning and decide you'd be totally different, did you? And even if you could make that decision, could you change so radically, or were you cursed forever to be who you were? Probably, that was what was most interesting about being here, I thought. Mrs. Brittany and her people would turn me into a different person, would re-create me, change me in ways I had never dreamed of, and give me a new name and a new identity. I wouldn't be someone Papa would love but probably just the opposite, someone he would hate more. However, after my training, I might very well love myself for real and not just out of some stubborn arrogance.

I knew how much I had failed back home and

in school. I knew I was heading for nowhere fast. I was Miss Persona Non Grata everywhere. I never had a substantial relationship with either a girl or a boy. Perhaps in the end, I had nothing to give either a girlfriend or a boyfriend—no friendship, no love, and no concern or compassion. I was some dark shadow haunting everyone with whom I came into contact, including my own parents and my little sister. I was a natural for this, a perfect candidate to become Mrs. Brittany's most successful girl.

Yes, I told myself, this was my chance to be re-born. My good looks and intellectual potential had come through for me. Admittedly, it was based on a lucky moment, but what difference did that make in the end? Didn't Mama believe almost everything in life was *bonne ou mauvaise chance*? I had some good luck, and I could make something of it. Mrs. Brittany wasn't wrong. It was up to me. I had to find the determination and the ambition. Those were two things I had definitely lacked until now.

Yes, I should be very, very happy tonight, I thought. *I should have no problem sleeping.* I didn't have to worry about whether the lock on the door would hold. I didn't have to hear sobbing and screams from other rooms. I didn't have to hold my nose to sleep or curl up, hoping nothing would bite me or infect me. I was safe. I should be happy. *Be happy,* I kept telling myself. It became more like a chant in a church, except that the church I was in now was the church of pleasure and wealth.

But I wasn't happy yet. I didn't even want to

think it, much less admit it aloud, but despite my bravado and defiance, I did miss my mother and my sister. Hell, I even missed Papa, missed his fury and his disappointments. There were also times when he was softer, even loving. He tried, but I didn't respond in the manner he had been hoping to see. There were many times when I caught him looking at me with disdain, I had to confess, if only to myself, that there were also times when I saw his lips soften and his eyes brighten, and I knew he was thinking, *She's beautiful, and she is my daughter.*

These thoughts made my heart ache, but I didn't sob. I squeezed my eyes closed tighter and took a breath.

Soldier on, I told myself. *Soldier on. The morning will bring a whole new life, a whole new world, and you will be a star in it. You'll never want for anything. You heard Mr. Bob. You'll find a new family here.*

But as if someone was listening to my thoughts, someone invisible, my second self, whispered in the darkness, *You'll find a new family, but you won't find the same love.*

I don't care, I chanted to myself, still in that church of pleasure and wealth. *I don't.*

What greater lies are there, the other voice whispered, *than the lies you tell yourself?*

I didn't want to listen to that voice. I closed my ears and willed myself to sleep.

6

I heard the sound of the curtains being drawn open, then the click of the lamp beside my bed. The light splashed on my face and popped open my eyes. When I focused, I realized Mrs. Pratt was standing there, gazing down at me full of disappointment and pity like someone looking at a body in a coffin. Her hair was the same, as was the modest makeup she wore, but this morning, she was dressed in a light gray tweed business skirt suit with a frilly white blouse. When I moaned, she clutched her hands against her chest and pursed her lips, now projecting a look of annoyance. For a moment, I forgot where I was. It had all happened so quickly yesterday that it seemed more like a dream. I pushed myself up onto my elbows and looked around the beautiful suite.

"What's wrong? What's happening?"

I had forgotten she had said I'd be up at six-thirty.

"Morning is happening," she said. "And I assure you that I won't be doing this every morning. Tomorrow and from now on, you'll be woken by phone. You don't have to do anything but lift the receiver and put it back, and the ringing will stop. I hope you will soon arrive at the maturity it takes to get yourself up without anyone else's assistance. Small but essential things like that will help convince Mrs. Brittany that you have what it takes to bear adult responsibility."

I rubbed my eyes and looked at her again as if I wanted to be sure she was really there and I wasn't trapped in a dream. Because of the expression on her face and the tone of her voice, I was tempted to salute her the way I used to salute my father to annoy him.

"I take it you slept well," she said.

"Yes, ma'am," I said. "I didn't hear a thing."

"Good."

She gazed with obvious disapproval at how I had left my new dress draped over a chair, my panties and bra on the chair, and my shoes beneath it.

"Why do you think you have a closet? Did you have a maid at home?"

"No."

"Your mother looked after you? Even at this age?"

"Look, I was excited and wanted to get into the tub to relax as you had suggested. I didn't expect to have a barracks inspection with the playing of reveille first thing in the morning."

She nodded like someone agreeing with her own thoughts. "I don't know," she said. "You have much to recommend you, but you might be too young yet."

"Well, I guess we'll know soon enough, won't we?" I countered.

"Yes, we will," she said. "Wash your face, or do whatever you need to do, and come down to breakfast. Portia and Camelia are almost dressed and will also be there."

"Why are they up so early? Are they just starting here, too?"

"Hardly," she said, now smiling at me, but with condescension, making me feel like a child, after all. "Anyone could see they are top Brittany girls."

"Well, this is the first time I've ever seen a Brittany girl, so I don't have someone to measure them by. Is Mrs. Brittany up this early, too?"

"Of course. Mrs. Brittany has to go to Boston for the day, and I have things to do for her preparation. We're all very busy here. I'll have your schedule prepared and bring it to you in the breakfast dining room."

"Where is that?" I asked, getting out of bed. "You didn't show it to me yesterday, or is that the same room for dining-etiquette instruction?"

"No, it is not. Why don't you see if you can find it yourself?" she said. "Show some early initiative. Mrs. Brittany likes that in a girl. Besides, you know where it isn't."

"Excuse me?" I asked, pausing.

She sighed. "If you get lost, there's staff all over the house, Roxy. Just go down and turn right this time."

I could see she was definitely going to be a hurdle I would have to get over if I was to win over Mrs. Brittany, but I wasn't in the mood to kiss up to her, now or ever. Was it my stubborn pride or my damned defiance, or was it because I had real backbone? I couldn't be my father's daughter without it, which was something he himself couldn't appreciate or understand.

She picked up my dress and my shoes and brought them to the closet. "This is the first and last time I will do anything like this," she muttered, as if she was trying to convince herself more than me.

I rose and looked out the window on the right. The view was magnificent. I could clearly see how much land Mrs. Brittany owned, and to the left, I could see the stables. Three horses were in a pen, all black and about the same size. Between the stables and the mansion was an oval pool with a cabana. Someone was setting out lounges and opening the umbrellas at the tables. When I shifted a little, I could see farther to the left and caught a glimpse of two tennis courts.

"I didn't realize how big this place is," I said, more to myself than to her.

"There's a lot you haven't realized, Roxy," she said, emerging from the closet. "You're just beginning to make interesting discoveries. At least, I hope they are interesting to you."

She had an impish smile. At the moment, she reminded me more of a commander of a prisoner-of-war camp than an executive assistant.

"I'm sure they will be interesting to me if they're interesting to you, Mrs. Pratt."

She mouthed a small laugh, looking like someone swallowing a bubble, and shook her head. "Fine. Don't dilly-dally. Move along," she said, and left my suite. The moment she walked out, I couldn't help it. I did salute.

"Yes, ma'am," I muttered, but I did rush to get ready. I ran a brush through my hair, but there was no lipstick for me. I wasn't sure what I was supposed to look like, but they couldn't blame me for anything in that regard. I was practically kidnapped. When I went downstairs, I turned right and was greeted by a maid coming out of Mrs. Brittany's office.

"Breakfast table?" I said, and she told me it was the last door on the left.

It was a light maple room with one side nearly all windows. There was a large armoire on the right filled with pretty blue and white china and a long wooden table a shade or two darker than the walls. Camelia and Portia were there already. They both had glasses of orange juice and coffee. Camelia was dressed smartly in a ready-to-wear Dior I had recently seen advertised, a coated-cotton blue jacket with a silk jersey T-shirt and soft lambskin baggy pants. She looked like the model in the magazine. Portia was in a sweatsuit not unlike mine.

"Roxy, right?" Portia asked when I entered.

"Yes."

"That's your place setting," Camelia said, nodding toward the one across from her. Portia sat at the head of the table. Before I reached the seat, a curly-blond-haired man with very dark brown eyebrows came through the door that opened to the kitchen, carrying a tray with two plates of poached eggs, toast, and jam and two small bowls of mixed fresh fruit. He was a good two inches shorter than all three of us and wore a black leather vest over a white long-sleeved shirt and black slacks. A gold bracelet dangled on his left wrist, and he had a diamond stud earring in his right ear. He widened his smile, revealing piano-key-white capped teeth. His rust-brown eyes brightened at the sight of me.

"Is this our new princess, then?"

"Herself, Randy," Camelia replied.

"Welcome, welcome, welcome," Randy said, with just a slight shift in his hips. He served Camelia and Portia and then hurried over to pour me a glass of juice and a cup of coffee.

"*Au lait?*" he asked.

"*S'il vous plaît,*" I replied.

"Ooh, I like her," Randy said. He poured some milk into the coffee. "Low-fat, you know," he said, winking at Portia. "All the fat here is low."

The girls laughed.

"Your breakfast will be just two shakes of a prostitute's bum."

He went back into the kitchen.

"What was that?" I asked, and they both laughed again.

"That was Randy Carr. He's been with Mrs. Brittany for nearly ten years," Camelia told me. "She stole him out of a restaurant in Key West. She's very fond of him, so watch what you say about him."

"One thing is for sure," Portia said. "He'll never say a negative word about her, and if you're smart, you won't say one in his presence, either."

"In anyone's presence," Camelia warned.

"Amen," Portia said.

"Everyone is so loyal to the queen," I said. "I feel I should genuflect in her presence."

Neither laughed.

"It's her castle. We live in her kingdom. Besides, everyone is paid well and treated well," Portia said. "Mrs. Brittany keeps her word when it comes to what she promises you. Don't ever worry about that. And if and when she accepts you, you'll have a very good friend for life."

"Before you know it, you'll be as loyal as we are to her, if not more," Camelia told me. She looked at Portia and then back at me. "Considering where you are and where she might take you, probably more."

"Where I am?"

"Assuming she gets the stamp of approval," Portia reminded her.

"Oh, she will win over Mrs. Brittany," Camelia said, smiling at me. "I think she has what it takes."

I drank some orange juice, pleased that it was freshly squeezed. Mama always served freshly squeezed orange juice in the morning. Having fresh fruit and vegetables was always a priority to her. I recalled how proud she was of how they ate in France, shopping at farmers' markets and rarely using frozen foods.

Why was it that even here, with all these distractions, I continually thought about Mama and Emmie and even Papa? Did this mean that deep down inside, I knew I couldn't do this and that I would end up at my family's front door, head bowed, begging to be permitted to come home? I pushed the thought out of my mind.

"She has barely begun her first day, Camelia,"

Portia reminded her. She kept her smile. "A little early for predictions, don't you think?"

Camelia shrugged. "I can remember my first day as if it were yesterday," she said. She began to eat.

I watched how daintily she cut into the egg and how carefully she spread jam on her toast. In fact, both of them ate as if they were in a competition to see who could drop the least amount of crumbs. They patted their lips after every bite.

"Oh, and how did yours go?" I asked.

"I think I was terrified," she said, turning to Portia. "Even though I never let anyone know it."

"I know I was, and I'm sure they knew it."

"Why were you two terrified?" I asked. I gulped the rest of my juice. They stared at me a moment and then smiled at each other. "What's so funny?"

"You drink like a teenager," Portia said. "Not very ladylike, and here you want to be very ladylike."

"I see that Mrs. Brittany has her work cut out for her," Camelia admitted, probably having second thoughts about my success.

"Yeah, well, maybe I'll surprise her. I can tell you one thing. I'm not terrified, and this is not an act."

"Too bad," Portia said quickly.

"Why?"

"You'll try harder if you're terrified of failure. I did, and so did Camelia."

I shrugged. "Five thousand dollars isn't a bad kill fee," I said, and they both laughed. "Now what's so funny?"

"Five thousand dollars is less than a night's work

for us," Camelia said. "To see that as a safety net or something and be satisfied after being brought here and seeing what you could have is ludicrous."

"She means ridiculous," Portia said.

"I know what it means. I'm not stupid. I don't know what you've been told about me."

"Not much," Portia replied, "and even if we had, we'd be D and D."

"D and D?"

"Deaf and dumb."

Camelia sat back, studying me a moment with a smile on her face.

"Now what?" I asked.

"You're one of Mr. Bob's Lana Turners, aren't you?" she asked.

"What?"

"You know who Lana Turner was?"

"Yes, a movie actress. Actually, one of my father's favorites."

I almost bit my tongue after I said that, but it was too late. However, I could see that neither Camelia nor Portia cared to hear about my father.

"She was supposedly discovered at a soda fountain in Hollywood. Part of it is myth, and part of it is fact," Portia said. "I'm one of Mr. Bob's Lana Turners, but I was discovered at a charity ball. Mrs. Brittany herself found Camelia."

"Where did Mr. Bob find you?" Camelia asked. "I hope he's not raiding high schools these days."

Portia laughed and said, "He'd raid a nunnery if he thought he had someone with potential."

"He wasn't waiting outside my high school. I met him in a restaurant."

"You were a waitress? That's a first."

"No, I was eating, and he approached me," I said. "I've never been a waitress."

"What have you been?" Camelia asked.

"A troublesome teenager," I said, and they both laughed again.

"Haven't we all," Portia said.

"Not like I was—am, I should say."

Neither spoke for a moment.

"Well, by now, Mrs. Brittany has confirmed whatever police record you have, and it's not been enough to toss you out," Portia said. "You can be assured of that. No one pulls the trigger faster on someone than she does."

"I'm sure you won't be a troublesome teenager here," we heard as Randy returned with my dish of poached eggs and toast and a bowl of fruit.

"Eavesdropping, Randy?" Camelia asked him. "That's very naughty."

"'Ear now," he said, imitating a Cockney accent. I 'ear what I 'ear."

Camelia and Portia laughed.

"Do you need anything else, princess?" he asked me.

"No, thank you," I said.

"Ladies?"

"We're fine, Randy, thank you," Portia told him. He winked at me and left.

"So where did Mrs. Brittany discover you?" I asked Camelia as I sipped some more coffee.

"In a dance studio in London," she said. "I was good, but she convinced me that I was not good enough. 'Why waste your best years?' she asked. It was as simple as that, and voilà, here I am, not wasting them."

Portia widened her smile. "I'll drink to that," she said, and sipped her coffee.

Camelia looked at her watch. "I've got to get going," she said.

"Where to?" I asked. I tried to cut my egg the same dainty way she had.

"London," she said, and rose. "I wish you luck, Roxy. But take my advice, get a little terrified," she added. "Take care, Portia." She blew her a kiss. Portia blew one back, and we watched her walk out.

"Camelia is real British upper crust. She has a number of royals as clients. I love her."

"I thought we couldn't mention who our clients were," I said.

"We can talk to each other, sweetie. We can't talk out of school, but we still don't mention names. And don't think Mrs. Brittany wouldn't find out if you violated one of her rules. She has eyes and ears everywhere, and I don't mean just Randy Carr. Let me give you some early advice, too. You'll meet others here from time to time. Don't ever think you can confide in anyone. Whoever it is, she'll betray you, if not to look better to Mrs. Brittany, then to protect the organization, which means protecting herself." She smiled. "You'll actually get to be the same way. If you make it," she added.

She sipped her coffee. I was getting tired of the big *if*.

"I'll make it," I said. "If I want to make it."

"More power to you," she said.

We heard footsteps in the hallway. I turned toward the door just as Mrs. Brittany entered, followed by Mrs. Pratt.

"Good," Mrs. Brittany said, seeing that I was finishing up my breakfast. "You're on schedule. Mrs. Pratt?"

Mrs. Pratt stepped up and put a card beside me. It was my training schedule. There were activities for me all day right up to dinner.

"I will return for dinner," Mrs. Brittany said. "Please keep in mind that every meal and just about every activity you do in this house is an education and a test."

"What isn't?" I asked. "I imagine someone is watching me sleep."

"Could be," she said.

I glanced at Portia, who kept her face locked in a tiny smile.

Mrs. Brittany looked at Mrs. Pratt and then back at me, nodding at the card. "That's your schedule for the foreseeable future," she said. She started out, then paused and turned back to me. "If you have any problems today, see Mrs. Pratt." They looked at each other, and she turned back to me one final time to add, "I suppose the big question to answer is whether you will still be here when I return."

"I'll be here," I said.

"Don't let us both down, then," she replied, and left.

"She likes you," Portia said immediately.

"You're kidding. If she likes me, I pity someone she doesn't like."

"Exactly. That was our point."

"How can you tell, anyway?"

"I've been around her long enough. After a while, you'll figure it out for yourself," she said, and finished her coffee.

I looked at the empty doorway.

There's a woman who would be a match for my father, I thought, and finally smiled, thinking about the two of them in the same room talking about me. I'd love to be a fly on the wall that day. My smile widened.

"What's so funny?" Portia asked.

"Nothing. Everything."

She widened her eyes and laughed.

So did I, but I wondered when I would laugh again.

7

Portia left before I finished my breakfast. She told me she was going for a morning swim and then, after a massage and a session with Claudine Laffette, who had promised to give her a new hairstyle that was the rage in Paris, she would have lunch and rest before dinner. She said she didn't expect to see me again until then.

"You'll be much too busy."

"I can see that," I said, indicating my schedule. "How long are you going to be here?" I asked before she walked out.

"I'm leaving tomorrow. You'll have the whole place to yourself for a while, I think, although we never know. Good luck," she said.

I looked at the clock on the wall. I had ten minutes. I finished most of the fruit in the small bowl, drank some more coffee, and then picked up my schedule card and rose just as Randy returned.

"All alone? They deserted you on your first day. How sad," he said.

"I've been alone a lot longer than this," I told him.

"Poor pretty thing," he said, and began to clear

the table. "Well, I hope that will end soon and forever and ever," he muttered like a silent prayer. I watched him carefully pick up cups and plates in small, dainty moves, as though he was trying not to make a sound. He smiled at me and shrugged his left shoulder. "I'll see you at lunch. Don't worry. I'll help you in any way I can during the training." He winked and returned to the kitchen.

Exercise was the first thing on my schedule, so I headed for the gym, where I found Lance Martin doing stretches. He saw me enter but didn't stop. I stood waiting and watching for almost five full minutes.

"Sorry," he said, rising off the mat, "but it's very important to begin with stretching and not break your concentration. I'm Lance Martin." He held out his hand.

"Roxy Wilcox."

It wasn't much of a handshake, more like just touching as if he was afraid he'd pick up some evil bacteria.

"Have you done much physical training?"

"None," I said. "Unless you count brushing my teeth every morning and evening."

He nodded without breaking into a smile. I imagined a sense of humor wasn't part of the program.

"You don't look much older than sixteen. Mrs. Brittany's going to market you as the ingenue, I imagine."

"Me? Sweet, innocent, and virginal? I doubt it."

That brought a smile. He had a very strong mouth

and deep-set hazel eyes. He was dressed now in a pair of swimming trunks and a tight-fitting T-shirt, and I could clearly see the perfect symmetry of his muscles. I couldn't see an inch of fat on him. He looked unreal, more like a mannequin created to depict the ideal manly physique. I thought he had a waist only an inch or so wider than mine. Tanned, with neatly styled short dark brown hair, he was one of the healthiest-looking men I had ever seen, but there was something almost asexual about him at the same time. I didn't feel any erotic excitement or attraction. It was as if everything about him, even his facial expressions, had been sanitized. He was the sort of man who worried about his own well-being and health so much he probably avoided sex with anyone except another health and fitness mannequin. Mrs. Pratt needn't have been worried about my seducing him or him seducing me, I thought.

"Ingenue," he repeated, looking me over. "It's a matter of marketing, not reality. You have your sports bra and panties on?"

"Yes, why?"

"Please strip down to them," he said, then reached for the tape measure he had lying beside a clipboard on the mat. He looked up at me, surprised, when I didn't take off the sweatsuit instantly. "Don't tell me you're bashful," he said. "If so, you'd be my first."

"Hardly," I said, and took off the sweatsuit. He stared at me a moment, walked around me, and then began taking measurements of my thighs, calves, waist, arms, back, and shoulders. He looked at my breasts for a moment. "Are you firm under there?"

"What?"

"You're not one of those girls who go braless most of the time, are you?"

"Not most of the time, why?"

"Old gravity has a say in what shape you'll take. You can be defiant and free like some feminist if you want, but stretching won't be attractive."

"Thanks for the advice."

Ignoring me, he moved quickly to measure my breast size and picked up his clipboard to write down the numbers he had taken.

"You're pretty good right now," he said. "But I can tell you're going to have a little trouble with your thighs. Your calves aren't as tight as I would like them to be, and your arms, especially in the triceps area, will be a problem later on if you don't keep them tight. They're a bit loose now for a girl your age, in fact. I guess you're telling the truth when you say you don't exercise much."

"You can't tell that way. Everything about me is a bit loose for a girl my age," I muttered, reaching for a funny double entendre, but he acted as if he didn't hear or care.

"Okay, let's get started with the basics of stretching exercises. Then we'll design a daily routine for you to attack the areas we need to attack, and we'll get you into the pool and start building your stamina and strengthening your shoulders and your trapezius muscle. We'll get you up to speed before we turn you over to Brendon in a day or so. Horseback riding is terrific physical exercise, too. Have you done much of that?"

"I rode a pony at some fun fair once, and I've been on a carousel—does that count?"

"Hardly. You can joke if you want. You may not appreciate it yet, but you have to be prepared for horseback riding. It will get you aching in areas you never knew you had. It's great for stimulating muscles in the dorsal and abdominal regions that are seldom used in everyday life. Most people don't understand that it's a great calorie burner, too. They think the horse does all the work."

I looked around the gym at the various machines, each specifically designed for one area of the body.

"All of this sounds exhausting," I said.

He smiled, but it was a smile of condescension. "After a while, you'll find it all invigorating, just as I do. When you're on your mark, it's as good as sex," he said, and I thought maybe for him, that was definitely true, but it would never be for me. I think he saw my thoughts and laughed.

"Just kidding. Don't panic. But I will tell you this," he added almost in a whisper. "Women who are in top physical shape are better lovers. Even sex requires some endurance. One other thing," he added, pulling himself up even straighter to emphasize his point. "We don't use any steroids. No drug enhancements here."

"Good. I don't want to grow a mustache," I said dryly.

He didn't even smile. Was it healthy to be so damn serious about your work?

"Let's get to the stretching," he said. "As I said, it's how we begin every day. I'm proud to say I haven't had anyone I train pull a muscle or strain a tendon."

I found the stretching to be more difficult than anything else he had me do in the gym. It was actually very painful. He told me I had to work through the pain to eliminate it. I couldn't imagine ever standing with my legs straight and stiff and placing my palms flat on the floor, but he guaranteed that I would be doing it in less than a week.

As he took me through his plan of exercises specially designed for me, I laughed to myself, recalling how uncooperative and defiant I had always been in PE class. This year, my teacher, Ms. Lecter, gave me so many demerits that I was a candidate for failing PE in my senior year after only the first week of class, and that was something that could possibly threaten my graduation. Eventually, when that consequence didn't change my behavior, she took to doing the same thing most of my teachers did: she ignored me and didn't even bother to send me to the dean.

Again, maybe because my father made such a big deal about staying in shape, especially when you were young, I was recalcitrant. That description of me was actually on my report card. I hated almost any form of exercise, and I knew it irked the girls in my class who did work out hard and didn't have anywhere near the perfect figure I had. They glared at me with such envy and hate. It was so unfair to them. Why was I so blessed? All the Miss Piggies looked as if they would enjoy beating me to death in the locker room and eating me for lunch.

I came back at Papa whenever he chastised me for not wanting to walk to the store to get something Mama needed or even something I needed. He was especially enraged when he saw the grades I was getting in PE.

"How can you be failing this?" he cried, waving my multicolored report card in the air like something forbidden he had found in my possession. "What do you do?"

"Nothing, that's why."

"You're making a fool of yourself and fools of us!" he bellowed.

I looked at him calmly. "Who are you to talk, Papa? You're not exercising the way you should anymore, are you? You have a sedentary job, and you don't walk to work."

Of course, he rattled on about how he was working hard to keep us all comfortable and wanting nothing. He did try to get to the gym every weekend, but he wasn't happy about how he had to eat while entertaining clients. I think he was drinking more than he should. It was the first time I seriously considered the possibility that he regretted the choice he had made, after all. Perhaps by now, he could have been a high-ranking officer. I knew he harbored the belief that he could have been a better soldier than his older brother, who was still only a lieutenant colonel, whereas their father had become a general by his age.

After my gym workout, Lance gave me two bathing suits to try on. Both were a little tight. I think he did that deliberately so I would feel bad about my figure. The first one fit better. When I came out of the bathroom, he gave me one of his energy drinks. He was drinking some himself. I sat at the small table and sipped it. It wasn't bad. I had been expecting it to taste like some sort of medicine.

"You are a little soft in the abdomen," he said. "Most women don't usually gain their weight there, but you look like you might have that inclination. Are your parents overweight?"

"No. Well, my father is now, but my mother has a terrific figure for someone her age and always did."

"So you take after your father more," he said. The way he said it irked me.

"I don't think so."

He laughed. "You mean you don't wish so, but your genetics have a mind of their own. There's just so much we can do about that. What do you usually have for breakfast?" he asked, grimacing as though he already knew my answer.

"Coffee and something sweet. My mother is French. *Petit déjeuner* is usually a café au lait and a sweet roll or croissant. My father often has oatmeal or eggs and bacon." I smiled to myself, remembering his complaining about my mother's breakfast habits. Her comeback was always, "Who has more obesity, the French or Americans?"

Emmie ate more like he did, which pleased him.

"Yes, well, you'll get a good nutritional plan here,"

Lance said now. "You probably won't change your breakfast habits after you leave, but at least you'll supplement them, and you'll soon see why you need to. So have you done much swimming?"

"Almost none," I said. "My school had no pool, not that I would have gone into it, and we don't go to the beach much. Well, I should say, I don't. My younger sister loves it, and my mother is a good swimmer. When she was younger and living in France, the family would summer in Juan-les-Pins, where an uncle had a beach house. I've never been there, but she often talks about it. My father grew up in a military family and was . . ."

I stopped myself. Why was I talking so much about my mother and her family and my father? I felt certain most candidates for Mrs. Brittany's company were as cut off from their families as I was and certainly didn't talk about them much, if at all. Lance's deadpan look confirmed how little interest he had in hearing any of it.

"No," I admitted. "I'm not much of a swimmer. In fact, I hate putting my face in the water."

"We'll change that," he said casually.

"Why is swimming so important?" I asked, practically moaning. I really wanted to ask if he knew I'd be going swimming with a client or something.

"It's great exercise. I think you'd like it better than running laps around the property," he added. "You don't look like you've played team sports."

"I haven't, and I was never in the Girl Scouts or the Brownies, either. Like Groucho Marx said, I won't join any club that would have me as a member." He didn't break a line in his face or relax a lip. "You've heard of Groucho Marx?" I asked.

He shook his head. "Something tells me I should add some self-defense training to your schedule," he said.

"I'm not bad in that area," I said. Despite the trouble I was to get into on playgrounds and in locker rooms, my father had taught me some self-defense when I was younger. It was part of his upbringing in a military family, where it was as important as toilet training. I didn't tell Lance any of this. The thoughts just flowed quickly through my mind and off into space.

"Okay, we're set for the pool." He stood up. "Shall we start? I want to see how you freestyle."

I looked at the rest of my drink. I didn't want to say I'd rather go to the pool outside and lounge, but it was sure in my mind. For the moment, I was afraid to complain about anything. I followed him out and across the hall to the indoor pool. As soon as I got in and started, he stopped me. He jumped in beside me and showed me how to hold my head in the water, how to take a breath, and how to be more graceful with my stroke. He had me do it repeatedly until he was satisfied that I had a better technique. Then he watched me struggle to do a full lap and shook his head.

"You don't smoke, do you?"

"On occasion, some pot, some cigarettes. Once a cigar just to drive some girls nuts."

"Well, your lack of exercise and that behavior all show. You'll have to be able to do at least ten laps every day," he said.

I groaned. "Ten? You're kidding."

"Mrs. Brittany is adamant about her girls being in top shape, and under my guidance, they all are," he said with pride. "They don't get to work for her until they are," he added as an incentive. "Let's go again. You'll do ten today, no matter how long it takes us."

By the time I was finished in the pool, I was ready to go up to my suite and collapse, but instead, I was introduced to Olga Swensen, who guaranteed me that she would restore my energy. I was surprised at how strong she was for a woman who was about five feet five and maybe one hundred fifteen pounds, but her fingers were more like my father's when she went to work on my muscles. She used her own body-oil formula. It brought heat and relaxation to me almost immediately.

"You are blessed with great muscle structure," she told me. "Is this your first massage? You seem very uptight about it."

"Yes."

"I'm sure you'll have them once a week after you leave here, and not because anyone orders you to."

I couldn't disagree. When she was finished with me, I was no longer feeling crippled. I showered and changed, but when I went to put on my sweatsuit again, I saw that someone had brought down one of the informal dresses I had seen in my closet. It was hung beside the chair, where another bra and fresh panties, socks, and a pair of flats had been left for me to put on. There was even a new hairbrush.

I got dressed and stepped out of the room. Olga was talking to Lance. I had the feeling they were talking about me when they both paused to look at me.

"How do you feel? Hungry?" Lance asked.

"Yes," I said, surprised myself. "What do I do about my sweatsuit? I left it in there."

"You don't do anything about anything, Roxy. Someone will always look after you here."

"Tell that to Mrs. Pratt," I said, and they both laughed.

"Anyway, you go to lunch now," Lance said. "Mr. Whitehouse is waiting for you."

"Oh." I wasn't going only to be fed. I realized I was going to another class.

"See you in the morning," Lance said. "And expect to be quite charley-horsed," he called after me, "even with Olga's great massage."

He sounded as if he would be happy about it. I heard them both laugh.

Without having realized it, I had enlisted in the army, I thought. Maybe this was a secret special-forces unit using only women, and they pretended it was an escort service. I feel more like a female James Bond than potential arm candy.

Mr. Whitehouse rose from the smaller table when I entered the dining classroom. He was a short, rotund man with very light brown hair and well-trimmed sideburns. He wore a bright blue sports jacket, a dark blue tie, a white shirt, and blue slacks. His eyes were a dull gray and round like two unpolished quarters under his thick, black-framed glasses.

"I'm Nigel Whitehouse," he said, extending his hand. I took it and felt how soft his palm was. It was like shaking hands with a large makeup pad.

"I'm Roxy."

"I know who you are, Miss Wilcox. Your proper response should be 'I'm pleased to meet you.'"

"I'm pleased to meet you," I said dryly. *Oh, no, not another stuffed shirt in my life,* I thought. He reminded me of my science teacher, Mr. Rumsfield, whom everyone called "Rummy" because he always had a red nose like that of an alcoholic and, in fact, was suspected of drinking alcohol from his coffee thermos between classes.

"No, that's not good enough, my dear. You have to say it as though you really mean it, whether you do or not. In the line of work you're hoping to begin, the face you put on, especially at lunches and dinners, is far more important than the face you really have. It's all a matter of pleasing someone in the end, isn't it? So let's try again. This time, give me a smile that tells me you mean it. Convince me. Make me feel good about myself."

I started to smirk at his lecture but stopped myself. He was still holding my hand. I had the sense that anyone along the way of the training gambit I was to run could give me a failing mark and have Mrs. Brittany send me on my way. All my life, I hated to kowtow to anyone, not just my father. I suppose all the men I had as teachers became my

father in my mind in one way or another; even some
of the female teachers reminded me too much of him.
But I now realized that defiance and tantrums were
two things I had to leave outside the door of this
mansion the moment I signed Mrs. Brittany's agreement in her office.

I took a deep breath, smiled with all the warmth
and charm I could muster, and hit him with the French
version of "pleased to meet you": "*Enchanté.*"

Now he smiled, satisfied. "Much, much better.
And it wasn't hard for you to do, was it?"

"No, just different," I said. "There are so few
people I've been pleased to meet."

He didn't laugh aloud, but I saw the delight in
his eyes. Maybe my independent spirit was refresh-
ing to him.

He pulled out a chair for me. "Miss Wilcox."

"Thank you, Mr. Whitehouse," I said.

"*De rien.*"

"Does everyone here speak French?" I asked as he
went around to take his seat across from me.

"Everyone has a smattering of it, I imagine. As
difficult as it is for an Englishman like me to admit,
it's the language of style, eloquence, and culture. You
are most fortunate to have mastered it as your second
language already at home."

"You know my mother is French, then? You know
all about me?"

"As much as anyone else knows about you, but
getting to know each other that completely isn't why
we're here at the moment," he said. He said it sharply,

but he kept his smile. He looked at the table setting. "Don't touch your napkin yet. In most of the finer restaurants, the waiter will unfold it for you and place it on your lap. Now, do you know why you have three forks and how you choose which to use?"

"This fork is for dessert?" I said, touching the fork above my plate. "This one on the far left is for salad. We go from left to right with our silverware."

"Precisely." He nodded, but I thought he looked disappointed that I knew that much. "Your family held formal dinners?"

"Not very formal," I said. "But my parents are cultured people and have entertained. Eating well and properly has always been important to my mother, especially."

"Really? Well, you're a rare bird, indeed. Many of my students came from homes where they eat with their hands."

My surprise made him laugh.

"I'm kidding, of course, although we did have a Moroccan girl recently, and that wasn't far from an exaggeration in her case. But I suspect—I hope—that with you, we'll have that much less to do," he said, and looked up as Randy entered. He went right for my napkin and then uncorked the bottle of white wine.

"We're having poached salmon today," Mr. Whitehouse said. "A sauvignon blanc goes best with it. We're having one of my favorites from the Bordeaux region, a Château de Roques."

Randy poured my glass first and stood back.

"Go on, let's see you taste it," Mr. Whitehouse said in a challenging tone.

I smiled to myself confidently. If there was one thing we all knew how to do in my house (even Emmie, as young as she was, had begun and enjoyed doing it to please my parents), it was how to taste wine.

I held it up and checked its color and clarity, then swirled it in the glass, sniffed it, and took a sip, rolling it around in my mouth before aspirating through the wine by pursing my lips as if I were going to whistle (Mama's directions), drawing in some air. Finally, I swallowed it. Mr. Whitehouse sat smiling throughout. Randy's smile was warmer, his eyes full of pride, as if I were his sister or someone he cherished passing an important test.

"Well?" Mr. Whitehouse asked.

"May I see the bottle, Randy?"

He moved quickly and turned the label toward me.

"I've had this wine," I said. "The year before this one was a better year for sauvignon blanc, but this is adequate."

Randy's eyes nearly popped.

Mr. Whitehouse sat back. "Adequate? Well," he said, looking at Randy, "I'm impressed. Aren't you, Randy?"

"That I am, sir," Randy said. He quickly poured Mr. Whitehouse his glass. "But I must say that the moment I set my eyes on this one, I thought, now, here's a winner."

"Let's have a toast, then," Mr. Whitehouse said. "To a very promising new Brittany girl."

He reached forward to clink his glass against mine, and we both took sips.

"Do you know why we clink glasses with lunch and dinner guests?"

"Yes," I said.

His eyebrows looked as if they had been attached to invisible wires and hoisted with his surprise. "Tell me," he said.

I recalled my mother's explanation years ago. "People used to drink from the same bowl passed around a table, with the host drinking last. Sometimes there was a piece of bread in it, and he would eat that, too. It reinforced trust and loyalty and friendship. When people began drinking from their own glasses, they toasted, clinking them, to share good feelings for the occasion."

"I see. And what if you are too far across from another guest at the table?"

"You just hold your glass up and make eye contact," I said. "Some clumsy people reach too far and knock something over," I recited, just the way my mother had.

He laughed. "Who taught you all this?"

"My mother," I said.

"She ought to be working here," he muttered, both in admiration and in disappointment. I could see there was so much he wanted to be the one to tell me. I imagined that not too many candidates could give him the answer. Maybe Camelia could have, I thought, maybe not.

How ironic this was. In a real way, Mama might

have prepared me for the new life I was about to begin. After all, she was a Parisian. She was always interested in fashion and beauty, stylish clothes, wonderful wines, and good food. I was sure she never realized how much of an influence she had on me. It was as if I was always looking at her surreptitiously. I couldn't explain why I was so unwilling to admit how much I admired her and in how many ways I wanted to be like her. My best excuse was my resentment of how devoted she was to my father, how obedient, and how careful she was in not riling him up when she attempted to defend me or disagree with something he had said. I think that had a lot to do with why I was so determined to be disrespectful and defiant, even to her.

Whatever, I knew she would not appreciate how I was going to utilize the sense of style and appreciation of the finer things in life that she had bestowed upon me. You separate from your mother when you are born. You separate from her again when you begin an independent life of your own. That's expected and understood. You still hold on to each other in so many loving ways, but what I was doing now was leaving her so completely and clearly that it would be as if I had never been born.

Probably, I would please Papa after all, I thought with a mixture of anger and sadness.

Mr. Whitehouse went on and on about different foods, ways to eat them, how to sit properly at the table, and, building on what I had said about toasting across the table, how not to reach for things. He stressed the importance of using my napkin, keeping my lips cleared of any food remnants. I was tempted to ask him if it would be all right to enjoy something or even to digest it, but I kept my mouth shut and listened, even though I knew a good deal about what he was saying. He made it clear that he would be at the dinner table tonight precisely to be watching to see what I had absorbed from this first lesson and what I had not.

When lunch ended, I realized it was the first time I had sat and taken so long to eat a lunch, even at home.

"We did a lot more here than is normal," he explained, "but one thing you never want to do is eat too fast, rush through a lunch or a dinner like so many Americans do."

"Yes, that's been one of my mother's favorite comparisons between us and the French."

"Really? Did she happen to include the English with the Americans or the French?"

"The Americans," I said without hesitation. "Her favorite way to put it is that in America, we eat; in France, we dine."

He looked a little annoyed, but then he smiled. "You've been lucky. You're a few kilometers ahead of most of the girls who come to me. I congratulate you," he added with a slight bow of his head. "Now, how would you end this today?" he asked. Randy had returned to take some of our dishes and the empty bottle of wine. He paused to see what I was going to say.

Again, I thought about Mama and the times when she and I had gone to lunch with one of her friends or one of the wives of the men Papa worked with at the firm.

"*Merci*, Mr. Whitehouse. I enjoyed our lunch very much, and I hope we'll soon have the opportunity to do it again."

He bowed his head in appreciation. "You make me feel like a vestigial organ," he said.

I raced through my vocabulary and smiled when I remembered what that meant: an organ that had lost its purpose, its function.

"I'm sure that's not true, Mr. Whitehouse. I'm confident that there is always something I can learn from someone like you."

He beamed with such pleasure that his cheeks took on a rosy tint and his eyes twinkled like a newborn baby's. "Beauty, culture, charm, and diplomacy, too. Mrs. Brittany has indeed struck gold," he said.

He made me feel the best I had all day. I thanked him again and left.

I had twenty minutes to refresh myself. I could either go up to my suite or take a very short walk outside. My next assignment was to go to the library. There was a two-and-a-half-hour block set aside for that, and I was looking forward to it even less than I had looked forward to swimming. I'd better get some fresh air, I told myself, so I wouldn't pass out in a stuffy classroom setting, and I headed out one of the patio doors to feel the warmth of the sun and smell the newly cut lawns. I always liked that scent. It made me feel fresh and alive, which was why I went to Central Park every chance I had.

I walked slowly, with my head down, until I remembered how Mrs. Pratt had chastised me for doing that and looking so insecure.

It was then that I first saw her—the young girl who would change everything for me here.

And maybe everything for me for the rest of my life.

8

She was walking toward the pool. She wore an ankle-length robe, and a maid was following her, carrying towels, a bucket with a bottle of something in it, and what looked like a book held tightly inside the crook of her right arm. For a moment, I thought the young woman was Portia, but then I saw that she was using a cane and limping as if her left leg was shorter than her right. Her shoulder-length black hair lay softly over the white robe. I stepped forward to get a better look at her when she reached the pool and the maid set down her things and helped her take off the robe. She wore a bikini and looked like she had a beautiful figure. The maid prepared one of the cushioned lounges for her, laying out the towels. She sat for a moment with her back to me before lying back and taking what looked like suntan lotion from the maid.

It was still spring in New York, so I didn't imagine the pool was warm enough, unless, of course, it was heated. There was, however, a cloudless sky, and the sun was strong. I guessed that the UV index was high, and I recalled the short lecture Olga had given me about the skin damage the sun could do. After the girl covered herself in sun protection, she lay back and opened her book. The maid opened a bottle of what looked like rosé wine and poured her a glass. She unwrapped some crackers and set them out with some cheese before leaving to head back to the house.

I decided to walk over and see who she was. How come she hadn't been introduced to me? Mrs. Pratt said that Camelia and Portia were the only other girls here. Was she one of Mrs. Brittany's girls whom a client had hurt? Had Mrs. Brittany lied about that? Was that why she was not there to meet me and why her presence was being kept a big secret?

She turned as I approached and put her book down.

"Hi," I said.

"Hello."

"The pool can't be warm enough, can it?" I said.

"Oh, it's heated, but I don't swim much, anyway," she said, nodding toward her left leg.

I looked. It was clear to see that it was a flesh-colored prosthetic. I smiled, hiding my surprise and shock, and looked at her book. "Oh, I know that book. My high school English teacher gave it to me for extra credit. I read it, but I never handed in the book report," I said.

She laughed. "You remember that?"

"It was only last month," I said.

"Only last month? How old are you?"

"Nearly eighteen. Actually, ten days away now."

Her smile brightened. "Oh, I love birthdays. Eighteen is a very special one, too."

"Yes, especially for me," I said dryly.

"You just get here?" she asked.

"Yes. My first day, actually. I'm not halfway through with it yet. I hope I live through it."

"Oh, is it that bad?"

"Tough, not bad," I said, realizing that the place was probably bugged by people who would bring my comments back to Mrs. Brittany.

"That's good," she said. I saw that what she was drinking was not rosé wine but some sort of carbonated juice. "What's your name?" she asked.

"Roxy, Roxy Wilcox," I said.

"You sound like you're from the East Coast."

"Yes, New York City."

Before she could tell me her name or answer any questions I might have, I heard Mrs. Pratt shouting for me. She was beckoning vehemently, too.

"Uh-oh. The drillmaster is calling," I said.

The girl laughed.

I glanced back at her and smiled. "Maybe I'll see you later," I said, and hurried toward Mrs. Pratt.

"What are you doing out here?" she demanded.

"I thought I had some time to take a breather," I said. I turned and nodded toward the pool. "It's a beautiful day, and I'd just started talking to that girl when you called. Who is she? What happened to her leg?"

"There will be plenty of beautiful days for you if you do what you are told," she replied, ignoring my questions. "You should be going to the library. Professor Marx is waiting for you, and it's very impolite to be late for a college professor. In fact, punctuality is very important to Mrs. Brittany. Our girls don't keep their clients waiting a minute too long."

"Sorry," I said.

"Just keep your head about you," she insisted, "and concentrate on why you're here."

Why was she suddenly so angry? I was sure everyone was giving me good marks so far.

I glanced toward the pool again and then started back into the mansion.

"Who is that out at the pool? Is she another one of Mrs. Brittany's girls? What happened to her leg?" I repeated.

"I don't see why any of that would matter to you. I warned you before. You don't have time to socialize with anyone, and when you do, it will be part of your training, part of your evaluation."

"Even that?"

"Yes, even that." She looked toward the pool. "Now, forget about that girl, and go on to the library," she said, then turned and left me looking out at the pool for a few more moments before I continued into the mansion. The girl was still looking after me. She waved, but I was afraid to wave back. Maybe there was a camera pointed at me, and Mrs. Pratt would claim I had defied her orders.

When I arrived at the library, Professor Marx was seated at a table with books opened before him. He looked up with an expression of disapproval. I was familiar enough with that look from my teachers.

"You're nearly ten minutes late," he said. "I don't mean to be stern, but we have a lot to do in a short time."

"Why a short time?" I asked as I approached.

"We don't have a college semester is what I mean," he said, his eyes wide with impatience. "Okay, please have a seat." He nodded at the chair across from him. "This is my technique," he continued before I settled on the chair. "I'm going to review current events and ask you questions. From your answers, I'll know how much you know about the background of the situations, political, economic, artistic, and historical. On the basis of that, I'll assign you things to read, and during the following days, I'll review those things with you to see what you've absorbed and how well you could discuss any of the topics. How well we do here together is entirely up to you."

"That seems to be the mantra of this place," I muttered. "Everything is up to me."

He had one of the most animated faces I had ever seen. All of his thoughts found expression in the movements in his mouth, his eyes, and the shifting muscles in his cheeks and jaw. It was clear that if something annoyed him, everything moved at once. He reminded me of a pinball machine, the thoughts rolling around and triggering brightness in his eyes, a groan in his throat, and a wavy motion in his lips.

"Well, it's as true here as it is anywhere," he said. "What kind of a student have you been in school?"

"The kind that visits most teachers in their nightmares," I said dryly.

The lines around his jaw deepened. He took a deep breath and blew air through his closed lips. "You won't be giving *me* any nightmares," he warned. "I can assure you of that. Let's begin."

He opened the *New York Times* and started with the lead story. I sensed that Professor Marx expected me to be a complete airhead. However, despite my sullenness at breakfast and at dinner in my family's house, I was unable to totally ignore my father's commentaries on current events, especially whatever affected the economy. He was always very emotional about his beliefs. Mama was his perfect audience, of course, showing her own amazement at the things that amazed him and showing her pleasure at whatever pleased him. Sometimes she looked toward me, hoping I would join her chorus and please my father. More often than not, however, just to annoy him, I took the opposing point of view by deliberately asking the simplest questions about the most obvious things that might challenge his beliefs. I never showed any real emotion or allegiance to anything that he criticized, but my merely taking that side of the argument brought the blood to his face.

In short, although I favored reading the rag newspapers and magazines more, the sort found at supermarket checkout counters, I wasn't totally oblivious to what was happening in our country and in the world. As I replied to his questions, Professor Marx's assumptions about me began to lose steam. He struck me as someone who didn't like to be proven wrong about anything. To get me, he had to go deeper and deeper into an issue.

My father, because of his work, favored a more laissez-faire approach to business. I understood that, and some of our hottest arguments were sparked by my concern for the less fortunate—the grunts, as his

own father, the general, might call them, the foot soldiers, the noncommissioned officers, the enlisted men,
who in my opinion did the most work and bore the
most pain and responsibility.

"If we lived and thought the way you do," my
father fumed at me, "we'd be out on the streets, too."

Well, I certainly could say to him now, "You were
right. Where did I end up?"

Once again, I thought it was ironic. My father
would never dream that his frequent political lectures
in our dining room would help prepare me to find success in this new life I was choosing for myself, a life I
was certain he would despise.

My biggest weaknesses were with the arts, theater,
opera, even stage musicals. Professor Marx pounced
on those areas, piling up the reading material for me.
I had taken an art class in my sophomore year but
failed. The teacher, Mrs. Faber, was one of those teachers who found the most attentive students early on
and put all of their effort into teaching them. The rest
of us could stay or leave as far as she was concerned—
mentally, of course. I did my best daydreaming in her
class, and now I was about to pay for it. The introduc-
tion to art textbook Professor Marx gave me was the
thickest. I thought it weighed five pounds.

He made it clear that I had to learn and be able to
identify famous arias from great operas and be somewhat familiar with their plots. He wanted me to have a
"decent knowledge of Broadway theater."

"You'll come in here and listen to them during
your free time."

"I have free time?" I asked.

He ignored that. "Many of the men you will escort will be much older. They won't be into hip-hop or Lady Gaga. They'll be pleased if you know Frank Sinatra, Tony Bennett, Dean Martin, and Sammy Davis, Jr. Do you know anything about any of them?"

"My father's favorite in that group is Tony Bennett, but he listens to all of them. My mother loves Edith Piaf."

"Oh," he said, taken aback. "Well, that's good exposure."

"Do you know Patachou?" I asked.

He bristled a bit. "I'm not here for you to interrogate," he said.

I shrugged. "I just thought you might know something about French music, since you seem to know Edith Piaf."

"Of course I know about French music, and I know about Edith Piaf. That's not the point. The point is what you know and what you have to learn, not what I know and what I have to learn."

I hid my smile behind one of the books he had shoved my way.

He then leaped across topics to deliberately make me feel inferior, I thought. He was on to geography, asking me questions like Alex Trebek on *Jeopardy!* There was no way I was going to do well identifying world rivers and capitals of countries other than the U.K., France, Germany, Russia, Spain, and Italy. I did remember Athens, but I was lost when it came to the Middle East and the Far East.

Before what had become four times worse than any of the classes I hated at school ended, he tossed mathematical concepts at me. I was practically silent. Finally, even he had endured enough. Ten minutes before our time was up, he decided to end it with a deep sigh.

"We'll meet tomorrow, the same time—only on time, please."

"You don't expect me to learn all this by then," I said, indicating the pile of material he had shoved my way.

"Not all of it, but enough to let me know you're serious and I'm not wasting my time and Mrs. Brittany's money," he replied.

"You won't be," I said, rising. Then I smiled at him. "You really ought to look up and listen to Patachou. My mother remembers her parents playing her records constantly when she lived in Paris. If you like Piaf, you'll enjoy her."

He just stared at me. I nodded and left the library, struggling to carry everything he had assigned me to read. Just as I entered the hallway, however, Randy appeared and came rushing over.

"Oh, you poor thing, turned into a beast of burden. Here, let me help you," he said, taking the pile out of my arms. "I'll bring this to your room. Where do you go next?" he asked as we started toward the stairway.

"I'm supposed to be at the salon in fifteen minutes. The only thing this place is missing is bells to signal the end of one class and the start of another," I said, and he laughed. I followed him.

"The first few days are always the hardest." He paused to turn back to me. "With anything," he added.

"Was that the way it was for you?" I asked when we reached the top of the stairway.

"Oh, yes, but for different reasons. When Mrs. Brittany found me, I had just broken up with someone. I had a shattered heart, but she knew how to help put me together again. That's her real talent, you know," he said in a whisper.

"What's her real talent?"

"Matchmaking. That's why she's so successful at this escort business. She knows exactly which one of her girls will be most successful with this one or that one."

"If she's so good at matchmaking, why didn't she ever remarry?" I asked.

"Oh," he said, smiling, "I can't imagine any one man with whom she would be satisfied for a long period of time. She's too . . ."

"Bossy?"

"Let's just say independent. It's a kinder term," he told me, and winked.

We paused at my door, and I opened it. He brought in my books and magazines and put them on the vanity table.

"This all right?"

"No. I'd rather they were locked in the closet, but I have no choice," I said. "That's my homework. I thought I had escaped all that."

He laughed. "You never escape all that." He looked around. "This is my favorite suite and I think

Mrs. Brittany's, too. She must think you have great potential if she's favoring you. One thing she hates most of all is wasting her time. She has a wonderful head for business, as does Mrs. Pratt. Between the two of them, with the special inside information they get," he added sotto voce, "they've built quite a little financial empire. She doesn't have to work another day of her life, but that woman loves what she does. I think she believes she is a female Cupid or something, destined to provide opportunities for pleasure and happiness, even love, as I can attest to."

"How is that?"

"She introduced me to Ron Carter. He's the house manager, in charge of overseeing just about everything here. At the time, he was going through a bad breakup, too. I'm sure you'll meet him soon. We stay in the west end of the mansion, as do most of the staff."

We started out of the suite.

"I saw a young woman today for a moment," I said. "She went out to the pool to sun herself and read. I noticed she needed a cane and had a maid carry out her things for her. When I went to speak with her, I saw she had a prosthetic leg. Is she another one of Mrs. Brittany's girls? Maybe to satisfy some weird fetish one or more of her clients have?"

"Oh, goodness, no. Heaven forbid. She's Mrs. Brittany's granddaughter."

"Granddaughter? No one mentioned a granddaughter. All I was told was that Mrs. Brittany married a man, a count or something, who was much older, and he had died."

"Yes, but they had a daughter, and she had a daughter, the girl you saw. Her name is Sheena. Mrs. Brittany disapproved of her parents naming her that, but she disapproved of most everything they did." He shook his head. "Sheena. What a tragedy there."

"What happened to her?" I asked as we started down the stairs.

"When she was only twelve, she contracted bone cancer. The hope was that surgery to remove the tumor would end it, but it didn't, and as a last resort, her leg was amputated."

"Oh. That explains it. How sad."

"Mrs. Brittany is arranging for her to have the most up-to-date prosthesis."

"So is she just visiting now?"

"No, no, she's lives here. She's in Mrs. Brittany's wing of the mansion. She's a very sweet girl."

"How old is she?"

"A little more than eighteen. Mrs. Brittany always blamed her daughter for what happened. Apparently, Sheena had been complaining for some time about pain, but her mother was not only a selfish bitch, she was also a heavy drinker. She neglected her so long that the options were limited when she finally did get to treatment. Mrs. Brittany's daughter became a severe alcoholic, left her husband—or he left her—and basically neglected Sheena while she was recuperating."

"What happened then?"

"Mrs. Brittany had her daughter committed to the Betty Ford Clinic in California, but she ran away from there and went off with some man she had met. If she's still alive, she's somewhere in Asia. So Mrs. Brittany took on the upbringing of her granddaughter."

"What about the husband, Sheena's father?"

"He remarried and has a new family. Mrs. Brittany blames him, too. Sheena is a very bright young woman and otherwise, as you saw, very attractive. She was basically home-schooled, however," he said softly, "and I'm afraid she's a bit socially retarded. She lives vicariously through the novels she reads and the movies she watches. Mrs. Brittany is overly protective of her. We rarely see her on this side of the mansion. She's never at dinner here. She's very shy and withdrawn. I'm practically the only one who has much to do with her.

"I'm telling you all this so you won't make the mistake of trying to have any more contact with her. That could be . . . fatal."

"Fatal?"

"To your ambitions," he said. "Oh, look at the time. I don't want to be blamed for causing you to be late. Enjoy your session with Madame Laffette."

I watched him walk off quickly, and then I headed for the salon, thinking after I had heard all he had told me that no amount of money, no position of power, nothing guarantees happiness, but this wasn't the time to become philosophical. I had things to do.

I was hesitant, even timid, about meeting Madame Laffette. I was afraid she would remind me too much of Mama, being that they were both Parisians. However, I had nothing to fear. Claudine was probably not more than ten years older than I was, if that much. She wore a turquoise cowgirl hat with sequins, a baggy white blouse, and a pair of very tight designer jeans. Spilling out from under her hat were slightly curled medium-length strands of blond hair. Her lips were too thin, but she had beautiful, even striking gray-blue eyes and a nose as small and perfect as mine. She shook her head the moment she saw me enter.

"Who has been doing your hair, *ma chère*?"

"No one," I said.

"It shows."

"I was already told that. What, is everyone given the same script?"

She laughed. "I know who told you. *S'il vous plaît*," she said, indicating the chair. "We have a lot to do." She looked at her watch. "*Mon Dieu*."

She ran her fingers through my hair.

"Dry, dirty, split ends. You American girls," she added, shaking her head.

"Not everyone has been through what I've been through these past days, and I haven't had time to do much more than run a brush through it since I arrived here."

I could have washed my hair the night before, but I was too lazy, exhausted, and overwhelmed. I didn't tell her that.

"Whatever. We will work a miracle, will we not?" she said, and turned on the water in her sink. "So, your mother, she is Parisian?"

"*Oui.*"

She gave me a look of disapproval. "A Parisian,

and she didn't bring you up to take better care of your hair?"

"No, she did. She would never let me go out of the house looking like this. I always took better care of myself before I left home, mainly because of her, but I have been on my own and not under good circumstances, *comprenez?*" I surprised myself at how vehemently I defended my mother.

"Ah, *mais oui*. Well, then, we will fix you up, make you the daughter of a Parisian again."

I didn't want to say how good it felt to have my hair washed, but it brought back the memories of all the times Mama would do it and, while she did it, talk about her own youth and her mother and the way she had taken care of herself, too. Claudine talked while she worked, but I barely heard anything she said. My eyes were tearing over, but I fought it back, hoping she wouldn't see. When she was finished, she stood back and looked at me a moment and then nodded to herself.

"You are perfect for this new hairstyle," she said.

"What new hairstyle?"

"What I have in mind for you," she said. I could see I had no choice in the matter. Mrs. Brittany obviously had full faith in her.

She began to cut, telling me she was cutting a foundation layer at the base of my neck, explaining as she went along. She cut it layer by layer, using a razor to provide texture and a softer modern edge. After that, she used a paddle brush with thick bristles to avoid a round, helmet look and instead make my hair look flat and shiny. She put in the mousse and brushed my hair down. When she finished blow-drying, she worked meticulously with her scissors to perfect the cut. She finished off by working some pomade into my hair. When I looked at myself from all sides, I was astounded by the change.

"You worked your miracle, Madame Laffette. *Merci beaucoup.*"

"I think Mrs. Brittany will approve," she said. "Now, sit at the vanity table, and we'll work on your makeup."

Mrs. Pratt came in just when we were close to finishing.

"Your dinner dress is on your bed," she told me. "The shoes are beside the bed. Mrs. Brittany has returned, and she also brought you some perfume to try. Dinner will be served in the main dining room in two hours. Mrs. Brittany will see you first in an hour and a half in her office. Besides Portia and Mr. Whitehouse at dinner, there will be a gentleman guest. He's an old friend, and Mrs. Brittany relies on his opinion about a great many things, not least of all her new girls."

"Am I supposed to be nervous?"

"Of course. How you behave when you are nervous is very important," she replied. She looked at Claudine. "*N'est-ce pas?*"

Claudine laughed. I looked up at her and then smiled myself. It seemed that even my breathing was being examined and judged here. I began to wonder if candidates for the CIA were more analyzed. Mrs. Brittany was one careful businesswoman, but looking around at what she had, I couldn't think of how to criticize her for it.

"By the way," Mrs. Pratt said, looking at me now, "you're very beautiful."

I didn't blush. It was more like something that took my breath away. Mrs. Pratt certainly had seen very attractive women around here. To find myself now included in that category filled me with more pride and happiness than I could ever have imagined for myself since I had left home.

"*Merci, madame.*"

"*De rien,*" she said, and left us.

"Well. If Madame Pratt approves of you, Mrs. Brittany usually will as well. Felicitations."

"I'm not there yet, Claudine, but *merci.*"

I rose, gazed at myself in the mirror again, and smiled at her.

Whenever anyone gave me a compliment in front of my father, he would always check his own happiness and tell me not to get a swelled head. Sometimes he would come back with something inane, like "Beauty is only skin deep." Once, a friend of his at work, Morty Kasner, retorted with, "Right, but who wants to go any deeper, anyway?"

It brought laughter to the table but not to my father. He just glared at me to wipe the satisfied smile off my face. *You can wash it off my face,* I thought, *but not off my heart.*

I was glad I had a little time to myself finally. It wasn't until I got up to my suite and flopped in the soft-cushioned armchair that the weight of all I had done that day announced itself in my legs and my shoulders. I thought I would just close my eyes for a few moments, but I didn't open them again until I felt someone shaking my shoulder.

"I had a feeling you might have dozed off," Mrs. Pratt said. "You should be getting into your dress. Mrs. Brittany wants to see you in ten minutes in her office, and don't forget to use the perfume she brought for you."

"Sorry," I said. "It's been a long day."

"And it's not over yet," she pointed out. "This is why you have to get yourself in better shape. Our girls don't peter out on their clients."

I nodded and took a deep breath to get myself up and dressed. I told myself I was only half joking when I compared what I was going through here with some army boot camp with someone like my father shouting orders and threatening KP duty. How did they expect me to go through all I had gone through and then attend a formal dinner, drink wine, and return to this room to do the homework Professor Marx had assigned? Was all of this designed to discourage me? Was this how they weeded out their so-called candidates?

I found the perfume, tested it, liked the scent myself, and sprayed it on. I checked my hair quickly, and then, literally nine minutes later, I was on my way down to Mrs. Brittany's office. I imagined I was about to get another lecture in preparation for this dinner. I knocked on the closed doors and waited to hear her give me permission to enter. She opened the doors herself and stood back.

Sitting there on the settee, wearing a very pretty turquoise dress and with her hair pinned up, was Mrs. Brittany's granddaughter. Surely she had told on me, I thought. Randy's words came rushing back: "It could be fatal."

I felt my heart sink.

Was it possible?

After all this, I had been brought here to get my walking papers.

9

"Don't just stand there in the doorway," Mrs. Brittany snapped. "Come in and close it behind you."

I did so slowly and looked again at her granddaughter. She was smiling at me, and not the sort of smile someone who had come to hurt you wore. It wasn't condescending or sly. It was soft, anticipating, making her look hungry to receive a smile back. I breathed some relief but still felt myself trembling inside, expecting trouble.

"Hi again," I said.

"Hi. Oh, look at your hair. I might not have recognized you. Yes, I would," she quickly corrected. "Oh, I never got a chance to tell you my name. It's Sheena."

"Please be quiet for a few moments, Sheena," Mrs. Brittany told her. She turned to me. "Sit," she commanded, as if she were giving orders to a well-trained dog. She walked around her desk. Since she didn't tell me where to sit, I sat next to Sheena, who looked delighted about it.

Mrs. Brittany wore an elegant beaded long evening dress with a diamond bracelet on her right wrist. All I could think was that she must have had a hairstylist on board whatever plane she had taken back from Boston. Not a strand was out of place.

"Sheena knows my rules about fraternizing with my girls in training," she began, giving Sheena a chastising glance. Sheena looked down but held her soft smile. "Normally, I remember to mention that to my trainees, but I forgot to do so with you. I didn't anticipate that you would have time to wander about the estate."

"I didn't wander about, Mrs. Brittany. I just stepped out for some air, and besides, I don't have infectious diseases," I said.

"Don't be insolent," she said sternly. Sheena glanced at me, and in that glance, she clearly told me to be still, too.

Mrs. Brittany's face changed to a much calmer expression. She glanced at Sheena and then back at me. "Some of this, perhaps all of it, can be attributed to your young age. Most of the girls who come here are older than you and have had more substantial experiences. In fact, you're the youngest girl I've agreed to take on. Technically, I could be accused of kidnapping, I suppose."

I wanted to agree. At times today, I had felt that way, but I didn't want to even imply it. "That's ridicu—" I bit down on my lower lip and stopped talking instantly.

She nodded. "Accordingly, I'm going to make an exception in this case, mainly because Sheena has requested it," she said. "Adamantly. Apparently, she sees qualities in you that I have yet to uncover."

I looked quickly at Sheena, who kept her gaze on the floor, her soft smile frozen.

"Frankly, I don't see where you would have any time to fraternize, anyway, but in the event that you do have some time, you have my permission to spend it with Sheena. While you still remain here," she added sternly. "Sheena understands that your time here could be cut short dramatically at any time."

Sheena looked up quickly, a bit frightened. I saw that it softened the expression on Mrs. Brittany's face quickly.

"However," Mrs. Brittany continued, "I have taken another thing into consideration. From the reports I'm getting, you have made a good first impression on everyone with whom you have been in contact, including Professor Marx, who I know can be quite difficult."

I pressed my lips together to keep myself from laughing. Difficult? His mother surely had second thoughts the day he was born. He had said something nice about me? It must have been through clenched teeth with fingers crossed behind his back.

"In that regard, Sheena might be of some assistance to you."

"Oh?"

"She happens to be an excellent student and might help you with your work with Professor Marx."

"I would welcome that," I said. "I would welcome any help with Professor Marx."

Sheena brought her hand to her mouth to smother a giggle. She looked more like a younger teenage girl, even a girl in grade school, and I recalled what Randy had said about her social skills and experiences.

"In short," Mrs. Brittany continued, "you have my permission to go to the east wing of the mansion, which is normally off-limits to everyone but the maids and Randy." She shot up from her seat. "For now, Sheena will return to her suite."

"She's not coming to dinner with us?" I asked.

Mrs. Brittany's eyes widened. "Of course not. Your dinner is part of your training. This isn't some party."

I nodded and turned to Sheena. "Well, maybe we can see each other tomorrow. I have all of my home-work in my suite," I added, and swung my eyes to communicate how much there was.

"I hope so," she said. "Good night, Grandmother, and thank you."

"I'll be up much later tonight, Sheena. I have some important things to address after dinner, so don't wait up for me," Mrs. Brittany told her.

Sheena looked at me, a little embarrassed by the way Mrs. Brittany spoke to her. I thought that despite what Randy had told me about her social skills, she didn't like being treated like a child. I immediately sympathized with her and winked. She smiled again and started out.

When she had left, Mrs. Brittany came around her desk and leaned against it.

"All right. There are things you have to know now. My granddaughter is a cancer survivor," she began. There would never be any equivocating when she spoke, I thought. The woman told everything like it was. This was what Mr. Bob meant when he said she suffered no fools.

I thought it was probably a good idea to play dumb and not reveal how much Randy already had told me, so I acted a little surprised.

"She developed a form of bone cancer. Initial surgery, chemo, and radiation did not stop it, and finally, the decision to amputate had to be made. We keep her carefully screened, of course, and until now, she's done fine. She is examined at least twice a year by the best doctors. She's adjusted to her . . . problem as well as anyone can expect a young, beautiful girl to adjust to such a thing."

"She is very beautiful."

"Yes. Anyway, because of her condition, she's been home-schooled. I wasn't going to submit her to any derision, even in a private school. I know how mean young girls can be to each other, especially girls who saw how beautiful she is."

"You're right about that," I said.

"I know when I'm right. I don't need to be assured of it," she snapped. She could use words like a bullwhip, I thought.

"Sorry, I just . . ."

"Just listen." Her eyes narrowed. "You had better start learning how to be quiet and listen. Don't be so eager to let other people know what you're thinking. That's a weakness I want you to lose and lose fast."

"Okay."

"Where was I? Her mother was a drunk. Her

father had spoiled my daughter rotten and made excuses for her constantly. She met someone not much better after they divorced, so I knew that relationship wouldn't last, either. Anyway, she's gone; he's gone. I'm all Sheena has."

"I understand." I pressed my lips together and then in my defense quickly added, "I just meant, I know what it is like to feel abandoned."

"Please, there is no comparison. You are a healthy young woman."

I nodded. "Sorry."

She didn't change expression. "This is a great deal more information than I intended to give you, to give any of my girls, but as I said, Sheena saw something in you today that she liked, and goodness knows, I want that child to have some pleasure in her life.

"So, tread softly here," she continued, her eyelids narrowing with threat again. "Be careful about what sorts of things you tell her. She's been very protected and is therefore very vulnerable. Do you get my point?" she asked sternly. "Or do I have to make it even clearer?"

"It's not necessary. I understand what you're saying, Mrs. Brittany. I'm not someone from the gutter. I admit I have been rebellious and defiant, but I've never really gotten into serious drugs or some other things some of my so-called well-behaved classmates have gotten into, including pregnancies kept hush-hush. The truth is, they always bored me with their ideas of what was exciting and what wasn't. I wasn't going to end up in any group therapy," I said.

She nearly smiled. "Yes, you were always a mile or so above them, I imagine. It's what I see in you. Don't prove me wrong," she said, with the lead weight of a heavy threat coating the words.

"I don't intend to."

"We all have good intentions," she muttered, and went to her office bathroom.

She kept the door open, and I watched her fix her lipstick and smooth some of her makeup on her cheek.

"It's time to go to dinner," she told me when she stepped out. "Don't slouch," she ordered when I stood up. "You do that when you feel nervous or insecure. You might as well announce it. The men you will be with want to see self-confidence in their escorts."

I straightened up.

"When you look at someone, look directly into their eyes," she continued. "Pull your shoulders back, and hold yourself as if you were a member of royalty. Men like that especially, even though they claim to be more comfortable with an airhead. That's good for a ten-minute ride but not for the ride we give our clients. Men of distinction, wealth, and stature like to know the women they are with will give them a full ride for their money, and it's significant money. Besides, it keeps them on their toes, challenges them, and makes them more competitive, and we all do better when we're competitive, *comprenez, ma chère?*"

"*Mais oui, madame*. I am ready to compete. Even with you," I said.

"*Touché*," she said.

We left her office.

"Now for the business at hand," she continued. "You are going to meet a man who is ridiculously wealthy. And too often ridiculous as well. You've heard the expression, 'He was born on third base but thought he had hit a triple'?"

"Yes, I've heard my father use it about some of his clients," I said.

"Well, Decker Farmingham was born on home plate and thought he had hit a grand slam. At the age of forty-one, he inherited seven hundred and fifty million dollars, much of it held in foreign banks. He's invested in everything from commodities to precious metals to private security forces. His father left a cadre of brilliant financial managers at his disposal, and his net worth is now off the charts. He has so many shell companies that it's impossible to determine how wealthy he really is. Somehow he's been able to remain outside the sweep of the Fortune Five Hundred. He's under the radar, as they say."

She looked to see if I was following her, and I nodded.

"He's like one of the medieval kings who married for either political or economic reasons and, of course, to have progeny. He's fifty-two now and has three sons in various executive positions in his businesses. You will never meet anyone who has been to more places, met more powerful people, and lived in more beautiful homes."

She paused to stress what she was going to say next.

"And who's been with more beautiful women.

He is my only business partner, a silent partner but a partner. When he's available and I have a new girl to consider, such as yourself, I invite him to meet her. However, I wouldn't tolerate anyone having veto power over any of my decisions. I do respect his opinions occasionally, and we're very fond of each other, despite his obscene wealth," she said with a small impish smile.

Moments later, we entered the formal dining room. It was the grandest room I had ever been in. Now that I saw it, I realized how ridiculous it was for me to think the classroom dining room was the main dining room. This was probably four times the size, with very large works of art on the walls and two enormous teardrop chandeliers over the long table that could definitely seat twenty-five or more people. There was a large red and black oval rug beneath and around it. On both sides of the room were beautiful matching armoires filled with dishware, glasses, and cups. Both sides also had tall windows with black velvet drapes. Portia and Mr. Whitehouse were on one side, and Mrs. Brittany's guest, Decker Farmingham, was seated on the other. The place at the head of the table was obviously reserved for Mrs. Brittany.

"You'll sit next to Decker," Mrs. Brittany told me as we approached.

The men stood. With a wide smile on his face, Randy stood off to the right, dressed in a tuxedo, watching us enter. He winked at me.

"May I say you look more beautiful than ever," Decker Farmingham told Mrs. Brittany.

"You may say it, Decker, but no one with half a brain would believe it. I know what's lost when we age," she replied, and he laughed. His eyes were on me. "This is our newest potential Brittany girl," she continued, "Roxy Wilcox. Roxy, this is Decker Farmingham."

He held out his hand for mine. He wasn't a particularly good-looking man. I thought his nose too long and his mouth too soft for a man. He had rather ordinary brown eyes and thick, styled dark-brown hair with just a touch of gray around his ears. The gray looked suspiciously dyed, something a man might do to appear older, wiser. I didn't think he was quite six feet tall. He was chubby-faced, with a little too much of a paunch. I recognized that he was wearing an Armani suit. Two rings glittered on his left hand, one a diamond pinkie ring and another that was probably a wedding band, also with tiny diamonds.

When I gave him my hand, he held it in his soft fingers and stared at me for so long before speaking that I was sure any other girl I knew would either giggle or turn and run.

"Don't memorize every cell in her body," Mrs. Brittany said.

He laughed but held on to my hand when he turned to her. "I think our Mr. Bob is a pure genius," he said, and then smiled at me. "Pleased to meet you, Roxy."

"*Enchanté,*" I said. I glanced at Mr. Whitehouse. He took on the look of a proud father, nodding at Mrs. Brittany to be sure he received some credit for my social etiquette. She ignored him and sat.

Mr. Farmingham pulled out my chair for me.

"*Merci*," I said.

"Well, well, well," Mr. Farmingham said, taking his seat. He looked at Mrs. Brittany. "Looks like you've borrowed a page from Nabokov. Might be a good idea."

He turned to me and smiled to see if I understood or appreciated his cleverness.

"I'm hardly Lolita," I said, and Mrs. Brittany laughed heartily. "At least, at the beginning of the novel."

"There's a bit of fresh honesty," she said.

Mr. Farmingham took on a shade of crimson. "Well, she doesn't look much older. I thought you were trying for that. Lolita is a popular male fantasy, you know," he told me. "I admit to having it myself."

I looked at Portia. She was staring with interest and amusement. I had the sense that she had gone through some similar initiation ceremony.

Randy came around to set my napkin on my lap. "You're beautiful," he whispered. I smiled and gave him a slight nod before turning to Decker.

"Yes, I know about that male fantasy, Mr. Farmingham. I often saw that fantasy working in the eyes of some of my high school teachers and even some of my father's friends. Let me say this about it. I am confident that I can be whatever Mrs. Brittany wants me to be."

He nodded, impressed. Portia widened her smile. Nigel Whitehouse looked a little overwhelmed.

"You have no reservations about fulfilling such fantasies?" Mr. Farmingham asked.

"Not really. It's a bit like being Cinderella, don't you think?"

"It doesn't always end at midnight, and you're not always with a prince," he countered.

I shrugged. "The point is, it ends," I said.

"Well said," he said. "I must admit that you women are a total mystery to me. The ones I think are simple turn out complicated, and the ones I expect to be complicated turn out to be simple."

"Maybe you should not go by first impressions," I told him.

"Well, now it seems I'm getting advice from Lolita."

"You asked for it," Mrs. Brittany said. She turned to Randy and nodded. The dinner service began. Two maids brought out our salads, and Randy opened the first bottle of white wine.

"I love what Claudine did with your hair," Portia said.

"Thank you. So do I. She had a lot to repair," I added, looking to Mrs. Brittany. If something I said pleased her, I saw it in her eyes first, and sometimes only there. Right now, she was keeping back any reactions to anything. What self-control, I thought. What power. Suddenly, I wanted to be just like her.

Randy came over to me with the opened bottle of wine. Apparently, Mr. Whitehouse wanted to show off my wine-tasting skills and had already arranged for me to be the one served first to do the tasting. He was probably taking credit for it, but I didn't care.

"Go on," Mrs. Brittany said when I hesitated.

Mr. Farmingham folded his arms across his chest

and sat back to watch. I went through it just as I had done with Mr. Whitehouse at lunch. And then I surprised them all.

"I think this is a bit too woody," I said.

Mr. Whitehouse looked shocked. Portia glanced quickly at Mrs. Brittany for her reaction, but Mr. Farmingham sat forward and lifted his glass for Randy.

He tasted it, thought a moment, and nodded. "She's right," he said. "Bring another bottle, Randy, from another case, please."

"Right away, Mr. Farmingham."

"It happens sometimes," Mr. Farmingham said.

I looked at Mrs. Brittany, too. She didn't smile, but she didn't seem angry. She looked more thoughtful now. Then she turned sharply to Mr. Whitehouse.

He raised his hands. "I can't take full credit. She knew a lot more about wine than most girls I've tutored," he confessed. "Her mother . . ."

"I'm not criticizing her, Nigel. I wanted to hear your reaction. That's all."

"Oh. Well, so far, quite impressed has been my reaction," he said, looking at me.

"Thank you, Mr. Whitehouse," I said.

"Well, now," Mr. Farmingham said, turning to me. "You should know that I own a few vineyards in France."

"Really? *Où sont-ils?*"

"Two in Bordeaux and one in Bergerac. Have you been to those regions?"

"No, only to Paris when I was much younger."

"Perhaps one day I'll give you a personal guided tour."

"I've been to your vineyard in Bergerac," Portia said.

He looked at her and smiled. "I heard. I was told after the fact, or I might have joined you and your company. Since I knew him, I should have—"

Mrs. Brittany cleared her throat specifically to end that discussion. Decker looked at her and sat back. I was impressed with the great care taken to hide the names of any client and any other details.

Randy hurried in with a new bottle of white wine. Everyone waited as he uncorked it and poured it into a new glass for me.

I tasted it the proper way, deliberately taking my time, and then nodded. "Much better, *merci*."

He poured Mr. Farmingham a new glass, and he had the same reaction.

"Well, with such a display of beauty and talent, I'd say you were on your way to becoming a Brittany girl."

"On her way," Mrs. Brittany said, fixing her eyes on me, "but not yet there."

"Of course. You can lose someone potentially very valuable by putting her out too soon. The same is true for a good racehorse, Roxy."

"Well, I've been compared to lots of things, Mr. Farmingham, but this is the first time I've been compared to a horse."

Portia and Mr. Whitehouse held their breath because I didn't sound amused.

"You'll have to forgive Mr. Farmingham, Roxy. He's been around animals too long," Mrs. Brittany said.

"Maybe because he's in high finance," I suggested, thinking about how my father described some of his clients.

There was a thick moment or two of silence, and then Decker Farmingham roared.

"I like this girl!" he cried. He pulled back and turned fully to me. "I'll give you my test. If you could take nine hundred thousand euros or a million dollars tonight, which would you take?"

I saw Portia smile. She was confident that I would not know the answer, but she did not know my father was in finance.

"With the exchange rate as it is right now, I'd take euros, of course, but I wish you would have offered Norwegian kroner as well."

His eyes widened. He turned to Mrs. Brittany. "How about I have a first go at this and take her to Nilo da Fonseca's party in Rio in July?"

"She won't be ready that soon," Mrs. Brittany said.

"Oh, I—"

"You just made the point with racehorses, Decker. You don't want to do anything prematurely, do you?" she asked, her eyes like cold steel. "I think I know best when one of my girls is ready and when she is not."

He nodded and put up his hands. "Who am I to challenge success?" he said. "Well, do keep me in mind when she is ready." He smiled at me, and we all began to eat our salad.

I could feel everyone's eyes on me, watching every bite I took, how I used my dinnerware, sipped my wine, used my napkin, and waited to swallow what I had in my mouth before I spoke. Before the main course was to be served, Randy brought out a bottle of red wine. I was surprised but happy to see that it was a familiar California pinot noir. My father used to tease my mother, comparing it to some of the better French pinot grapes in Burgundy. A California wine had won a major tasting contest against some of the best French wines, in fact.

Once again, I was given the task of approving the wine. It was as good as I recalled, and I said so. The main dish was a pork tenderloin with a reduction sauce. It was better than any I had eaten at home or at the finer restaurants Papa occasionally took us to in New York. Everyone thought it was delicious, and Gordon Leceister, Mrs. Brittany's chef, was brought out to be congratulated. Mr. Farmingham threatened to steal him away.

"I'll pay you twice as much as she pays you," he told him.

Mrs. Brittany sat silently, looking forward.

Gordon glanced at her and smiled. "Yes, but I hardly have time to spend the money I make here," he said.

"You practiced that response," Decker Farmingham accused, pointing his forefinger. He turned to me. "What do you think, Roxy? Doesn't it sound like they prepared for me? Rehearsed every answer?"

This was surely my lucky day. My mother's

favorite movie was *Casablanca*, probably because of all the French background and material in it. We had watched it together at least a dozen times. My father thought it was too soapy and romantic and usually read or left the room.

"I think he stole Sam the piano player's line from *Casablanca*," I said. "You know, when Signor Ferrari tries to steal him away from Rick's Café."

No one spoke.

Decker Farmingham stared at me a moment and then nodded. "She's right," he said. "I remember that now. If you don't make it here, Roxy, you'll come work for me in one capacity or another."

"If she doesn't make it here, you'll forget you ever met her, Decker," Mrs. Brittany said between clenched teeth. "It would be wrong to suggest anything otherwise and build her hopes." Her angry reaction almost shook the chandeliers above us.

He took one look at her and raised his pudgy hands. "Just kidding, just kidding!" he cried. "Of course. Don't send me to the gallows just yet."

Portia and Mr. Whitehouse laughed, hoping to lift the heavy cloud off our discussion, but the look Mrs. Brittany gave me frightened me. Somehow I had displeased her by being too perfect at the dinner table. She had been upset with me before we entered the dining room. I understood that she still wasn't happy that her granddaughter wanted to pal around with me. Now this had happened.

I began to wonder if I would last another day, and I began to consider what I would do with the five-thousand-dollar kill fee. I would have to wait a few more days for my eighteenth birthday, but after that, I wouldn't have to come up with lies and excuses for why I was on my own. I'd have enough money to buy some decent clothes and go somewhere to start anew, maybe some college town where I could learn to work in a restaurant and perhaps take some GED courses and get my high school diploma. No matter what happened here, I told myself, I was determined that I was still going to be better off than I was two minutes before Mr. Bob looked across that restaurant and feasted his eyes on me.

After dinner, everyone but me was to go to the living room to have an after-dinner cordial. I was sent up to my suite to do some of the reading Professor Marx had assigned. Because of the little tiff at the dinner table between him and Mrs. Brittany, Mr. Farmingham said as formal a good-bye to me as he could manage, but I thought I saw him wink before he turned away. I was sure I would be a topic of conversation.

Portia walked out with me. "I'll be going early in the morning," she said. "You did well, much better than I did at my first dinner here. I wouldn't worry too much about the looks Mrs. Brittany can give you from time to time. She's foremost a good business-woman. If she thinks you'll earn money, she'll overlook a lot more than she claims she would, but don't test her too much just yet. You've got to, as they say, make your bones first."

"Thanks for the advice. Will I ever see you again?"

"Maybe," she said, smiling. "Good luck."

She gave me a hug and hurried off to join the others.

I went up the stairs, wondering how I would read or learn anything after that dinner. All I wanted to do was crawl into that marvelous bed and soak myself in a good sleep, but when I opened the door, I was startled to find Sheena sitting in her robe at my vanity table, perusing the books and papers Randy had put there for me.

"Oh, hi," she said. "I've got this figured out for you. I've gone through it and underlined what's important and what's not."

I just continued to stand there in the doorway.

"Come in, silly. It is your suite," she said.

"Sorry, you just surprised me. I thought you had said, 'See you tomorrow.'"

"Good. I love surprises. When they are good surprises, I mean."

"You're a good surprise," I said quickly.

She smiled. "Why don't you get into your pajamas or whatever and get comfortable?" she suggested. "It's a pretty dress, but you look like you were in a spotlight or something and can't wait to relax."

I laughed. "That's exactly the way I would put it, a spotlight." I unzipped the dress, took out a pair of pajamas, and headed into the bathroom to wash off the makeup. She came in with me.

"My grandmother wouldn't want you to tell me about your dinner, but you can if you want. I won't tell her you told. I never had anyone I could share any secrets with, and I've never had a friend over, have you?"

I looked up at her. Here I was almost finished with my first day, and I was placed once more in what Mama would call a delicate situation. Sheena wanted me to hold her in my confidence. She wanted a friend, probably desperately, but if I was revealing and she slipped up and mentioned something I had told her, I'd surely get my walking papers. Nevertheless, I could see the need, almost the pleading, in her eyes. Because I was the youngest girl to be brought to the Brittany mansion for training, I would probably be most likely to befriend her.

"Actually, no," I said, which obviously surprised her.

Ironically, even though I wasn't put in the same situation by something as devastating as bone cancer, I had been and still was almost as much of a loner. The difference was that I never felt as much of a great need to have a close friend as she did. Maybe I simply didn't want to trust anyone or believe in anyone. The girls I witnessed struggling to be liked or to have a close friend most often than not looked pathetic to me. Usually, I would tell one of them that she looked ridiculous and sounded pitiful and wretched. I drove them to tears. Maybe I was cruel; maybe it was wrong to expect any of them to be as strong as I was when it came to rejecting any groveling. The girls who wanted to talk to me usually did so to get something from me. More than half of the girls in my class were simply afraid of me.

But if there was any honesty in me, I would have to admit that there was a part of me that wanted to be liked, wanted to be like Sheena, and wanted to have the need for a close companion, someone to share secrets with and explore what this whole journey into womanhood meant. Looking at her standing in my bathroom doorway, waiting for some sign, some indication that I was ready and willing to be her friend, did get to me. Yes, I was hard, and my recent disgusting life in the bowels of the city had hardened me even more, but the softness and innocence in Sheena's eyes brought me memories of Emmie and my mother whenever we could be . . . just friends.

"The food was fantastic."

"Oh, was it?"

"I've got to tell you," I said. "Your grandmother has a magnificent chef."

"Yes. I know," she said, welcoming my excitement.

I described the menu. She looked as if she was hanging on every word. I wondered if she knew Decker Farmingham, but I thought I shouldn't mention his name.

"Was everyone stuffy? So many of my grandmother's friends can be stuffy."

"A little," I said. "But I unstuffed them."

She laughed. "I wish I could have seen that."

"I had to be the wine taster," I said.

She came farther in.

"Wine taster? You mean you had to drink it first and decide if it was good or not?"

"Exactly."

"How did you know what to do, what to say? Did you learn all that today?"

"No, I knew all that. My mother taught me a lot about wine. She's French, a Parisian," I said.

"French? Have you been to Paris? I was there with my grandmother, but she assigned a special guide to take me around while she did business. I liked what I saw, but I hated all the boring things he told me. We went to great restaurants, but I didn't go up the Eiffel Tower or go on the big Ferris wheel, did you?"

"Actually, no," I said. "I was too young at the time to appreciate most of it. Someday I'll go back."

"I wish I could go with someone like you and not a professional guide."

"Maybe someday."

"You really think so?"

"Who knows? Two days ago, I could never even imagine I'd be here in this beautiful place talking to you, right?"

"Right." She thought a moment and then lost her smile as if it literally evaporated. "I'd be terrible to travel with. I'd slow anyone down, and I'd be gawking at everyone and everything, and everyone would gawk at me. And there is so much I don't know about . . . the real world," she said. "You'd hate it."

"I would not, and you will learn everything you have to learn about the real world, as you call it."

She shrugged. "Once, when I described all the things I wanted to do, my grandmother said, 'Just be grateful for tomorrow, Sheena.' That was right after I was very sick, but I never forgot it. I hate being grateful for tomorrow. Only very old people are grateful for tomorrow, right?"

"No. We should all be grateful for tomorrow," I told her, "sick or not."

She smiled again. "I drink some wine, whatever my grandmother says I should, but honestly, I don't know the difference between one or the other."

"No one has ever offered to teach you?"

She shook her head.

"Perhaps one day, I'll be able to show you what I know. If I ever get real time off, maybe we can have our own special lunch or dinner."

"Would you?" she said, her face bursting into a smile that reminded me of Emmie's smile when she opened her birthday presents. "That would be wonderful. I always feel so silly when the waiter asks me what wine I would like. Grandmother orders quickly for me, of course, but someday, I might go to a restaurant without her."

"You never have?"

"No. There's never been anyone else for me to go with. I certainly wouldn't go with Mrs. Pratt. She makes me nervous. Does she make you nervous?"

"I suspect she made her own mother nervous the day she was born," I said, and Sheena laughed.

I worked on my face.

"Did you always know how to make up your face?" she asked.

"Not like this. But I'm learning."

"I really like what was done to your hair. I wish mine was done the same way."

"Doesn't your grandmother permit the beautician to do your hair, too?"

She shook her head.

How could that possibly be a no-no? Sheena lived here, but somehow Mrs. Brittany kept her sheltered from what was really happening. It made me wonder how much her granddaughter did know about the escort business.

"I mean, she'll take me someplace to have it cut and styled when she thinks it needs to be."

"Not when *you* think it needs to be?"

"Oh, my grandmother knows so much more than I do about all that. She's a very sophisticated, worldly woman. She knows princes, queens, kings, and senators."

I nodded and rose to slip out of my bra and panties and put on my pajamas.

"You're beautiful," she said.

"Thank you, but you have nothing to complain about," I replied, and immediately felt like an idiot. "I mean, you're very pretty, too, Sheena."

She smiled. "I know," she said. "I just don't know why I was given a pretty face. It seems to me it was a great waste." She retreated into the bedroom.

Maybe, I thought, I was getting in too deeply, and not only would I drown but I would also hasten her drowning, and there was no question how Mrs. Brittany would feel about that.

Actually, it was hard, if not impossible, for me to imagine myself being helpful to anyone these days, especially someone as innocent and vulnerable as Sheena.

But maybe, just maybe, if I helped someone else, I would help myself.

The thought sounded too much like something Mr. Wheeler might tell me.

Suddenly, however, that didn't devalue it the way it might have only days ago.

Perhaps I could change.

10

"You shouldn't think like that, Sheena. The beauty in your face is not a waste," I said when I walked into the bedroom. She was sitting at my vanity table again, looking at the books and pamphlets.

She looked up at herself in the mirror.

"I can't help it, Roxy," she said. "I know I have an attractive face, but it's almost as if a terrible joke has been pulled on me, don't you think?"

She turned to me before I could answer.

"Everywhere my grandmother takes me, people tell me I'm beautiful. Most of the time, I think it's because they feel sorry for me and want to make me feel better or because they respect my grandmother or want something from her." She pulled up her robe to show me more of her prosthetic leg.

"I bet most of those people never noticed your leg."

She smiled and shook her head at me as if I were the naive one and not her. "I used to dream of that and pretend it, too. Even if I wear jeans, they still can see my false ankle, and even if they couldn't, they still see me limping or walking with the cane. Roxy, I've stopped pretending or dreaming. Grandmother tells me she is working on getting me a far better . . . what should I call it . . . device? One that resembles a real human leg and feels like real skin and muscle so that people will actually wonder if it is or isn't. But I won't ever wonder, will I?"

"Anyone who judges you on only one part of you isn't worth your attention, anyway. They have to be willing to know all of you."

"And how will that happen? Do you know I've never even danced with a boy? Sometimes, when I'm alone, I dance, but I feel foolish, even though no one can see me. I've never gone on a date just to have a hamburger or pizza or something. Actually, I've never even held hands with a boy.

"Oh, I know all about what it's supposed to be like," she continued. "I've read so many romance novels it would make your head spin. I have even read all the scientific information about sex. I probably know as much as any doctor or therapist, but I don't really know what a kiss is like, I mean a real kiss on the lips." She paused and then smiled. "How many times have you seen *Gone with the Wind*?"

"Only once, I think. Why?"

"Rhett tells Scarlett she should be kissed, and often. I love that scene. I pretend I'm Scarlett O'Hara. I've pretended to be lots of characters in romantic movies. Half my youth has been spent talking to myself and embracing imaginary characters. When no one is around, of course, but at least I get kissed on the lips in my imagination."

"Well, I've kissed a few dozen lips recently, and I can tell you, all but one time, I'd rather I had kissed a duck."

She laughed.

"I'm serious," I said. "Most boys don't even know how to kiss. They do it to get something over with so they can get to groping you and slipping their hands under your clothes, panting like some wildcat. I once broke a boy's pinkie because he put it where he shouldn't."

"You didn't!"

"That was quite a mess. My father ended up paying the doctor's bill. I tried to explain, but he believed the boy, who said I encouraged him. Well, maybe I did a little," I admitted.

She laughed again. "That's what I like about you. I saw it right away."

"What?"

"You'll tell me the truth . . . about everything, no matter what."

"No, no. I'm not your best authority when it comes to the truth. I majored in lying, in school and at home. I might even be in that *Believe It or Not!* book by now for telling the most lies for someone my age."

"Yes," she said, smiling like a little girl who expected she would get her Christmas presents no matter what, "but I'm sure all that lying was to protect yourself. You don't have to lie to protect me, so you won't. As Grandmother told me, you've been around the block."

"Is that how she put it?" I shrugged. "I would have thought she would simply say I was promiscuous or undisciplined."

"She saw something good in you, or you wouldn't be here, I'm sure."

"When did she tell you I was promiscuous?"

"When she was trying to talk me out of hanging out with you. She said you weren't the sort of girl I would find interesting or admire because you weren't a good student and had nothing to be proud of. She said she had a lot of work to do with you, on you."

"She's not wrong. I haven't done much in my life except mess up."

"I know, but that's exactly why I want to be your friend and want you to be mine. I've never been down the block, much less around it. I want to hear all about it. You must promise never to be ashamed of anything you've done, especially so ashamed that you wouldn't ever tell me. People aren't always what they seem to be, anyway. If you give them half a chance, you'll see first impressions are more the result of prejudice or false information. You've got a lot to share, especially with someone like me who sees the world through the rose-colored glasses my grandmother had fitted on my face. I have to know about these things, or I'll be a little girl when I'm thirty. So you see, you'll be tutoring and helping me as much as I will be helping you."

"Oh, boy," I said, sitting on my bed.

"What?"

"You're a lot smarter than everyone, including your grandmother, thinks you are."

"Why?"

"You didn't just volunteer to help me with all that," I said, nodding at the material Professor Marx had given me. "You want a little quid pro quo."

I lay back on my bed. *I'm in trouble,* I thought. Mrs. Brittany wanted me to have a G relationship with her granddaughter, PG at most, and she was looking for at least an R.

"No, I want more," she said.

"What more?" I asked, sitting up quickly.

"I want to be you, get into your mind, your memories, so well that I feel . . ."

"Feel what?"

"That I've been around the block," she said.

"I thought you might have picked up that it's nothing I'm proud of, Sheena."

"It brought you here, didn't it? You want to be here, don't you?"

I stared at her a moment. This could work in reverse, too. If she drew honest answers from me, she could feed them to her grandmother. For a fleeting few seconds, I wondered if that was really Mrs. Brittany's reason for permitting Sheena to be friends with me. Could Sheena be her grandmother's little spy, making periodic reports about candidates? Maybe without her even realizing how she was being used? On the other hand, according to Randy, Brittany girls weren't permitted to get to know Sheena. Should I have believed him? I couldn't help feeling as if everything I did and anyone I spoke to on this estate was in one way or another not to be trusted.

"I think so," I said, trying to sound as neutral as I could. Again, I wondered how much she actually knew about her grandmother's business. "It's too early to tell. I've not exactly benefited a hundred percent from the decisions I've made for myself, Sheena."

She nodded, but I didn't think she was listening to me.

"I always wonder if my grandmother would have wanted me to work for her, too. I mean, if I didn't have this," she said, indicating her prosthetic leg. "What do you think? Would it be that much of a hindrance? If I wasn't my grandmother's granddaughter, would I have been discovered like you? You said I was pretty. Unless you felt like you had to say it to please my grandmother."

"Well, you know now that I'm a good liar, Sheena, so I don't know how to convince you that I'm telling you the truth."

"Maybe . . . maybe we can double-date or something. Does my grandmother permit that while one of her girls is in training?"

Anyone could see she was fishing to find out more about her grandmother's girls, I thought. Because I never worried too much about what I said, I found this to be quite a challenge.

"I can only talk about myself, Sheena, and I can assure you, your grandmother wouldn't want me going on any dates while I was here." I thought a moment. She had to know most of it. "You know who Mr. Bob is, I imagine."

"He works for my grandmother, but I don't know what he does, exactly," she said. "I've met him only a few times, and when I'm around, they talk about everything but what he does, I think. What does he do, exactly?"

Here I go, putting my foot into it. If I didn't tell her things, she might get depressed and cry to her grandmother, and Mrs. Brittany would be angry, not only at me but at herself for permitting this to start. She wouldn't have had to if I hadn't been so damn nosy and gone out there to meet her. If I told her something Mrs. Brittany didn't want her to know, she'd also be angry, maybe even more so. Was this some sort of test, too? A challenge?

I saw the look of hope in Sheena's face, hope that she would finally have a girlfriend, someone who wasn't afraid to tell her intimate things and hear intimate things. Maybe I was flattering myself too much, but I suddenly saw myself as the sister she never had. I wasn't going to hurt her any more than she had been in her life. If Mrs. Brittany couldn't see that, then good riddance to her and this whole idea.

"Mr. Bob is the one who brought me to your grandmother. He's a kind of agent, like an actors' agent who discovers new talent."

"How did he discover you?"

Now we were really getting to the nitty-gritty, I thought.

"A short while ago, my father threw me out of our house, and Mr. Bob found me when I was about to give up on myself."

"Really? Your father threw you out?" she asked, now looking shocked. Maybe this would end the attempt at any friendship. Maybe this was for the best. I'd tell her everything, and that would drive her away. "I can't imagine a father throwing out his own daughter."

"Yes. I was thrown out. I've been in trouble all the time. He simply gave up trying to change me, and he was worried about my influencing my younger sister."

"Oh. How old is she?"

"She's about nine years younger."

"Did you, I mean, do you have a good relationship with her, anyway?"

"We hardly know each other," I said.

She looked more shocked. "Why?"

"Our age difference, for one reason, and for another, my father has done his best to scare her away from me. I can count on the fingers of one hand how many times I've gone somewhere with her without either my mother or my father tagging along. The last thing I did that you might call sisterly was give her a charm bracelet that had been given to me."

"What about your mother? Is your mother still alive?"

"She's still alive, but she . . . she's given up on me, too. I told you I was no angel. I've been in one pot of hot water after another. I guess I exhausted them, and they're terrified I'll spoil my sister. She's perfect in their eyes, whereas I'm all that's bad."

She thought a moment and then surprised me with

a smile. "Well, I've never been in trouble. I can't wait to hear what you did to cause your own parents to think you were all bad."

"I don't know if I should get into all that with you, Sheena."

"I do. You should. I won't go blabbering to my grandmother, if that's what you're afraid of," she said, "or anyone else. You can trust me with any secret you have. I want to trust you, too."

"I'm not talking about just being a bad student, breaking school rules, or staying out too late and going places my parents forbade me to go to, Sheena."

"Good. There's nothing extraordinary about that. All that sounds like simple immaturity or being spoiled. Boring stuff," she sang.

Was there anything I could say that would keep her from wanting to befriend me?

More important, perhaps, did I want to do that?

"I want to hear about your love life."

"I haven't had a love life, except with myself," I said.

She laughed. "Okay, your sex life, then. As I told you, I've read about anything and everything you've done, probably. I just want to hear about it from someone who's actually done it. Maybe what I've read isn't so accurate. Maybe it's too made up or too . . . hopeful. All right?"

"Okay. We'll see," I said.

"Yes, we will, but I'm not being fair." She turned back to the books and papers. "It's getting late, and

I haven't given you any pointers yet. I'm sure you're tired. C'mon," she urged. "Let's go over some of this." She laughed as she opened the fat art textbook. "I'm sure it will help you fall asleep."

She was right. After nearly an hour, my eyes began to close, and we decided it was enough, but she did home in on the information I would need to impress Professor Marx the next day. Before she left, she told me she was going to ask her grandmother if I could have dinner with her and spend time with her in her suite studying afterward.

"She has to agree to give you a day off, doesn't she?"

"I don't think she believes in the concept."

"Oh, she does. I'll work on her."

"Don't work on her too hard, or she'll just ship me off," I warned.

"I know how to handle my grandmother," she whispered at the door. "I got her to let you see me, didn't I? Don't worry about it. I have all kinds of things I want to show you, including some clothes I want you to try on. We're almost the same size in everything, I bet. Okay?"

I saw the desperation in her face. On this great estate with almost anything anyone could want at her beck and call, Sheena was hungering for the simplest thing of all, some real companionship.

Maybe I was, too.

Maybe escaping loneliness was the reason we did everything we did in this life.

Maybe my father was lonelier than I had ever imagined. Maybe my mother was, too.

Now Emmie would be.

And despite what my father hoped for now, no one would be happier because of what had happened.

"Okay," I said.

Sheena leaned forward to kiss me on the cheek. "Sweet dreams," she said.

I don't know why, but as she walked away, limping, I felt like bursting into tears.

Only I didn't know if I would be crying for her or for myself.

I closed all the books and crawled into bed.

In the morning, the phone woke me just as Mrs. Pratt had promised. I felt like throwing it against the wall, but I sat up quickly, lifted the receiver, and put it back as she had instructed. Groaning and moaning from the charley horses Lance had predicted with such glee, I got myself into a hot shower and then shifted to icy-cold water to wake up every cell in my body.

This time, when I arrived at the breakfast nook, there was no one there. Randy informed me that Portia had already left.

"She had to fly to Los Angeles," he revealed, and then pretended to zip up his lips.

I ate my healthy breakfast and then reluctantly rose and went to the gym.

"Stretching," Lance called the moment I entered. "You know the routine."

Yes, I knew it.

They'll kill me before I have a chance to be approved for anything, I thought, but the workout wasn't as bad as I'd feared. Lance did know what he was doing, just how much to push me and when to give me rest. We returned to the pool afterward, and according to him, I swam better. I didn't get a massage this time but was told to go to the library to see Professor Brenner, the man who was going to work on my elocution.

Unlike Professor Marx, he was jovial from the start and seemed genuinely amused at the way I pronounced some of my words. He wore a western-style tie and jacket, jeans, and boots and had a well-trimmed rust-red mustache. I didn't think he was more than fifty years old and wondered why he was a retired professor.

He pounced on my slurring of consonants and what he called my lazy tongue.

"You've got that New York thing, saying 'mounain' instead of 'mountain,'" he said. "Also, just like most people your age today, Roxy, you speak too fast. Do you know what a caesural pause is?"

I remembered Mr. Wheeler talking about it and said, "Sort of a pregnant pause?"

Professor Brenner laughed. "Exactly. You capture your listener's attention with it and elevate the importance of what you're saying next. Think about that, and it will help you slow down. You'll sound more . . ."

"Educated?"

"Yes, but I was thinking more mature," he said.

He gave me lessons to practice with a recorder, and then I went on to lunch with Nigel Whitehouse. Later that afternoon, I impressed Professor Marx with what I had mastered, thanks to Sheena. By the end of the afternoon, I felt more confident. Mrs. Pratt informed me that I was to have a private dinner with Mrs. Brittany. Again, clothes were brought in for me.

"It's all right for you to spend an hour or so with Mrs. Brittany's granddaughter," she added. I could see in her face and hear in her voice that she wasn't happy about it. She told me exactly where to go in the east wing of the mansion.

I set out as soon as she left and followed the corridor past the stairway. There was something about this wing of the mansion that seemed more homey. The colors were far more subtle, the paintings smaller, with depictions of rural scenes, lakes, and beautiful valleys. There was one portrait of significant size. It was of a handsome man in what looked like garb worn by royalty, with epaulets on his shoulders and some medals under his breast pocket. He wore three jeweled rings and was captured with a soft smile. *Has to be Mrs. Brittany's husband,* I thought, and turned the corner to knock on the first door on my right.

Sheena opened it instantly.

"Oh, it's you. I was hoping it was you. Guess what? My grandmother said I could go horseback riding with you tomorrow when you take your first lesson. Come in. Come in," she said, stepping back.

Her room wasn't quite as large as mine, but it was far cozier. She had posters of her favorite movie stars and singers on the walls, and dolls on a shelf and one on the bed. As I gazed around, I thought it was more like the room of a young teenage girl. Her four-poster light maple bed was smaller than my bed and wasn't as high. I saw a pile of CDs and a large pile of DVDs on a dresser, books on another, and many magazines. There was a built-in large-screen television on the wall across from her bed and what looked like a stack of audio equipment in a glass-framed closet beside it. In short, it had the look of a room for someone who was mainly a shut-in. I plopped onto the oversize chair to my right.

"You're exhausted," she declared with a wide smile.

"Yes. This is the first minute I've had to myself. Thanks for your help with the homework. Professor Marx was pleased."

"Oh, we'll do more tonight. After you have dinner with my grandmother, I mean. Yes, I know your schedule. I wanted to be there, too, but she says it's part of your training. But," she added, clapping her hands together, "we can have dinner tomorrow night without anyone else. She said we could even go out. Of course, she would choose the restaurant, but we'd go in her limousine. If I count our horseback ride together, it would be like spending the whole day with each other. Well, not really, I know. You'll be busy until you go for your lesson, but still, it's more time than I've spent with anyone this year. Or last year," she added with a laugh. "Maybe this coming weekend, she'll let us go to a movie. I don't know what we should go see, but just going would be fun, wouldn't it? And afterward, maybe we could go for pizza or something. Whatever you think is fine with me. My grandmother said she would let me accompany you and her when she takes you shopping next week. Of course, she'll buy me things, too."

It seemed she would talk incessantly, behaving like someone who was afraid of a moment of silence or any sort of disappointment.

"That all sounds great to me, and it's news. I didn't know I was to go shopping next week."

"Oh, it doesn't matter. It's not a top government secret or anything. You've got to see this dress she bought me last week in London. I wasn't there, but she brought it back. Don't move."

She stepped into her walk-in closet. I laughed to myself, thinking of how I was with the girls in my school when they started talking about all the things they had and all that their parents did for them. If they were looking to impress someone or make someone envious, they were always disappointed in me. On the contrary, I would invariably mock them or criticize what they were given and make them feel small and stupid. Most girls didn't mention such things to me after a while.

However, I wasn't being friendly and pleasant with Sheena simply because she was Mrs. Brittany's granddaughter. I had never met someone Sheena's age who seemed so innocent and pure, so vulnerable and delicate. There was a part of me that wished I were just like her. For sure, I would have gotten along much better with my father and my mother. Girls like Sheena needed a grandmother like Mrs. Brittany or a friend like me to watch over them. They wouldn't recognize evil, envy, or just plain meanness when they confronted it.

After a few moments, she stepped out in her dress. I nearly gasped with surprise. Mrs. Brittany bought her this? It was a backless silver glitter dress with long fitted sleeves and strong shoulders, in a stretch fabric that hugged every curve. It was a good six inches above the knee, too. Where would she wear such a dress? I would have thought she would have found her a dress that was at least ankle-length for obvious reasons.

"Don't you like it?" Sheena asked.

"I'm overwhelmed. You're stunning in it," I said. For the most part, she was, but the prosthetic leg added an incongruous element, making her look a little bizarre. I mean, she was sexy yet odd.

Why did Mrs. Brittany buy this for her? Was she trying to get her to forget about her leg?

"I haven't worn it anywhere yet. Do you think I should wear it when we go out to dinner?"

"Absolutely."

"You can borrow it anytime," she said.

"Thanks."

She turned in a circle and then laughed. "I wouldn't put it on until now. I knew it would be all right to show it to you."

"You could show it to anyone. Don't worry about that."

"Silly," she said. "Of course, I would worry." She looked down at her prosthetic leg.

"Anyone looking at you will be looking at the rest of you more. Believe me," I said. "You have a better figure than I do."

She widened her smile. "I have other dresses I never dared to wear. I'll show them all to you, but not now," she added. "That's too boring." She sat on her bed and faced me.

"It's not boring."

"No, no. I don't want to waste precious time. I know you have to get ready for dinner with my grandmother, and I know how nervous you'll be about it."

"How do you know that?"

"I know. I've watched other girls when she didn't know I was watching. I could see how nervous they were. I'm a little bit of a Peeping Tom—or Thomasina." She laughed and then lost her smile. "I know you think that's sick or something."

"No, I don't."

"It is," she insisted. "I'm always looking through something to see what's really happening, looking through windows or through television and movie screens or just peering at life through words in a book. But not now, not with you here. You're a living person my age, who's been places I dreamed of."

"No, I haven't."

"Yes, you have."

She sprawled on her side and propped up her face with her left hand.

"Tell me what it was like. Don't leave out a detail, and don't worry about how I might react or anything."

I leaned forward, smiling at her. "What *what* was like? Where do you think I've been?"

"You've been there," she said, nodding. "Or you wouldn't be here."

I sat back. "Sheena?"

"Tell me about the first time. Start from the very beginning, especially when you realized you were going to do it. Then tell me exactly what it felt like. I don't believe what I read in my novels, and I don't get anything out of the textbooks.

"Oh, and tell me what he was like," she added, "and if you ever saw him again or if that mattered."

I started to shake my head, saw the disappointment creeping into her face, and stopped. "I was only fourteen," I began, "and it wasn't long after I had my first period."

"Menarche," she said, nodding. "I was only twelve, and my mother was furious because I didn't tell her. She didn't know it until she saw my panties and what I had stuffed in them. Did you tell your mother right away?"

I thought for a moment. That should have been something a mother and daughter shared. It should have been a remarkable moment.

"No," I said softly. "I was prepared. I've always been prepared."

And then something hit me like a snowball in my face.

"I've never really been a little girl," I said.

We were both silent. I saw how fearful that made her, so I quickly smiled.

"He was a pimply-faced sixteen-year-old," I said, "but he had been around the block."

She perked up, and I got so involved in my story and how grateful she was to hear about it that I nearly forgot to get ready for my dinner with Mrs. Brittany.

And that was surely at the top of the list for fatal mistakes.

11

Having dinner with Mrs. Brittany was intimidating enough, but just the two of us in that grand dining room made me feel I was on a larger stage and in a brighter spotlight. The room seemed cavernous without any other people present. As I walked over the tile portion of the floor, the echo of my footsteps in the new high heels sounded like spikes being driven into it. I tried to step more lightly.

She sat at the head of the table and watched me approach, her eyes like X-rays examining every turn and twist in my hips as I walked. I don't think anyone could make me more self-conscious of my every move, my every breath. As soon as I had entered the grand room, I corrected my posture and kept my head up. She seemed to grow larger and more intimidating as I approached, while everything around her seemed to diminish.

"Did you look at yourself before you left your bedroom?" she asked the moment I reached the table.

"Yes."

"You put your lipstick on too thickly. It's off your lips on the right side, in fact."

"Oh." I reached up to wipe it clear. "I guess I was in too much of a rush."

"Don't do that. You'll only smear it more."

She opened the purse she had hanging off her chair and handed me an ivory case that opened to a small mirror. I saw what she meant, and using a tissue she handed to me, I wiped away the excess lipstick. I thought she must have microscopes for eyes to have picked up on this so quickly. I looked at the case when I closed it.

"Beautiful."

"It was a gift from a member of the president's cabinet," she said, taking it back. She nodded toward the seat on her right, and I sat. "If there is one thing I never want you to rush, it's preparing your appearance. Every Brittany girl takes pride in how she looks, not only to the person she is accompanying but also to herself. That's why I bring in experts in makeup, coiffure, and style. What good is all that if you don't take great care? Always be sure to leave yourself enough time. If you appeared before one of our clients who was paying top dollar and looked like that . . ."

"It won't happen again," I said.

Maybe to come to my rescue, Randy hurried out with a bottle of white wine chilling in an ice bucket. He set it down quickly. I saw that it had been opened.

"There was no need to test you on that again," Mrs. Brittany said when she saw me looking at it. Randy pulled out the cork and poured us each a glass. "You can bring our salads, Randy," she told him.

He glanced at me, smiled, and hurried back to the kitchen.

"How far away is the kitchen?" I asked her.

"Now you're worried about Randy working too hard? What's happened to the self-centered young girl who arrived?"

"Maybe I've become a bit bored with her," I replied. "She was just one note." I saw in the way her eyes sparkled that she liked my response.

"You continue to get high praise from members of my team," she said. "But don't think that's convinced me yet. As was just demonstrated, you have a long way to go."

"I understand."

"Do you? Most girls your age these days want instant gratification."

"I'm not most girls my age these days," I fired back. If I had been brought here to be slowly cooked over the hot coals in her eyes, she had a surprise coming.

She nodded, clearly seeing the fire in my eyes, too. "Okay. Let's put that all aside for now. Tell me more about your family, why things became so difficult for you and for them, and what you expect will happen with them in the near future, as regards you, I mean," she said, relaxing.

Randy brought out our salads. I waited for him to serve and leave before I began to describe my parents and what life had been like for me growing up in the house my father ruled like a commanding general. I gave her as much detail as I could, but I didn't blame everything on him. I confessed to as many of my indiscretions as I could recall, elaborating on some of the bigger incidents at school.

"I'm surprised you weren't sent off to some behavior-modification camp," she said.

"So am I, although that was probably coming if I remained there any longer. I think my father thought it was too late even for that, however. If I stepped out of myself," I said, "and took a good look, I don't think I'd want me around, either."

As I spoke, I knew she was listening keenly but also watching how I ate my salad and talked without food in my mouth. Nigel Whitehouse, as if he knew what to prepare me for tonight, had made a big deal of the way people conversed at lunch and dinner tables. He referred to it as "the delicacies of gracious living."

"It will give you the aura of sophistication that the men you will be with appreciate, look for, and actually demand. It's part of what justifies their cost, *comprenez*, my dear?"

"*Mais oui*," I told him.

A week ago, I might have come close to spitting in the face of someone who told me I looked gross the way I ate or sat, but it was as if another window on the world had been opened for me, and when I looked through it, I saw what lay in wait for someone who had more than just a modicum of class. When I had first arrived, I was skeptical and indifferent about the value of all this cultural training, but that skepticism was dying away. I wanted to do well now. I wanted more.

I saw from the expression on Mrs. Brittany's face that I was passing this particular test. She concentrated now on what I was saying and not so much how I was saying it. She really wanted to know more about me, and I knew she wouldn't take interest in anyone she thought would not succeed with her. When I was finished with my description of what my life had been like, she signaled for Randy to take our dishes.

"Give us ten minutes before bringing out the entrée, Randy," she said.

"Yes, ma'am," he replied, and winked at me. I gathered this was not a bad sign. I wasn't going to be read my rights and sent off.

She was silent for a moment, and then she leaned forward and spoke in the softest tone I had heard her use. "Normally, I am averse to involving myself, my company, and my associates with young women who come from such troubled backgrounds as yours. Frankly, if it wasn't for Bob's insistence, I wouldn't have agreed to your coming here at all. I don't like to start with someone who carries so much baggage. It takes too long to unload it, and I'm never confident that some of it won't rear its ugly head later on when I most need that not to happen.

"However," she continued, leaning back, "I also rely heavily on my own instincts. I believe, and so far you have shown, that you have the wherewithal to improve yourself, make the necessary changes, throw off the baggage, and blossom. I do not intend to blow up your ego with these remarks. In fact, most young women, even many I have in my employ, have difficulty handling compliments. One can get too confident, if you know what I mean, and I think you do.

"I like the way you have treated Sheena, and not only because she is my granddaughter. It has shown me something important about your character, something that supports my own instincts about you. I don't think you're as selfish and spoiled as you believe you are, but that's something you will learn for yourself in time.

"Now, then," she said, taking a more formal tone again, "the day after tomorrow, we will go to one of my favorite boutiques in Manhattan to start your personal wardrobe. I'm sure Sheena has told you something about it. She's coming along with us."

"Yes," I said. "She was very excited about it."

I had made up my mind never to lie to her or pretend ignorance of anything anymore. It wasn't worth the risk, and she was too perceptive to miss any deceptions. I used to think I was good at that, but I realized now that I was sitting alongside a master.

"From time to time, during your stay here, I will have other guests. I want them to meet you. I rely on some of them for their impressions, but as I told you, I never depend on any of them—on anyone else, in fact—to come to a conclusion about any of my girls. We'll have dinner parties, cocktail parties, even some sort of picnic as the weather continues to improve. I'll be taking you to Broadway shows and concerts, here and in other cities, in time even in other countries. I intend to cram a great deal into your head very quickly before I send you out into the field, Roxy, but by the time I'm finished with you, any resemblance between you and the errant young woman Mr. Bob brought here will be difficult to discover. I have a feeling that won't upset you in the least."

"No, it won't," I said.

She nodded and turned her head just slightly to signal Randy, who hurried out with our dinner, a delicious branzino, something I'd never had. She went on to describe it as a silver-skinned fish found in European seas and saltwater lakes.

"Some call it European sea bass, spigola, loup de mer, robalo, or lubina," she said.

As I listened to her talk about gourmet foods, wonderful restaurants in world cities, her travels and cultural experiences, and some of the castles she had been to, I found myself growing more infatuated with her. The hard shell I had first encountered seemed to melt away. More and more, I realized how much I wanted to be like her. She would rapidly become someone I would idolize. She was rising higher on my list of women to emulate.

For a few moments, I felt terribly guilty about that. Once, when I was very young, I wanted to be like my mother, but as I grew older, I couldn't tolerate how subservient she was to my father. He loved her, I was sure, but he was blind to how firmly he controlled even her emotions, forbidding her tears, sweeping away her protests and complaints, retreating from any compromise that might overtake him and cause him to be more reasonable.

Mrs. Brittany would be a formidable opponent

for him, I thought. She would bend him. He wouldn't be so eager to rage in her face or throw ultimatums and commands at her like rice at a bride. I laughed to myself, imagining a day in the future when I would introduce them. It was a pipe dream, of course, but an amusing fantasy.

We didn't have any dessert. She wanted me to attend to whatever material Professor Marx had given me and to work on the elocution lessons Professor Brenner had assigned. We walked out together and paused in the hallway to say good night.

"Is it really all right for Sheena to go horseback riding with me tomorrow?" I asked. "I mean, considering her physical condition and all. I don't want you to think I put her in any compromising position or . . ."

She smiled. "No. The question is more like, is it all right for you to go with her? You haven't had proper lessons. She's a seasoned equestrian. She's overcome many things, but she needs her confidence strengthened. I suspect the two of you will do that for each other. Good night," she said, and walked off to join Mrs. Pratt, who waited for her outside her office.

I hurried up the stairs. My heart was full of hope. This private dinner with her had gone well. I was going to do well. I was confident that I was going to leave that—what did she call me?—errant young woman behind. I hadn't felt this happy for some time, and it was all because I was growing stronger, not just physically but also in my belief in myself. If *mon père* hadn't thrown me out, none of this would be possible.

Yes, I'm in the right place, I thought, and hurried to meet Sheena in my suite and go over the work Professor Marx had given me. She was waiting there, sitting at my vanity table and dabbling with her hair and eyebrows. She spun around quickly when I entered.

"I'm sorry. I didn't mean to use your things."

"That doesn't matter. Don't be foolish."

"Oh, I was so worried about you," she said.

"Why?"

"I thought . . . you were taking too long. I was sure my grandmother was lecturing you, and maybe you were angry and saying bad things, because she can be so difficult, and you would hate her and would want to leave right away."

"No, it was a wonderful dinner. And I like her," I said. "I like her very much."

Her face blossomed with a wide smile.

"But I'd better not let her down," I said, warning myself as much as Sheena. "I have to keep doing well, or she'll banish me from her kingdom. There is no doubt about that. She won't tolerate failure."

"Oh, yes. Right. I've been through your assignments again. Let's start with that. I'll listen to you practice your speech assignment, too. I've had similar lessons. I know what to listen for. Let's not waste time." She smiled. "After all, there's so much more I want to learn from you, too. What did you call it, that quid pro quo?"

"Yes," I said, laughing.

We did my work. She was a stern and diligent tutor, sometimes taking on expressions that reminded me of her grandmother when I made mistakes. After-ward, I knew we were up too late talking. Actually, I was doing most of the talking. I told her about some of the different boys I had been with, finishing with Steve Carson. She was most intrigued by a young man his age being as much of a virgin as she was when I had first met him.

"And shoplifting just to get his attention," she added, feigning a little disapproval, when I could see the whole story excited her.

"I wasn't all that surprised at his innocence. Just about all of the boys I've known weren't too sophis-ticated when it came to sex," I told her. "Most of the time, it wasn't remarkable. As a matter of fact, I told Steve that making love to him was like brushing teeth, something just necessary. Needless to say, it was an-other great disappointment."

"Maybe that's good. Maybe sex shouldn't be just another thing we do," she said. "Maybe it cheapens us. At least, that's what I read in a novel recently."

She waited to see what I would say.

"Our bodies should mean more to us, don't you think?" she added when I didn't answer.

I saw how worried she was that she might have hurt my feelings, but I didn't answer quickly, because one of the changes that was coming over me involved exactly that idea about sex. In the world I was enter-ing, it seemed that most things I once considered mundane and ordinary suddenly had great value and importance, whether it was how I ate a sandwich, walked, or held a conversation. And certainly with whom I had sex. Mrs. Brittany and her staff were isolating every little thing I did and showing me how it could define me, express who I was, or, as Mrs. Pratt had put it, service me. Yes, Sheena, in all her innocence, was right. She didn't need all my experience to sense what was instinctively true.

"Sex should be special. 'Friends with benefits' is not all it's cracked up to be," I told her.

Her eyes widened. After some of the things I had described myself doing, I understood why she was so surprised at this answer. "You really believe that?"

"I do now. It's like my vision has cleared," I told her. "When you put such little value on yourself, others will, too. And what about later, when you want it to be special, when you do find someone you love and respect? Won't it be too late to be able to make him feel special or convince him you are special?"

She stared at me with her mouth slightly open.

"I know," I said. "I know. Just listen to me. I can't believe I'm saying these things, either. I sound like some jealous wallflower. My mother tried to instill these values in me, but I was always too stuck on myself to listen or care. I think I made love out of spite more than out of desire. Maybe that's why, even now, I don't have many great memories. In fact, I'd like to forget it all ever happened. I'd like to go to a clinic and get back my virginity. Too bad you can't unring a bell."

She laughed. "I love listening to you, Roxy. You make me feel . . . okay, like I haven't missed all that much and shouldn't feel so sorry for myself."

"I can tell you this, Sheena. The only thing I'm freely giving away from now on is advice, and even that will sometimes cost something."

She laughed again and said, "I'd better go and let you get some good sleep. You have a lot to do tomorrow. Don't forget your horseback riding. You'll need your energy and strength. The horse doesn't do all the work. Go on, get to bed. I feel responsible for you now." She concluded sounding like my older sister or even my mother. After she closed the door, I had the best laugh I'd had in days and the best night's sleep, too. And she was right. It was important that I did.

She was there at the riding stable already saddled and waiting the following day. Brendon Walsh was a short, slim man, not quite as small as a racetrack jockey but not much taller or heavier. He had curly red hair and freckles sprinkled over his cheeks and forehead like flecks of red pepper. He was very serious about his instructions but patient with me.

I felt a little silly in the riding outfit Mrs. Pratt had sent up for me. Sheena was wearing a similar one, but she looked very good in it. I could see the confidence in her face as she sat waiting on her horse. One of the things she had told me the night before was that horseback riding made her feel complete.

"The horse and I become one," she had said. "I have healthy legs again. But every good rider feels that way about it. Brendon says that's when you know you are comfortable in the saddle and, more important, when the horse is comfortable with you there."

I had no idea what she meant when I first began, but it wasn't long before I did.

Lance had been right about the new muscles I would be exercising, too. They let me know the next morning, but Brendon told me I couldn't stop just because of some aches and pains. He wanted me riding every other day. Sheena was delighted, and by the end of the week, I was doing well enough for the two of us to take a long ride through trails they had developed on the property. I never truly understood how large a tract of land Mrs. Brittany owned until we rode horses from one end of it to the other.

We talked a great deal during the rides. Sheena felt confident enough with me now to describe what her life had been like with her parents. As I listened, I couldn't believe a mother could be so indifferent to her child's pain and illness. Sheena tried to excuse it all by blaming her mother's binge drinking and her father's anger about that. I understood that she didn't want to believe her mother could care so little about what she was enduring or that her father was blind to what was happening to her. Into this scene she described came Mrs. Brittany, who, from the way Sheena described her, swept in quickly to take complete control once she understood what was happening.

"It was the first time I saw my grandmother act like a powerful queen."

"So you never hear from your parents?" I asked.

"No," she said. "I think about them often, though," she confessed. When I was silent, she added, "But I am glad for my grandmother."

"Hearing what you've told me, I think I might be almost as glad for her as you are," I said, and she smiled.

"I hope that when you go to work for her, Roxy, you'll still remember me."

"Of course I will. And you'll visit me wherever I am."

"Will I?"

Maybe I shouldn't be making promises without first checking them out with Mrs. Brittany, I thought.

"Let's only think of good things for ourselves now," I told her as a way of assuring her.

She nodded, and we rode on, both captured for the moment by our own fear of what tomorrow would actually bring.

In the days that followed, with Mrs. Brittany's blessing, Sheena and I did draw as close as sisters. Just about every novel Professor Marx insisted I read, she had read and was ready to discuss. That also included plays. She was really a very bright student and expressed so much joy in sharing her knowledge that I couldn't help but want to learn and understand. What a student I might have been if I had been friends with her while I was going to school, I thought.

We had been permitted to go out to dinner, and Mrs. Brittany promised her we would be able to go to a movie together very soon. Although it was true that because of my companionship, she took on a new glow and *joie de vivre*, I was getting almost as much out of it as she was. For the first time in my life, I had a real friend.

Our shopping sprees with Mrs. Brittany were probably our happiest times together. After the first trip to Manhattan, when I was overwhelmed with the money Mrs. Brittany laid out to start my wardrobe, the planning of another shopping trip always brought great excitement and anticipation. It wasn't just what she would buy for me and for Sheena, but also the places she would take us to for our shopping.

We'd be flown in a private jet to Palm Beach to shop on Worth Avenue, or taken to Boston or Chicago because of some designer Mrs. Brittany had heard about. Sometimes she was sent a photograph, even whole portfolios of new fashions. There was always something she wanted to try on me. She took us to runway shows and many private showings in New York. People she admired or trusted brought back pictures of fashions being designed in Europe and the Far East.

One of her favorite fashion designers, Pierre Beaumont, came from Paris to stay at the mansion for a weekend and arranged for models to come and demonstrate some of his creations. Mrs. Brittany wanted me to listen to him and learn what made clothing exciting. He was very knowledgeable about the history of fashion. I learned a great deal from him at our lunches and dinners together.

It seemed to me that she had the whole world at her beck and call. Sheena was right to describe her as being like a queen. She could pick up the phone and call so many important people directly or reach any famous person who had anything to do with what was glamorous.

Sometimes at night, after a full day of training and exposure to something cultural, I would feel as if I had been lifted onto another level on our planet, a level far above the ordinary world, where people like my father and my mother lived. I began to sense what Camelia and Portia were trying to tell me, why they felt so special and were so special.

"If you think poorly of yourself, you will get others to think the same," Mrs. Brittany told me. "You don't want to be so arrogant that you make others feel inferior, even if they are," she added with a smile. "You want them to admire you for your self-confidence, but also for the respect you give them. They won't say it, but they'll feel blessed to have you treat them well, and you won't even have to look or act superior to have them do it. Do you understand?"

"Yes," I said. "I do."

She gave me that look that told me she believed me. I couldn't help feeling that now she not only had confidence in my becoming one of her girls, but she had also developed a genuine and sincere affection for me. Maybe it was just wishful thinking, but it helped me to keep going, study harder, read more, master every task I was given, and win the admiration of every instructor or gentleman to whom I was introduced. It was all going so well that I couldn't imagine anything that might stop me from becoming as successful as she had promised.

Perhaps that was because I was a little too arrogant now. That was something she had always warned me about, too. She described it as someone walking a tightrope way above the ground.

"As long as she keeps her eyes forward, she's fine, but when she looks down to celebrate how high up she is, she loses her balance. I'd like you to remember that."

I could blame only myself for forgetting.

12

Mrs. Pratt stepped into the library and interrupted my lesson on current events to tell me Mrs. Brittany had to see me immediately. There was no way to tell from her expression what this crisis was about, but it was clear that whatever it was, it was something serious. I raked through my recent memories to find something I had done wrong, something I might have said to one of the staff, or, worse, something I had told Sheena and Sheena had told her. Perhaps I had been wrong to be so revealing about myself and the things I had done. That first fear I had when Sheena and I started hanging out together reared its ugly head. I had been too R when I should have been PG. Mrs. Brittany had warned me about this. Would she just end my relationship with Sheena, or would it be even more devastating for me?

Life here over the past months had been so all-consuming that I'd had little time lately to think about my family and from where and what I had come. Sometimes thoughts about Mama and Emmie would sneak into my head just before I fell asleep, but I usually lost them under the dark vision of Papa's face the day he pointed to our front door and said, "Get out." The possibility of returning to them and having to explain where I had been and what I had been doing was too much to even consider.

I excused myself and rose from the table. Professor Marx said nothing, but he looked genuinely afraid for me. I knew that all his initial impressions of me had been wiped away and he was sincerely enjoying our tutorial sessions now. Sheena continued to help me in the evenings, but I had taken more control myself, using my free time wisely to read the books and articles Professor Marx assigned and suggested.

Recently, I had occasion to discuss current events and some other subjects with some of Mrs. Brittany's guests, and I could see from the expressions on her face and theirs that I was coming off well. One man, a hedge-fund CEO, blurted out that I had brains and beauty, the unbeatable combination. He was so excited about me, in fact, that he asked Mrs. Brittany what name I was going under.

"We're not quite there," she told him. "Close, but no gold ring just yet."

"I think I can be of some help when the time does come," he told her, looking mostly at me.

"Of course, you can, Gerard," she said. "You wouldn't be here otherwise."

He laughed at how easily Mrs. Brittany could make someone feel used but not insulted about it. Even I had to smile at her brutal honesty. She gave me an appreciative look, and for the first time, I felt as if we were working as a team. Wasn't that enough?

Didn't she feel that, too? Couldn't I have that gold ring now?

As I left the library to walk with Mrs. Pratt to Mrs. Brittany's office, I could feel the trembling start in my legs and reverberate up my spine and around my heart. Could it be that I had come all this way and now would be asked to leave, my kill fee in hand? What would I do? Where would I go?

I called upon that raging, defiant spirit I had brought along with me that first day. If I was thrown out, I wouldn't return home, and I wouldn't go to any roach hotel, either. I'd find my way. I'd make them sorry they'd dismissed me.

Mrs. Pratt opened the office door for me and stepped in with me. Mrs. Brittany had her back to us. She was looking out the window. Her office had a view of the small pond on her property and some of the wooded area that separated her land from the closest neighbor's. About a half dozen grounds people were cutting the grass and trimming hedges and the bushes around the pond. The dull hum of engines was just barely audible. I saw what looked like a flock of ducks lift off the surface of the pond when something frightened or disturbed them. She waited for them to disappear before turning to us.

"Sorry to interrupt your work with Professor Marx," she began. She nodded at the red bullet leather chair in front of her desk. Mrs. Pratt sat on the settee. Whatever this meeting was about, her advice was obviously going to be appreciated. I had been in meetings she had attended before, and I realized that Mrs. Pratt wasn't just an echo. Her opinions carried weight. I hoped I hadn't done anything that had offended her.

I sat and waited. The pause and the silence could be just another test of my nerves, I thought. I was always under glass here.

Mrs. Brittany opened a folder on her desk.

"I have a copy of your birth certificate. You didn't lie about your age. It was one of the first things I checked, of course. Even though you began here underage, we thought we could slip under the wire, so to speak."

She glanced at Mrs. Pratt, who nodded.

"When your parents didn't follow up on your disappearance, I, like you, thought you had a father who was so headstrong and cold that he was able to write you out of the family without any regret. It's not that unusual. Blood isn't always thicker than water. It gets thinned out for various reasons," she said.

"We know that for a fact," Mrs. Pratt said.

"Yes, we've had some interesting examples of it during our journey. For example, there are parents who disown their children because they show homosexual tendencies and those who disinherit children because they marry the wrong people, people from other races, cultures. There is no shortage of reasons or examples of blood losing its adhesive qualities. Ruth—Mrs. Pratt—was disowned when she refused to marry someone her father had chosen."

I looked at Mrs. Pratt. During all the time I had been there, my interest in her was so small I never asked any questions about her. In my mind, she was almost a piece of the furniture, something that came with the whole picture. I never thought of her as someone with a past, with pleasures and disappointments separate from Mrs. Brittany's. I saw now that I had underestimated her importance.

"Anyway," Mrs. Brittany continued, "we were cautious about you. Mr. Bob and I anticipated the possibility of starting you out and having to abort because of your age and your family or your father regretting his actions. We didn't want to get in the middle of that, and we were prepared to send you on your way every day until your eighteenth birthday. When that came and went, we were more confident and willing to invest more in you."

"What's happened to change that?" I asked, unable to balance myself much longer on my roly-poly anxieties and fear.

Mrs. Brittany's response was to lift a page from a newspaper out of my folder and pass it to me.

There was my picture just under the headline on the page describing my disappearance. My mother had apparently finally gotten her way and initiated a search by the authorities. Some ambitious young reporter had tracked down some of my history of bad behavior, Papa's work and firm, and went on to describe the halfhearted effort to find "a girl neither her school nor her father is that keen on seeing return." That take on it had obviously initiated a bigger discussion about lost children, especially teenagers. There were references to upcoming radio and television talk shows that would have it as the main topic.

Mrs. Brittany passed me another article from

another city newspaper that had picked up on the story and revisited the Pulitzer Prize–winning narration about "America's Forgotten Children" living on the fringes, young people who were ripe fruit for drugs, crime, and prostitution. My picture was reprinted there, too. And in another article, there were two different but relatively recent pictures of me.

"We understand," Mrs. Brittany continued, "that the *New York Crier* magazine is going to do a five-page article on all this, highlighting your disappearance. These pictures and a few others will appear. Your mother is turning over whatever she has to build it up. Your picture won't be on milk cartons, but it could turn up on the sides of city buses and taxis advertising the magazine article."

"I never thought . . . I mean, I never expected . . ."

She reached for the articles, and I handed them back to her. She placed them in the folder and closed it. I glanced at Mrs. Pratt. She mirrored Mrs. Brittany's look of deep concern. My heart began to thump. What was coming next?

"We're not blaming you for anything. Our taking you in is totally our responsibility," Mrs. Brittany said. "Obviously, however, if anyone managed to connect the dots, it would bring some serious negative attention to us."

"No one knows I'm here. I haven't violated your rule about contacting anyone. I had no one to contact. I've never even tried to speak with my mother since I've been here, and you know I wouldn't try to speak with my father."

"Yes. And I'm not concerned about anyone who has come here and met you," she began, sounding more like someone thinking aloud. "The places I've taken you, shops and so on, should be fine. However, no one can predict if someone who saw you and read these articles would make the connections. We can only hope not. And we would hope, or assume, that anyone working here who saw you, even if he or she could make any connection, would simply not do so.

"But," she continued, "I do not like being dependent on the discretion of too many . . . underlings. We're risking too much by parading you around on the outside."

"I don't need anything else, and I can wait to see shows or go to more museums."

Again, I looked to Mrs. Pratt, hoping to see her nod, but she was stone-faced.

"That's not going to solve our problem," Mrs. Brittany said.

"So you want me to leave?" I asked, dreading the answer. I held my breath.

"Yes," she said.

I felt a cold chill come over me. It was like being thrown out of my home and driven from my family again. I didn't know whom to blame more, myself, my father, or Mrs. Brittany. I think what hurt me most was the feeling that my father was going to win after all. All this training, this education I had been enjoying, the hope and the new self-confidence I had developed, would be snatched away. The vision of myself on the streets again actually turned my stomach.

"I would never say you kidnapped me or anything stupid," I told her. I looked at Mrs. Pratt, too, so she could see how sincere and determined I was. "And no matter what, I wouldn't reveal anything about your company or the other girls or . . . anything."

"We know that, but more often than not, things happen, good intentions are lost."

I could feel the tears come quickly into my eyes. They came more quickly than I could remember happening before. When Mr. Bob first brought me here, I was a much harder, more tightly wrapped person, I thought. Rarely was my father or even my mother able to bring me to tears. I hated the idea of revealing what I really felt inside. Besides making me feel weaker and more vulnerable, something I detested, it gave whoever was criticizing me or chastising me a sense of superiority. It got so I could keep from changing expression when a teacher or the dean at school bawled me out. My expressionless face invariably drove them back and forced them to get me out of their sight. I always left a confrontation feeling victorious even if the results were bad grades, behavior demerits, suspensions, detentions, or being sent to my room.

Once, my father was so frustrated with my indifference he screamed, "She's like the devil. You can defeat him in a battle but never destroy him."

Then stop battling me, I thought. *Leave me alone.*

He couldn't. I couldn't be his perfect daughter. Or even his daughter, for that matter, and so I was here, sitting in front of Mrs. Brittany's desk, feeling as if I were back in school, where I had been called to face the dean so he could discipline me for some rule I had broken, some fight I had been in, or some nasty remark I had made to a teacher.

"What do you want to do with me?" I asked.

"I'm sending you out of the country. You'll be flown to Nice in my private jet today, and you will stay at my home in Beaulieu-sur-Mer. It's a beautiful villa overlooking the sea. There are servants to care for everything, and since you speak French so well, you won't be uncomfortable."

"For how long?" I asked, now feeling some hope. This wasn't a dishonorable discharge. She was planning something strategically.

"I don't know for sure. We'll have to wait until this all dies down and see how long your parents, probably your mother, continue to appeal to the media. It might not be a matter of only a few weeks, Roxy. If you don't want to go through this, we'll understand. I'll double your kill fee, and we'll arrange for you to return home. Maybe things will be different for you now that they've shown a desire to get you back. Who knows?"

"No, they'll never be any different. He'll only hate me more for having put them through this," I said.

"Well, the choice is yours."

"I prefer to keep hoping I can join your organization," I said. "I'm willing to do what you want."

She nodded slowly. "Good. As you see, I'm not exactly giving up on you. I'll visit you as soon as I can and as often as I can, as will Mrs. Pratt."

"What about Sheena?" I asked.

"What about her?"

"Can she visit, too?"

"We'll see. I think for now, it's better that you don't tell her about this and . . ."

"And give her any false hope," I muttered.

"I'll explain things to her. I'll tell her I have you overseas for some necessary training and education. And you will have some important and beneficial experiences. I have a trusted associate in Monte Carlo who will look after you, Norbert Davies, a distant relative of Daphne du Maurier."

"The author of *Rebecca*?"

"Yes. He's very interesting, but he can exhaust you with stories of the family, the famous actors and writers. He handles some of the Principality of Monaco's business affairs. He'll do a good job watching over you. I trust him with you completely for many reasons.

"I'm going to ask Professor Marx to draw up a list of reading for you and have the books and materials sent over. The villa has a small exercise room and an infinity pool, so you'll continue to follow your physical regimen. You have enough information to know how to develop your own program. Norbert will arrange for your beauty needs. There's a limousine and a driver to service you, although you won't be going around anywhere on your own. When I can't respond to anything you need quickly enough, Mrs. Pratt will arrange for it," she added. Mrs. Pratt nodded.

"So, do I go pack or . . ."

"Everything's been packed that you're taking, Roxy. You'll have the opportunity to get whatever else you need there."

"Been packed?"

"We've been working on this all morning," Mrs. Pratt said.

I nodded. "So I leave . . ."

"Immediately, if you choose to do what I'm asking," Mrs. Brittany replied.

I looked from her to Mrs. Pratt. Neither broke into a smile or even changed expression.

"Just like that? Just get up and walk out of here, dressed the way I am?"

Mrs. Brittany finally smiled. "You came with nothing and easily left whatever you had," she said.

"I had nothing, but can't I at least say good-bye to Sheena?"

"I told you I'd rather you not," she said. "Let me handle that."

She rose.

"The car's waiting," Mrs. Pratt told her.

What a strange feeling it was to know that you could go off and take nothing with you and that you could literally disappear from anyone you cared about or who cared about you. It made me feel light, airy, invisible. I stood, looked at Mrs. Pratt, and started out.

"Head up," Mrs. Pratt snapped.

"Don't dare feel sorry for yourself, Roxy Wilcox," Mrs. Brittany said. "You're not being shipped to San Quentin. You're going to be in the lap of luxury at the height of the season on the Riviera."

She walked along with me.

"Norbert will see to it that you attend some wonderful concerts and events in Monte Carlo. I have a friend who will be sailing his yacht into Villefranche-sur-Mer in about a month. We might join him for a luxurious weekend."

I looked from side to side and into rooms as we headed for the front entrance. With both of them on either side of me now, I felt as if I was being escorted off the premises, and they were making sure that I could speak to no one and no one could speak to me. The stretch limousine was right outside. Jeffries had completed whatever packing needed to be done. He closed the trunk, and the chauffeur got out quickly to open the door for me.

For one frightening moment, I wondered if this was all a ruse and I wasn't going off to the French Riviera but being carried off to some other form of disposal so I would never be a threat to Mrs. Brittany and her powerful, rich organization again. Maybe she could see the thought pass across my eyes. She took hold of me at both elbows and turned me around.

"This is more of a test than I had envisioned for you, Roxy, but if you can come through this and continue to grow and develop, I am sure you will be one of my top Brittany girls. You know I don't say such things lightly."

"Yes," I said.

For a second, I thought she would actually kiss me on the cheek, but she let me go and stood back.

"Please tell Sheena I didn't want to leave without saying good-bye, at least."

"I said I'd handle it. Don't worry."

"We'll see you soon," Mrs. Pratt added. "Remember, keep a very low profile. We don't expect anyone to connect the dots over there, but American tourists will be there. Don't speak to any strangers, ever."

I felt like saying, "Yes, Mommy," but kept my lips sealed.

"Since you will be in France, you might have the temptation to contact your mother's family. That would be very, very foolish," she added. I looked at Mrs. Brittany to see if she had the same thought.

"I definitely won't do that, Mrs. Brittany. You have my word."

"I expect you to keep it. I am hoping that you have what it takes to be on your own like this, Roxy. Don't disappoint us. Don't disappoint yourself," Mrs. Brittany told me just before the door was closed.

I looked out at the two of them. Neither waved as we pulled away. They wore identical looks of concern and skepticism. I had the feeling they had debated doing this, with Mrs. Pratt probably taking the view that it would much easier just to turn me loose and forget me. *I'll prove her wrong,* I thought.

As we turned down the long driveway, I looked toward the east side of the mansion and Sheena's room. I imagined that she was going through some of her clothing, planning what she would wear on our next night out together, which, I realized, was supposed to be tonight. How would Mrs. Brittany explain this, and would she make it clear how much I hated leaving her? I hoped Mrs. Brittany realized that Sheena might see this as another betrayal.

I felt a real tear on my cheek. It shocked me until I realized that I was crying inside for Sheena as much as for myself.

We drove on. I sat back. The description Mrs. Brittany had given me of her villa and what awaited me should make me happy, I thought. After all, she was continuing her investment and faith in me.

But when I analyzed what this was about, I realized that I was still running away from my father.

Would that ever end?

13

Everyone, from the chauffeur to the pilots and the flight attendant on Mrs. Brittany's private jet, was overly solicitous. I had the sense that anyone who represented Mrs. Brittany would be treated as if she were Mrs. Brittany. My comfort was foremost. I learned that the food that had been brought onto the plane had been prepared by Gordon Leceister. Even my silk pajamas and robe were there for me when I wanted to sleep. The plane had every amenity someone would enjoy in the first-class cabins of the best airlines. I doubted that anyone involved, however, knew anything more about me than that I was Mrs. Brittany's guest. In minutes, it seemed, we were on our way, and I hadn't had to show anyone a passport or go through any security check. I began to wonder who had more power in this world, the president of the United States or Mrs. Brittany. She snapped her fingers, and I was being whisked off to southern France.

Because of the time difference, I arrived at midday. Her friend Norbert Davies was waiting at the airport to rush me away to Mrs. Brittany's villa the moment the plane landed. My luggage was quickly transferred to the limousine, which had been brought right up to the airplane.

"*Bienvenue*," Norbert said as soon as I stepped off. He was a tall, dark-complexioned man with ebony hair but surprisingly blue eyes. I didn't think he was more than thirty or maybe thirty-five. He wore a light, silver gray Armani suit with gold cuff links and one of the more expensive Rolex watches. He looked as if he had just done a *GQ* cover.

"*Enchanté*," I said.

"Please." He indicated the inside of the limousine. "We are having some unusually warm weather," he told me as an explanation for why he wanted me in the air-conditioned vehicle as quickly as possible. "The whole Côte d'Azur is smoldering, with temperatures in the forties."

"Forties? That's not hot."

"Celsius," he said, smiling. "You're here now, and when in Rome . . ."

"*Exactement*," I said, realizing that, of course, Europe was on Celsius, not Fahrenheit. "*D'accord.*"

He got in beside me. He was a George Clooney–handsome man but with an aristocratic air about him that made him seem untouchable. He was immaculately dressed, with hair so accurately cut I doubted there was a strand too long or too short.

"How is my godmother?" he asked.

"Mrs. Brittany is your godmother?"

"*Mais oui*. My mother and her late husband were cousins, but even if not, she would have been my godmother. When she lived in Europe, they were all very close. She was there for me after my mother passed away. I owe her a great deal. She was instrumental in my getting a good education and the position I hold now in the Principality of Monaco. I can never do enough to repay her, but I can't say this assignment is any burden. I look forward to making you comfortable and looking after any of your needs."

"*Merci*," I said, and wondered how much he actually knew about me and my situation. If he did know all of it, he was very discreet. He talked about my stay as if it was nothing more than a welcome vacation.

"I understand your mother is French and you've been to Paris but never the Riviera."

"Yes, that's true."

"Then it will be my pleasure to show you as much of its charm and beauty as possible while you are here, but I won't exhaust you with historical sites, museums, and endless churches. That's a promise," he said. "I have never forced anyone to do anything I wouldn't want to do."

"Then you've done something like this before?" I asked.

"Not for Mrs. Brittany. For other family friends."

I nodded. Perhaps I shouldn't ask too many questions, I thought. It all made me nervous enough as it was. I would wait for him to volunteer any information.

As we drove to Mrs. Brittany's villa, he pointed out the famous beaches of Nice. The hotels along the promenade had sections with lounges and umbrellas across from them. Every part of it looked crowded. There were streams of people walking along the promenade. Motorboats pulled water skiers and the more adventurous tourists who wanted to ride the parachutes. There was a luxury ocean liner crossing the sea for some destination Norbert said was probably in Italy, maybe Sicily. When we passed the port of Nice, I saw very large private yachts. He recognized some owned by Arabian princes and major industrialists and described what they were like inside, how many people had to be employed, and how expensive they were to operate.

All around us, young and even middle-aged people wove in and out of traffic with their motor scooters, almost all of them carrying two passengers. The risks they took to edge past other vehicles were sometimes shocking.

"Grandmothers ride them, too, and are just as reckless, if not more so," he said, smiling when I commented on the close calls.

The hustle and bustle made it seem as if I had been dropped into a great ongoing celebration. The wealth I saw not only in the yachts but also in the villas and grand hotels he pointed out made it all seem surreal. It wasn't that long ago that I was sleeping in a slum and witnessing filth and poverty all around me. Now here I was in the playland of the rich and famous. From what Norbert had told me, a day's operating expenses on one of those luxurious yachts could support a dozen homeless people for a year. It seemed unfair, even callous, that so few could live so well while so many suffered, but when I asked myself where I would rather be, there was no doubt in my mind.

Everywhere along the ride, we had breathtaking views of the sea. I especially enjoyed looking out on the bay of Villefranche-sur-Mer with Cap Ferrat on one side, a peninsula Norbert described as particularly the home of the super-rich. He rattled off the names of famous celebrities, fashion designers, and Middle Eastern monarchs who had private villas there.

Not long after that, we entered the small French village of Beaulieu-sur-Mer, and after passing through the main part of town, we veered off to the right and wound our way down to Mrs. Brittany's villa. There was a private gated entrance, but the property itself, although beautifully maintained, was not even one-twentieth the size of Mrs. Brittany's estate on Long Island. Nevertheless, the landscaping was lush, with its small palm trees, beautiful red and white bougainvillea, and rosebushes. I saw the swimming pool off to the right as we came to a stop at one side of the villa itself.

"Mrs. Brittany bought this nearly twenty years ago," Norbert explained, "and just recently had it refurbished and modernized. She didn't change a thing about the outside, but she redid the floors and updated every appliance. There are only three bedrooms, but each has a loggia facing the sea. There is a small guesthouse off the right side. Ian and Margery Dance live there. They are the caretakers. Margery is your cook. They are lovely people from London who have been with Mrs. Brittany almost from the very beginning here. They speak fluent French, but they'll be pleased to speak English, although British English sometimes seems like a totally different language from American."

As if they had heard themselves being introduced, they appeared to help with my luggage. Ian was short and a little stout, with a robust jolly face that needed only a white beard to have him play Santa Claus. His wife was a little taller, leaner, with hair a shade grayer than his. She wore it pinned up, but it looked as if when it was down, it would reach the middle of her back. They were both all smiles.

"They're happy to have someone to care for," Norbert whispered. "Margery will tell you that an empty house invites ghosts."

He stepped out and reached in to help me emerge.

"*Bonjour*, Ian, Margery," he cried when I stepped out. They hurried over. "This is Mademoiselle Roxy Wilcox. She can speak French, too," he added, as if he wanted to warn them not to say something behind my back in French.

"Welcome, dear," Margery said.

"*Bienvenue*," Ian said. "We've been here so long, we drift in and out of languages. Margery says she's dreaming in French these days."

"Oh, I did not. He's Mr. Exaggerator," she declared. "A pound's never quite a pound if not a pound and a half. And don't listen to his weather predictions, either. It's never going to rain, according to him."

"You ignore the devil, and he gets bored and goes away," Ian said in self-defense.

"Oh, don't start talking your nonsense, Mr. Dance. Let's get her things into the house."

"Yes, sir, Madame Dance," he replied.

"I'll give her the tour," Norbert said, and reached for my hand.

Was there a difference between the way a man held a woman's hand and the way a father held his daughter's hand? Was it even something any woman could sense? When Norbert took my hand, I didn't feel anything other than that he wanted to lead me into the house. In fact, I didn't think he held me firmly enough to keep my hand from slipping out of his unless I held his tighter.

I didn't see any wedding ring on his finger, but of course, he could have a girlfriend, maybe even be engaged. Or maybe women weren't his choice. What I didn't want to do was start asking him personal questions and give him the impression that I was interested in him. Despite his good looks, I was still too much in a daze to think about anything romantic. Everything had happened so fast and continued to happen fast.

He took me around front so we could enter the villa by going up the stone steps, pausing at the front balcony, where we had an unobstructed view of the Mediterranean. There were two chaise longues and a table with six chairs. The table had an umbrella. Sprinkled across the vista were sailboats, motorboats, and that luxury liner we had seen in Nice moving slowly against the horizon. Now it looked still, more like a

piece on a movie set. In fact, I had arrived so fast and
it all looked so unreal I felt as if I really had wandered
into a movie.

"There is a path that leads down to the shore,"
Norbert said, "where there is a small dock and where
Mrs. Brittany's boat is usually kept, but it's being ser-
viced at the moment."

"Beautiful view," I said.

"Yes, one of the best in this area. Well, let me show
you the house."

We entered the villa. It was simply furnished with
traditional French country antiques, and the tiled
and wooden floors looked brand spanking new. Ian
and Margery were carrying my luggage up the short,
slightly winding stairway.

"Downstairs you have the kitchen, the dining
room, the living room, an exercise room, and the
downstairs bathroom," Norbert catalogued as he led
me about.

The living and dining rooms were bright and airy,
and the kitchen looked updated, with beige granite
counters. The exercise room had some weight equipment, a treadmill, a large ball like the one Lance had
shown me how to use, and a stationary bike.

"The three bedrooms are upstairs. You'll have the
guest bedroom on the right. Mrs. Brittany's room is
in the middle, and there is a second guest bedroom on
the left. All have en suite bathrooms."

"It's very nice," I said, gazing at the paintings of
French villages and countryside scattered on every
available wall.

"Comfortable, cozy," he said. "The pool is right out those sliding doors, where you will find a patio, chairs and chaise longues, and umbrellas. Mrs. Brittany wanted me to give you a day or so to settle in and then come around and take you perhaps up to Èze first. It's a small village with cobblestone walks, shops, and restaurants. At the top is a garden, and the views are spectacular. We can have a nice lunch there.

"Next week, there is a concert at the Auditorium Rainier III in Monte Carlo. The Saint Petersburg Philharmonic will be performing. Mrs. Brittany says you shouldn't miss it."

"*Merci*," I said. "Then I won't."

"Let me show you to your suite," he said, and indicated that I should go first to the stairway.

Margery was putting away my things. Ian was hanging up my clothes. It was half the size of my suite at the estate but elegantly appointed, with patio doors that opened to a private balcony. The bed was king-size but without a canopy or posts.

"It's very beautiful," I said, and walked onto the patio. Norbert followed and stood just behind me as I looked out at the sea. "It will be easy to relax here," I said, mostly to myself.

"I'm sure. You are from New York?"

"Yes," I said, turning to him. "Were you born in France?"

"Yes, Normandy. My parents moved to Monte Carlo when I was just twelve. Since I resided in Monaco for more than ten years, I was able to apply for citizenship, but I wasn't approved until I began to work for the royal family, so that is another reason I am grateful to my godmother."

"Mrs. Brittany does have influence in many places," I said.

"I don't think she subscribes to the philosophy of 'It doesn't matter what you know but who you know,' however," he said. "She still wants to see people earn what they get."

"As we say in the States, you have to make your bones with Mrs. Brittany."

"'Make your bones,'" he repeated, smiling. "I like that. Is there anything I can get for you, do for you, at the moment?" he asked.

"I think I'm pretty much set," I said. "*Merci.*"

"You shouldn't eat your first dinner alone here," he said. "With your permission, I'll return with someone to join you."

"*Absolument, s'il vous plaît,*" I said. He was right. I didn't want to be left alone so quickly.

"I'll inform Margery," he said. "She's a very good cook. I'd advise you to get some rest. Jet lag can be sneaky." He started to leave the room and paused. "You're sure you're up to company? We can wait until tomorrow night. It was a long journey for you."

"I'm fine. I did sleep some on the plane. Besides, I don't know what time it is, and I have a feeling I don't want to know," I said.

He laughed, made a slight bow, and went to tell Margery about dinner. I sat in the chair next to the small table and just looked out at the sea. I couldn't help but feel like a fugitive. People were looking for me now, and I had fled. I was hiding out. Not once during the meeting with Mrs. Brittany and Mrs. Pratt or during my trip over here had I asked myself why I wasn't returning to my family. It was clear from what was happening that even if for only a short time, Papa was sorry and wanted me found and brought home. Perhaps, with the way I felt about myself now, I could have returned and gotten along with him. I might even have done so well in school that I could think of going to college. In short, I could have my family back. I did think of Emmie often. It would have been nice to be her big sister again, but this time for real. Being with Sheena had brought that thought home to me. Perhaps I was too quick in rejecting Mrs. Brittany's offer to turn me out and give me that kill fee so I could return to my family.

All the work I was doing, having my days so full, and developing my relationship with Sheena had pretty much kept me from even dreaming of a reconciliation with my father, but now that I was thousands of miles away, alone with nothing to do but amuse myself, I had time to reconsider my choices and actions. I didn't want this idle time. I hated even thinking of regrets, but the thoughts and feelings I had successfully kept dormant were sprouting around me like weeds determined to crowd out any bright flowers of hope and happiness.

"Excuse me," Margery said. She was standing in the patio doorway smiling sweetly. "Would you like a cup of tea, a cold drink, a glass of wine, or something to eat?"

"Maybe a glass of white wine," I said. "I'll come down." I started to rise.

"Oh, no need. I can bring it up here if you like. You might want to relax and maybe take a nap. No matter how easy it was, it was still a long journey."

"Yes," I said, feeling tired now. "You might be right. Thank you, Margery."

"*De rien*," she said, and than laughed at herself. "Oh, for a moment, I forgot that you speak English, too. Better start doing that before I can no longer converse with my relatives."

She hurried off. I sat again. *Converse with your relatives*, I thought. Would I ever do that again? However, I didn't miss that when I was living at home. Why should I miss it now? And yet I wondered if I was going to have a great empty place in my life, no matter how many luxurious and wonderful things I filled it with.

Below, Margery had put on the radio. I heard a familiar French song and fell into a melancholy, remembering my mother humming "La Vie en Rose" to herself and then, when I was younger, singing an old French nursery rhyme to me as she did her housework and I smeared finger paints over a canvas. My father used to say I was taking out my aggression with those distorted images.

I was lost in my memories until I heard the phone ring, and moments later, Margery returned to tell me Mrs. Brittany was calling. I got up quickly and went to the phone by the bed.

"Hello."

"Are you settled in? Did my godson take good care of you?"

"Oh, yes. You didn't tell me he was your godson."

"It wasn't necessary to tell you," she said sharply. She wasn't someone who accepted any criticism easily.

"He's returning to join me for dinner," I said, to make sure she would approve.

"Good. You just relax and forget about the situation for now. I'll call you if there are any other significant developments."

"How's Sheena?" I asked quickly, sensing that she was about to hang up. "Did you explain?"

"She's fine. She understands. I'm taking her to the clinic for her annual review, anyway, and then seeing about a new prosthetic leg. Don't worry. She'll be occupied. Worry about yourself for now," she ordered. "I'll check up on you from time to time. You're in good hands there."

"Okay, thank you."

I guess my small voice caught her rarely felt sense of compassion.

"Everyone here sends you his or her best. You have made a very good impression, Roxy."

"Thank you."

"Yes, but let's not veer from our course, not now," she warned. "Be careful."

"I will."

When I hung up, Margery brought me my glass of wine and some cheese and crackers. I returned to the patio and sat for nearly an hour before I felt my eyes closing. Moments later, I was in my new bed and fast asleep.

Fortunately, people on the Côte d'Azur didn't eat dinner until eight or nine, especially during the summer, when daylight lasted so long. I didn't wake up until seven and then leaped out of bed to shower and dress. I wore a simple off-the-shoulder peasant dress. It was still quite warm, but I could feel the temperature moderating as the sun began to drift toward the horizon. The patios all faced northwest, so I imagined there would be wonderful sunsets. *Stop feeling sorry for yourself, Roxy Wilcox.* Few fugitives had as wonderful a hideout, I told myself.

When I went down, I found that Margery had set up a cocktail table on the main patio. Ian assumed the role of waiter. He was dressed in a pair of black slacks, a white shirt, and a black vest. There was a bottle of champagne in a bucket at the center of the table.

"*Bonsoir, mademoiselle.*" He nodded at the champagne. "A welcome gift from Monsieur Norbert."

Moments later, the doorbell rang, and Ian went to let Norbert in. Accompanying him was a younger man with light brown hair styled almost the same way as Norbert's and a well-trimmed goatee. He had a firmer, more athletic build and was a few inches shorter than Norbert. His features weren't as perfect, but I thought he was handsome in a more rugged way.

"*Bonsoir*, Roxy," Norbert said. "I'd like you to meet my good friend, Paul Lamont. Yes, of the Lamont cosmetics line," he added before I could ask.

"Do you have to embarrass me instantly?" Paul

asked him. "*Enchanté*," he said, turning back to me and taking my hand to kiss. "You'll find that Norbert enjoys having his friends at a bit of a disadvantage."

"It's hardly a disadvantage to be part of the Lamont cosmetics line," I said. His smile widened.

"Ah, finally someone you can't confuse," Paul told him.

"Thank you for the champagne," I said to Norbert. "Shall we?"

I led them out to the patio, where Ian was opening the bottle.

"I had forgotten what a view you have here," Paul said. "I was here once before with Norbert to meet Mrs. Brittany."

"Breathtaking," I said.

"Save your breath. There are many breathtaking places to visit on the Côte d'Azur."

"Norbert should be in public relations. I know no one who can do a better job of selling the Riviera to first-time visitors," Paul said.

"Does it need anyone to sell it?" Norbert said.

Ian handed us each a glass.

"Thank you, Ian," I said.

"Let's toast to what I hope will be the beginning of a memorable visit," Norbert said.

"How could it be otherwise?" I replied.

Paul's smile widened, his eyes brightening with an almost childlike delight. We sipped our champagne, and then we all sat.

"Norbert seems to know nothing about you," Paul

said. "Or else, he refuses to reveal anything. You're a young woman of mystery."

"Do you like that idea, a woman of mystery?"

"Oh, yes."

"Then why ruin it with my telling you too much?" I asked.

Norbert roared. Paul looked lost for a moment and then laughed, too.

"Okay. We'll bore you to death by talking only of ourselves," he told me.

They did, but I wasn't bored. Paul had recently graduated from the Sorbonne, where he earned a dual degree in economics and tax strategy. It was clear from the way he described his youth and his education that his family had a great deal to do with whatever choices he made.

"Like a prince being schooled in what is necessary for him to rule a kingdom, my friend is being groomed to be CEO of Lamont Enterprises," Norbert said.

Paul didn't deny it. He seemed resigned to the fact that his life had been prearranged.

"Even down to whom he will eventually marry," Norbert added with a slight twist of his lips.

"My family is quite old-school," Paul offered in explanation. "My parents' marriage was prearranged, but both claim it worked out perfectly."

"And your father has no interests on the side?" Norbert teased.

"I didn't say that, but maybe that's what makes his marriage perfect."

Norbert laughed. I was astonished at how honest

they were being about themselves, especially with someone they had just met who wasn't being the least forthcoming about her own life and past. It wasn't long before an instinctive feeling about Norbert was confirmed. He was gay. His partner was busy tonight, so he had brought Paul. I didn't have a chance to find this overwhelming. All of it came too fast, one thing after another, before I could react. But our dinner was wonderful, with both of them entertaining me. Afterward, we had some ice wine from Germany, a very expensive wine that I knew.

We sat talking on the patio. Yachts and smaller boats dazzled us with their lights, which sometimes looked like stars that had fallen into the sea. Way off on the horizon, I could see the ghostlike silhouette of a barge, and later, we saw another ocean liner all lit up.

"It's heading for Barcelona, I'll bet," Norbert said.

"Have you been on a cruise?" Paul asked me.

"No."

"A yacht?"

I shook my head.

"Well, maybe we can arrange for that this coming week. My family's yacht is in Monte Carlo."

"I thought your social calendar was full this month, and tonight was your only free night," Norbert told him.

"Yes, it was," he replied, keeping his eyes on me. "But that was before you brought me here."

"I see. Be careful, Roxy. He's a heartbreaker. That was really his major at the Sorbonne."

"I've racked up a few of those myself," I said, and they both laughed.

It all seemed so incredible when I considered how quickly I had traveled, not only from New York to southern France but from the roach hotel to an elegant villa to be entertained by sophisticated wealthy men. I was confident that I was more than holding my own with every topic, too, every bit of repartee.

Suddenly, it occurred to me that this could be Mrs. Brittany's way of testing me in the field. I wondered again how much Norbert really knew about her business and especially my upcoming role in it. Was Paul telling the truth when he said that Norbert knew almost nothing about me? It was difficult to know how I should behave, what I should say, and, most important, what I should agree to do with either of them. Decisions weighed me down.

"You look like you're falling asleep," Norbert said. "Paul, let's let her catch up."

"Okay, but only if she agrees to my helping you show her around," he said.

"Why wouldn't I agree? Two for the price of one?"

They both laughed. I walked them to the door.

"*Bonne nuit*," Paul said. He kissed me on the cheek. Norbert did the same.

I watched them walk to the car, and then I closed the door and hurried up to my room. I felt as if I would fall asleep on my feet if I didn't get into bed soon. It was a comfortable bed, and despite all that had happened so quickly to bring me there, I was feeling good about it now. I had really enjoyed my dinner with Paul and Norbert, and I was looking forward to doing all the things they had suggested. I was confident that even if this was another one of Mrs. Brittany's tests, I would come through it with flying colors.

Yes, how far I had come.

Smother any regrets or second thoughts, I told myself. There was no turning back for me now.

14

Margery woke me when she brought me a cup of wonderful French café au lait, a small orange juice, a croissant, and jam.

"To start you off, *petit déjeuner*," she said.

"Yes, I know. My mother still sees this as breakfast."

"Oh, your mother is French, then?"

"Yes."

She smiled. Even though I could see that she was bubbling over with questions, she kept her curiosity chained. She must have cared for other guests of Mrs. Brittany, perhaps other Brittany girls. Maybe even Portia or Camelia had been here. I was sure she knew how Mrs. Brittany felt about gossip.

"I looked in on you twice," she said. "I didn't want to wake you, but I thought you might want to be up by now. It's nearly noon."

"Is it? I haven't slept this late for months, maybe years," I said, sitting up.

She placed the tray on the bed table and rolled it over. Then, without my asking, she placed a second

pillow behind me so I could be more comfortable sitting up. I certainly didn't mind being pampered, not
after what I had been through.

"There now. Comfy, are you?"

"Yes, thank you, Margery."

"I can make you eggs and ham, if you'd like."

"This will do fine for now. Thank you, Margery."

"My pleasure. Just call if you need anything else,"
she said, then hesitated a moment as if she was decid-
ing on another question to ask, thought wiser of it,
and left.

I sighed and looked around at my cozy, bright,
and warm room. I hadn't noticed the pastel painting
of two little girls building a sand castle on the beach
and the embossed pewter candleholders on the walls.
When I finished my *petit déjeuner*, I pushed the table
aside and sprawled out again, letting myself sink into
the soft mattress and oversize pillows. After months
of training and education at Mrs. Brittany's estate, this
sort of lazy day was wonderful. There was no phone
ringing to wake me up, no one pouncing on me to
move quickly and not keep someone waiting.

I deliberately took a lot more time doing everything. By the time I started downstairs, it was nearly
one-thirty in the afternoon. Ian was working on the
grounds, cutting grass and trimming bushes. Margery,
after bringing me some of her homemade lemonade
out on the patio and asking me if I wanted anything
else, went up to do my room.

It wasn't as warm as yesterday, I thought, but
the sky didn't have a cloud in it. Brittany girls were

forbidden to get too much sun. Our tans, if we were to have any, were to come from creams. Claudine Laffette had told me that Mrs. Brittany expected her girls to look young and beautiful well through their early forties. Early wrinkles were as deadly for us as they were for vampires who realized they were reaching the end of their so-called immortality. Mrs. Brittany's skin was still youthful-looking, although she had surely had some plastic surgery, and she did use certain skin creams and treatments. I had some of her latest newly developed miracle creams in my makeup bag with instructions.

"You're never too young to worry about that sort of thing," she had told me. "Get into the right habits now, and you'll be happy about it later."

By now, I was feeling like all the others under her command. I would probably walk over hot coals if she told me it was necessary.

I sprawled on a chaise in the shade and sipped a glass of Margery's cool natural lemonade. She left the radio on for me. After all the tension during the last thirty-six hours, it felt wonderful to continue just drifting and relaxing. I had nearly fallen asleep again when I heard the doorbell. Margery hurried to see who it was, and I sat up, listening.

Moments later, Paul Lamont appeared on the patio. He wore a light blue short-sleeved shirt and light blue pants and was sockless in blue boat shoes. His hair was as perfect as it had been last night. Everyone always looked different in the daytime, I thought. Imperfections were always more visible, but if anything, he looked even more handsome today.

"I hope I'm not disturbing you," he said.

"Oh, no. Please," I said, nodding at a chair. "Would you like some fresh lemonade?"

"Looks good." He poured himself a glass, sipped some, and smiled. "Perfect." He stared at me a moment. "I woke up this morning thinking about you, how delightful and attractive you are."

"Oh?"

One of the things Mrs. Brittany had taught me was that most people feel obligated to return a compliment with a compliment even though they don't feel or believe it. "If someone lavishes a compliment on you, accept it gracefully," she told me, "but don't do or say anything that isn't authentic. Really discerning men and women will know you were just being polite, but it also makes you look as if you don't believe you deserved the compliment they gave you. Be tight and firm with your emotions. Never lose control, and the easiest way for that to happen is to permit someone to stroke your ego."

"I didn't wake up this morning. I slept until nearly noon, so I had no time to think of anything or anyone," I said, hardly acknowledging his lavish flattery.

"Well, that's understandable, the time change and all, especially how long we kept you up talking."

"I'm not complaining about myself," I said. "I wanted to be lazy. I intend to be as lazy as I can."

He laughed.

"Beautiful, bright, and honest. You are indeed unique, especially for the social world you'll find here. You might feel out of place."

"I am what I am," I said with cold conviction. "I'm not going to change to fit any setting, anyone."

"And full of self-confidence, too. I'd love to know how you were brought up."

"No, you wouldn't," I muttered.

He laughed nervously. There was a short moment of uncomfortable silence.

"My life isn't that interesting yet," I added to soften the pause.

"I like that you added 'yet.'" He looked around. Ian was clipping hedges but occasionally sneaking a glance at us. Paul nodded at him before turning back to me. "So you had breakfast late, I take it?"

"*Petit déjeuner*. Fashionably late."

"Yes, of course. Anyway, I thought you might want to have lunch at the Café de Paris. Three's a good time," he said, glancing at his watch. He tilted his head to the side and added, "I did check with Norbert first to see if he had other designs on your time. He thought he would be free, but he's tied up with business for the Principality. I mentioned that I'd be glad to step in where you were concerned. He did suggest that I might be being a little too pushy, and I should let you get acclimated to your new surroundings. I told him I didn't think you were so old that you needed the time for such a thing. Was I wrong?"

"Actually, I am getting hungry. Where is the Café de Paris?"

"The one in Monaco is in Monte Carlo, right near the casino." He sounded surprised that I didn't know.

"Oh, right. Well, let me throw something else on, perhaps."

"No, you're fine like that."

"Then let me run a brush through my hair and put on some lipstick," I said.

"You're fine like that," he repeated. "At least, as far as I'm concerned."

"Don't you know that women look good for themselves first and for a man last?"

He laughed. "Not the women I've met."

"Maybe you need to expand your acquaintances."

"That's exactly what I intend to do," he replied with an impish smile.

As I walked out and up the stairs, I laughed to myself. Wasn't I the little coquette? Before Mrs. Brittany, whenever I met a boy I was interested in or who was interested in me, I was crudely honest about my intentions. I was changing, and I liked the change. When I stood before the mirror and fixed my hair, I paused as a ripple of concern washed across my mind.

Wasn't this happening a little too quickly? Norbert brings him along, and then Norbert steps out of the picture. Mrs. Brittany was testing me for sure. Was she testing to see how quickly I would socialize? Was she testing to see if I would be careful? Or was this actually going to be my first foray into the field? Would she get a report from Norbert and Paul? Should I have been so eager to go with Paul? I had decided that I would always be a tougher critic of my behavior with men than Mrs. Brittany would be. Should I have played harder to get, turned him down but suggested perhaps another time? Was it too late to change my mind? How would that make me look?

How conscious of my every action, every word, I had become. Did that make me careful or just plain neurotic? *Whatever,* I thought. *If I've been tossed into the game, I'll play it as best I can, and if I fail, I fail.* Maybe it was a good idea to find out if I could do this, be a full-blown Brittany girl, sooner rather than later, not only for her but for myself. Why should either of us waste any more time?

He was waiting for me at the base of the short stairway, looking up at me with such admiration in his eyes he made me feel like Venus descending.

"You still look terrific to me," he said.

"I didn't think I'd look worse after brushing out my hair and putting on some lipstick."

He laughed and held out his hand for mine. This time, I was being gripped with some interest. I looked back and saw Margery standing in the kitchen doorway staring at us.

"Shall I prepare dinner tonight, Miss Wilcox?" she asked.

"We'll call you," Paul answered for me. He looked to see what I would say or do about his answering for me so quickly.

"I'll call you if there is any change in my plans," I told her, stressing "I'll."

He nodded. "Pardon my enthusiasm, *s'il vous plaît.*"

"Enthusiasm isn't bad, but every woman surrounds herself with her own minefield. Be careful. First learn the terrain," I warned with a small smile.

He sucked in his breath and straightened up quickly. "Yes, ma'am," he said. He started to raise his hand toward his forehead.

"Don't salute me, please, Paul. That's the kiss of death."

"Okay," he said.

We stepped out.

Paul had a gold Lamborghini.

"Oh, you have the Murciélago," I said.

"You know what this is?" he asked, his voice full of genuine surprise.

"*Mais oui*. Like all Lamborghinis, it's named after a famous bull."

"You know cars?"

"A little," I said. Mrs. Brittany's advice was to always be modest and always permit the man you were with to believe he knew more, even if he didn't.

"The male ego lacks vitamin C," she'd said, half in jest. "It's easily bruised."

The truth was, I did know a lot about cars. One of my requirements with Professor Marx was to learn about expensive automobiles. I actually knew the ten most expensive ones and could discuss their engines and their accessories. Most rich and powerful men loved their expensive toys and appreciated someone who could share their enthusiasm for them.

Sometimes when Mrs. Brittany was trying to share her male-female wisdom with me, I would stop and think that a man, any man, was at quite a disadvantage when he was with one of her girls. There were so many contrivances, manipulations, all done subtly so that they weren't aware of how under control they were.

Paul looked at me and nodded.

"What?" I asked.

"You really are an amazing young woman."

"You mean you didn't mean it before when you said it?"

"Well, yes, but . . . what are you, nineteen?"

Another Brittany quote came quickly to mind. "It isn't the time you clock, it's what you clock in the time you've had," I told him.

His eyes widened, and then he laughed. "Well said, well said. I think I'll use that on my father when he lectures me about something and stresses how young and inexperienced I am."

"Be sure to give me credit."

After I got into the car, which was obviously brand-new, he asked me about the famous bull for which his car was named. "I mean, I know they do that when they name cars," he said, "but I don't know why one bull is more famous than another."

I wasn't sure if he was telling the truth. Was he testing to see if I really knew anything? I said, "Murciélago was known for having survived twenty-eight sword strokes in a bullfight. The crowd called for his life to be spared, and the matador did just that."

"Have you been to a bullfight?"

"No, but I've read about them, and I read Hemingway's *Death in the Afternoon*." It had been one of the books on Professor Marx's required reading list.

"Really? I've heard about it, but I haven't read it."

"Well, now, since you own a car named after a bull, maybe you will."

"I'll buy it as soon as possible. And then maybe you and I can discuss it."

"Have you ever discussed a book with a woman?"

He shook his head, smiling. "Hardly."

"Then it really will be a new experience."

"Yes." He started his engine and patted the steering wheel. "Well, thanks to you, I'm even prouder of my vehicle now."

"Good, but you don't have to survive twenty-eight accidents," I said. He laughed and drove onto the Basse Corniche, which he explained was the lower highway that would take us to Monaco.

"There are three main roads here: the Basse Corniche, the Moyenne Corniche, and the Grande Corniche. I like this route. It's more scenic."

It was. The views of the sea were awesome. We went through a short tunnel cut out of a rock and cruised through the village of Èze-sur-Mer, where I saw fruit and vegetable kiosks at the side of the highway. It reminded me about how proud Mama was of the freshness of French food. I didn't realize how quiet I had become when I thought about her, but once again, I realized that I was in France, closer to Mama's family and where she was born than I had been for a long time.

"You okay?" Paul asked, noting my long period of silence.

"Oh, yes. Fine. I'm just enjoying the scenery."

"So, woman of mystery, what will you tell me

about yourself? I must have earned some information by now, don't you think?"

"I'm crazy about dark chocolate," I said.

"We'll make sure you get some of the best Belgian chocolates today, then. You're from New York?"

"I was born there, but it's up for grabs where I'm from," I said.

He shook his head. "This is really going to be a challenge."

"Would you have it any other way?"

"No," he said.

"Yes, you would," I retorted. "Like any man, you want everything to be easy when it comes to a woman."

"Oh, I do, do I? Where did you get all this experience, or should I say clock it?"

"How many times do you have to put your finger on a hot stove before you realize you shouldn't do it?"

"Is that what you think a man is, a hot stove?"

"No, not all. Some are cold soup."

"Well, that's not always so bad. There's gazpacho."

I smiled. *Let him win his point*, I could hear Mrs. Brittany whisper. *If you continually frustrate and defeat the man you're with, he won't be with you long.*

"*Touché,*" I said.

Despite how vague I was about myself, I could see he was feeling more relaxed with me. As we drove into Monaco and Monte Carlo, he pointed out various highlights, the palace and the museums. Once we turned up toward the world-famous casino, I was impressed with how pristine everything was. I tried not to be a bug-eyed tourist, but I had not been out of New York and America very much and only when I was much younger. I couldn't help but be excited and struggled to keep from sounding unsophisticated. I didn't want him to know anything about my past if I could help it.

Everyone seemed to know him at the Café de Paris. He had what I assumed was his favorite table, off in a corner. Most of the clientele looked as successful and wealthy as he was. Everywhere I turned, women and men were in stylish clothes, bedecked with expensive jewelry, and exhibiting that *joie de vivre* that came with having no real worries. The music in this restaurant was laughter. Smiles glittered. Everyone was on his or her own stage, asking the rest of us to look at him or her and be envious.

"You were right," I said. "Three is a good time for lunch."

"Oh, it gets crowded when the cruise ships come in, but I knew there was none in today," he told me as we were seated. "You like rosé wine?"

"For lunch? Absolutely."

"Any favorites?"

I looked at the wine list and chose a particular Côtes de Provence rosé I knew. Once again, he looked impressed. Was everything I did being checked off? I felt as if Nigel Whitehouse was sitting at the table to our right, watching my every move. Would I always feel that way, always think that someone from Mrs. Brittany's world was looking over my shoulder, evaluating every gesture I made, every word I spoke?

We ordered our food. Because I had mentioned Hemingway's *Death in the Afternoon*, our conversation centered on books and the theater. Just recently, Professor Marx had gotten me up to speed on the London theater scene. Paul was unaware of a particular playwright's new production and was once again surprised at my knowledge.

"How do you keep up with all this?"

"Like anyone else, newspapers, television. That's no mystery."

I turned the conversation to business, his company, cosmetics in general. He was surprised that I knew his company was on the New York Stock Exchange, but my father had been touting the stock to his clients for some time. We discussed what affected the rise and fall of some company stock value. I felt grateful to my father for his constant lectures about the economy at our dinner table, especially when I considered that economics was Paul's major at the Sorbonne. I could almost feel his first good impressions of me growing stronger with every passing moment. It was like watching the mold of a beautiful statue harden with its eyes full of you.

I looked around, nudged by my paranoia, which was rapidly becoming my new shadow, clinging to everything I said and did. I wasn't nervous, however. In fact, I was surprised and pleased at how quickly my self-confidence was growing. If this was my first test in the field, I would ace it for sure.

"So how do you know Mrs. Brittany?" he asked me as we finished our dessert. We were sharing a tiramisu.

"A friend introduced me to her," I said, thinking of Mr. Bob.

"I never quite understood what she does, how she came into so much money. You should hear Norbert talk about her. He thinks the day practically starts and ends with her."

My alarms were sounding. If there was any question designed to test me, this was the chief one.

"She's his godmother," I said.

"Yes, I know all about her and her husband being related to him, but I had the impression they were poor royalty. That villa you're in is worth more than eight million dollars."

I shrugged as if I had been in multimillion-dollar villas all my life. Besides, it was easy to see that a million dollars to the wealthy here was like a hundred dollars to the people back home.

"Mrs. Brittany is an enterprising woman," I said. "She enjoys her success and uses her wealth wisely."

"How?"

"Excuse me?"

"How did she get this wealth?"

I couldn't imagine Norbert not telling him anything, but then again, perhaps he was as loyal to her as anyone who worked for her. Did he work for her, too? Did he send her clients from this world of wealth and glamour?

Once again, I shrugged. "She's an even bigger mystery than I am," I replied, and he laughed.

"Okay, we'll go back to talking about me."

"Good idea." I leaped on the opportunity. "Is your marriage really prearranged?"

"That's what my soon-to-be fiancée thinks."

"What about you?"

"I'm still thinking about it," he said, but not very firmly.

"Well, what is she like?"

"She's not unattractive, but I can guarantee she doesn't know much about cars or books or theater. I know she's not too informed about stocks and bonds, either."

"What do you talk about when you're with her?"

"Our families, her latest fashion purchases, hot new pop stars. She, unlike you, hasn't clocked that much experience in the so-called real world. She's attended a charm school and went to a liberal arts college, but I think she was, how shall I say it, helped along?"

"How often do you see her?"

"When our families get together, which is monthly these days."

"So when will you be formally engaged? If you agree, that is."

"I don't know," he said, starting to become visibly upset. "I changed my mind. Let's talk about something else rather than me."

"Why will you do this if you're not in love with her?" I pursued. I knew it was a no-no to make the man you were with feel uncomfortable about anything, but I was genuinely interested in him now, and it was still possible that he wasn't part of any test of my new abilities.

He studied me a moment, and then, after taking a

breath, he said, "It's more of a merger than a marriage. I could end up running the whole game. As you know, we're an international company, just making inroads in Asia, in fact, and with her family business tied to ours . . . we're talking huge numbers. And I would be the man in charge."

"Ambition, tragic hubris," I said in a playful tone of warning, recalling my discussion of *Macbeth* with Professor Marx and the work Sheena and I had done with the play. We had read it aloud, with each of us playing multiple parts and enjoying our over-the-top acting. I thought I would make a very decent Lady Macbeth.

"I'll be fine," he said. "All kidding aside, what are your interests? How come you're here? How long will you be staying? Are you in school? Will you be going to school, college, maybe in Europe? Please. Tell me something about yourself, anything besides the chocolates you like."

I laughed. If I didn't give him something, I thought, this might be the last time I would see him, and I did want to see him again.

"I don't know how long I'll be here yet," I began. "I've been treated to a vacation. I'm interested in most things. No, I'm not in school at the moment. I'm in between. How's that?"

"I don't know any more about you than I did before your answer," he said.

"Well, is this the last time we'll see each other?"

"Better not be."

"Okay. Then as time goes by, you'll learn more about me."

He smiled. "What were you planning to do with the rest of your day?"

"Nothing much. Maybe take a swim."

"Want company?"

"I thought I had that," I said.

He signaled for the waiter. "*L'addition*," he told him. "We can stop at a store just out here that carries the best chocolates in Monaco."

"I was just kidding. That's not important."

"Okay. Then let me stop by my house and pick up a suit. That way, I can, as Norbert would say, impress you."

"Oh, not another mansion," I said, and feigned a yawn, pretending to be bored with the idea. He laughed and paid for our lunch.

His family home was above the Grande Corniche. It looked more like a castle, with its turrets and walls. When I said that, he told me it *had* been a castle.

"It was my father's dream to turn it into a livable modern home. It took nearly five years to redo and modernize with plumbing and electricity. There's an elevator, too, not that either of my parents needs one."

"Are you an only child?"

"My sister says she is," he replied, smiling. "There's just the two of us. She's older and married and living in Switzerland. She's one of those Greenpeace types, so my parents and she don't see eye to eye on most things. Her marriage was a disaster as far as they're concerned. They tolerate my brother-in-law, but they're not fond of him. Consequently, my sister isn't here much and has nothing to do with our family enterprise. What about you? Any brothers or sisters?" He waited to see if I would answer.

"I'm on my own," I said. It wasn't really an answer, but it was true.

"Okay."

We drove through the opened gate and into a wide courtyard.

"Dad says there was a moat here, but he's just kidding, of course."

I got out, now very curious. "Are your parents home?"

"No, they're on a trip with some friends. They're on the yacht. But they'll be back this week, and I can take you for a short trip, maybe a day or so, if you like."

"Maybe," I said. I thought I would absolutely have to check with Mrs. Brittany first, and perhaps then I would know if this had all been prearranged or if it was just happening. Even if it was just happening, I wasn't sure how she would react. Maybe she would think I had already gone too far.

"My father wanted to preserve the stone exterior. The house has a history. It was a nobleman's castle in the seventeenth century," Paul explained as we stood looking up at the walls around the front entrance. "Of course, such structures were cold and dreary inside, so part of the renovation involved widening windows to get more sunlight. There are twelve bedrooms. He kept the structure so that all of them are perfectly round. If you want to go around in circles, this is the place," he joked, and opened the large, tall oak front door to reveal another, smaller courtyard. The more modern entrance with large glass windows was at the other side of that.

"Voilà," he said. There were wooden benches, small ponds and fountains, beautiful flowers, and some statuary in the inner courtyard. "I'm on the third floor," he said. "You've got to see the view."

"Isn't that what the fox told the hen?"

"Not quite, but close."

I followed him over the stone walkway to the actual entrance. A woman in a light blue uniform appeared as soon as we stepped into the long, wide entryway. She looked to be in her late fifties or early sixties.

"Ah, Mrs. Luden. We're just here to pick up a bathing suit. No need to interrupt whatever you're doing."

"Very good, Mr. Lamont."

She looked hard at me but turned quickly and returned to whatever she was doing.

"Been with the family for years," Paul muttered, and led me to the circular stairway.

"She didn't look like she approved of my being here," I said.

He looked after her. "Maybe not. She's always been a bit of a prude, but good servants are always also deaf and dumb." He paused and nodded at the grand tapestries draping the walls, the paintings and large furnishings. A skylight had been cut in one ceiling, and sunlight rained down, spotlighting the statuary in niches and the artifacts on tables and shelves. "Think you could live in this place?"

"So far, yes," I said. "There's nothing cold or dreary about it now."

"Yes, home sweet home," he said, and reached for my hand so we could continue up the stairway together.

A round bedroom was unique. There were no corners. His television was hanging from the ceiling. He showed me that it could be raised or lowered by pressing a button on the wall by his bed's headboard. All of the furniture had been constructed with rich mahogany and had been custom-made to fit into a round room. There were oval dressers and a curved desk. The flooring consisted of marble and a white area rug.

The en suite bathroom had the same marble floors and a slightly darker shade of marble tiling for walls. There was a large round Jacuzzi and a circular, very large shower that had five different showerheads, including the rain head. Paul explained that the shower converted into a steam room, again by pressing buttons on the wall. The only noncircular area was his walk-in closet, which was a wide rectangular shape, everything very neatly organized, from dozens of shoes on shelves to a row of sports jackets and suits with a half dozen different tuxedos at the end.

"What do you think?" he asked. "Make you dizzy?"

"A little. I'm surprised you don't have a circular bed. Isn't Hugh Hefner famous for having that?"

"I thought about it, but the truth is, it's rare that I have anyone up here to share my bed."

"What about your soon-to-be possible fiancée? Not here?"

He lowered his head and raised his eyes.

"We have some other properties, a farmhouse in Mougins and a chalet in Switzerland, to name two."

"Norbert will be upset. I am impressed," I said. "He warned me about you."

He laughed, opened a drawer to find a bathing suit, and then opened the curtains, which were motorized.

"I think you have more switches and buttons in here than an air-traffic controller in the JFK tower."

"I have a better view than they do. Come." He beckoned, and I joined him at the window to look down at the seaport of Monte Carlo. Because of the clarity of the day, we could see far toward the horizon. He had a telescope and pulled it over for me to gaze out at some of the vessels and sailboats in the distance and also down at the port.

"Feels like we're on the top of the world."

"Just like the slave who stood next to the Roman generals and whispered in their ears, I have to tell myself constantly that I'm only a man," he joked.

He stood very close to me. Our eyes seemed to lock, and then, as if we had magnets in our lips, we drew closer and kissed. It was a soft kiss, but he paused only to take in a breath and kiss me again, harder, more demanding, his hands sliding up the sides of my body and pausing at my breasts. He kissed me on the neck.

"I regret that I don't have a round bed, but this one is no slouch," he whispered, edging me toward it.

I stopped firmly. "Fox and the hen," I said.

"Neither complained."

"I think it's best if we walk before we run," I told him, inching away.

The look of disappointment and surprise shifted quickly to amusement. "How about we swim before we run?"

"That was the plan," I told him. There was no doubt or hesitation in my voice.

He laughed, scooped up his suit, and held the door open for me.

On the way out, I thought Mrs. Brittany would be proud of me. I had hit all the marks.

One way or another, I was sure it wouldn't be long before I would find out.

15

❦

"Not that I don't appreciate you taking me places and spending time with me, but don't you ever have to work?" I asked him on our way back to the villa.

"A good CEO creates his own schedule. I have some very good assistants, too."

We heard his mobile phone vibrate. He looked at me.

"Maybe I spoke too soon. Paul Lamont," he said into it, and listened. Then he looked at me and smiled. "Yes, we went to lunch at Café de Paris. Now we're returning to the villa for a swim. Well, why don't you ask her?" He handed me the phone.

"Hello," I said.

"*Bonjour*, Roxy. It's Norbert. Is everything all right?"

"Yes, everything is fine. I was introduced to the playland of the rich and famous," I said, smiling at Paul.

"I'm sorry I've been too busy to call. There was a little crisis here. I will call you again later, and you have my mobile number if you need anything until then."

"Yes, *merci*, Norbert. Don't worry," I said. "I never completely let go of the handlebars."

"Pardon?"

"Nothing. I'm fine. *Merci*."

"Let me have Paul again, *s'il vous plaît*."

I handed him the phone.

"Yes, Dad?" he joked, and listened. "I understand. I'm on my best behavior. *D'accord. À bientôt*," he said, and closed his mobile.

"I guess you really do have a reputation," I said.

"It's hard to say what worries Norbert more, you being upset with me or Mrs. Brittany being upset with him."

"Probably one and the same," I told him.

He looked at me strangely, the impish smile gone. "If she were Italian, I would think she was the head of some Mafia family or something."

"She's not Italian."

"Yes, I know. How long have you known her?"

"Not long," I said.

He nodded.

"How long have you known Norbert?" I asked him.

"Oh, well over fifteen years. I think you might have picked up that we don't exactly travel in the same circles, however."

"Some of my best friends are Chinese."

"Pardon?"

"Nothing, it's a joke my father used to use," I said, and immediately regretted it because it nudged open one of those doors that I wanted to keep tightly shut.

"Oh? What does he do? I assume he still works?"

"I don't like talking about my father," I said, so sharply I could feel the air freeze between us.

"Oh, sorry, but you just brought him up, and I thought . . ."

"I was trying to make a point about you and Norbert still being friends even though he's apparently gay."

"Ah, yes, yes. I see. He's actually my best friend," Paul said. "There's a lot more in life to share besides sex."

"You might get kicked out of your gender for making such an outrageous remark," I told him, and he roared.

Moments later, we turned into the villa's driveway and parked.

"Before we go in, I'd like to settle something between us," he said.

"What?" I asked, anticipating something about my being so elusive when it came to answering questions about myself, my family, or Mrs. Brittany. I was prepared to tell him to stay in the car and not bother anymore. But he surprised me.

"Dinner," he said. "Margery will be hovering over us, and I'd like to get that in cement."

I laughed, but then I wondered if I should call Mrs. Brittany first and tell her what was happening. Would she think me cautious and wise to check with her before going too much further, or would she think I was too insecure?

"We'll go close by. I have a favorite restaurant

in Beaulieu, Les Agaves. You'll love the food, the ambience."

My hesitation was confusing him.

"All I want to do is walk a little more before we run," he added with a smile.

I had to smile, too. "Okay," I said.

We got out and went in to change into our bathing suits. I had a new bikini Mrs. Brittany had bought me on one of our shopping sprees. He took the guest room and was waiting for me below as I descended. I saw the smile on his face blossom even more as he drank me in with his thirsty eyes.

"You're a very beautiful woman, Roxy. I mean that."

"I hope so," I said, as unimpressed as I could sound. "I hate insincerity, especially when it involves something concerning me."

He lost his smile. "You don't accept compliments too easily. Why so cautious?"

"Compliments was the way Lucifer got to Eve in the Garden of Eden."

"I'm not Lucifer."

"We'll see," I said. "Let's go swimming. We both have to cool off."

He took my hand as we walked out. Either Margery or Ian had set up the chaise longues with towels and placed a bottle of white wine to chill in a bucket beside them. I looked around but didn't see either of them. My paranoia began to seep in again. This felt like some sort of setup. Everything was so convenient, so easy and encouraging.

I went right to the pool and dived in to start my laps. When I had completed four, I saw that Paul was still standing at the edge of the pool watching me.

"What?"

"You're the first woman I've been with who really meant swimming when we went swimming."

"Try it," I said, with a challenge in my voice, and continued my laps.

He got in and swam beside me, but after ten more, he stopped to catch his breath and hold on to the side of the pool. I did another five before pausing.

"How old are you, really, Roxy?" he asked.

"Why?"

"I want to find an excuse for myself."

"You're not that old, Paul. Have you ever read *The Great Gatsby*?"

"Oh, no, another book I missed. Why?"

"There's this famous quote from it you should know. 'Let me tell you about the very rich. They are different from you and me. They possess and enjoy early, and it does something to them, makes them soft where we are hard,'" I recited, recalling how Sheena and I had discussed the novel.

"Well, I'm not becoming poor just to keep up with you in the pool."

"I don't want you to be poor."

"So you want me to be hard. No problem," he joked.

I started to get out, and he reached for my hand and pulled me to him. He held me, dripping wet in his arms. We kissed again.

"I'm glad you agreed to go to dinner with me," he said softly. "I don't want this day to end."

"Don't you believe in tomorrow?"

"Not unless you're in it," he said.

I smiled, kissed him on the tip of his nose, and went to a chaise to get a towel.

"Some wine?" he asked.

"Sure?"

He poured me a glass. I sipped it and watched him pour his own. Then I sprawled on the chaise and closed my eyes.

Was this what it was always going to be like from now on, I wondered, escorting one wealthy man after another, enjoying the best food, going to the most luxurious places, never having to think or worry about anything but my makeup and my hair?

"Excuse me. I have to make a call," Paul told me.

"It's okay. I'm going to drift off on a cloud," I said.

He leaned over to kiss me softly on the lips and then went to the rear of the patio to make his call. Before he returned, I was fast asleep. When I woke up, I heard voices and looked back into the villa to see Paul talking to a young man who was delivering some fresh clothing for him to wear to dinner. I checked the time, subtracted the difference between here and New York, and rose to call Mrs. Brittany. I had decided she wouldn't be critical of my checking in with her. This was, after all, the first time I was on my own since I had been with her. Surely she would see it as intelligent and even loyal.

"It's getting late," I told Paul as I passed him. "I want to take a shower, wash my hair. Can you amuse yourself?"

"No problem. I'll shower and dress, too, and spend the rest of the time waiting and thinking of you."

"Such a romantic. Who are you, Maurice Chevalier?" I kidded, comparing him to the famous French actor who was so well known for his charm. Again, I knew about something thanks to my mother.

He laughed and watched me walk up the stairs. I hurried to my suite and closed the door. I went right to the phone and called. Mrs. Pratt answered.

"Everything all right?" she asked when I asked to speak with Mrs. Brittany.

"Yes. Everything all right with you?"

I heard her blow into the receiver and smiled to myself. Moments later, Mrs. Brittany was there.

"I have nothing new to report yet, Roxy. It's far too soon. Besides, I would have called you if there was something."

"I'm not calling to find out about that. I know it's too soon."

"Why are you calling?"

"Norbert brought a man with him to dinner last night. I went to lunch with him at the Café de Paris, and he came here to swim with me and asked me to dinner tonight. His name is Paul Lamont. He's of the Lamont cosmetics family."

"I know all about the Lamont cosmetics family. So?"

"I don't think it's brain surgery to figure out that he wants to get more involved with me."

"I'd be pretty stupid to be surprised about that," she said dryly. "And very disappointed to hear otherwise."

"I wanted to be sure that you thought it was all right."

"What was all right?"

"For me to be seeing him like this while I'm here," I said.

"It's all right if it's all right with you, if you handle everything correctly and carefully. Perhaps he'll fall in love with you, and you won't have to come back," she added. "Would you like that?"

"We've only known each other for twenty-four hours, but he probably is in love with me," I told her.

She laughed. "One of you is," she said.

"Yes, but you have no worries. He won't ask me to marry him. He's in one of those arranged relationships."

"He doesn't have to offer marriage," she said.

There was something about the indifference in her voice that sparked suspicion in my mind.

"This is a test, isn't it?" I asked. "It's all prearranged."

"Everything you will do from now on is a test, Roxy, whether I arrange it or not. Get used to it. I've got to go. Make your own decisions now. We'll see you in about ten days. Unless something makes that unnecessary," she added. "*Au revoir, ma chère*," she said, and hung up.

I sat there with the dead receiver in my hand, thinking. Was everything pure coincidence, or wasn't it, and if it wasn't, did that mean Paul was part of it? Would I be disappointed if that was so? Would I feel manipulated, my emotions tapped and prodded, with everyone waiting to see what I would do?

"Make your own decisions," Mrs. Brittany had said. *All right, I will. Right now, I'll just shower and wash my hair, and then I'll make my first decision since we spoke. I'll decide what to wear. None of this will intimidate me,* I told myself. I really should have told her that, made it clear. Right from the beginning, I should have done what she said, assumed everything was a test in one way or another. I didn't need her to confirm it. I'd never need her to confirm it.

I wasn't sure what made me more enthusiastic and excited, my defiance, my growing affection for Paul, or my desire to learn the truth. What would I do with that truth if and when I learned it, anyway? Would I pout and then quit, demand my kill fee, and go off on my own? Would I just swallow it and keep it to myself? Would I laugh in their faces and claim that I always knew?

"Everything is an experience," Mrs. Brittany once told me. "Treat it all that way. Feeling sorry for yourself after a distasteful or disappointing experience only blinds you to what lessons there are and how you can benefit."

Now was the time to take her advice, I thought. Maybe I wasn't just discovering things about Paul and Mrs. Brittany and everything and everyone else around me. Maybe I was discovering more about myself. What was I made of, fragile and delicate little feelings that crackled and popped or feelings covered with thick, strong skin that helped open my eyes more and trained me to confront any problem courageously?

How many times after I had left home did I stop to feel sorry for myself? Each time I was tempted to surrender, to go crawling back. If I had done that, what would have become of me? I could hear the derision in Mrs. Brittany's voice. *So you think you're being tested? Poor girl. If you think this is a test, wait until you're really out there.* I was so angry at myself the more I thought about it that I nearly stomped out of my room and ripped off the banister as I descended the stairway.

Paul was out on the patio having some wine. I paused to look at him, unseen. He had freely admitted that he was committed or was in the process of being committed to another woman, primarily for business reasons. Would he toss that aside for someone like me, someone who had nothing but herself to offer? Was it the musings of a romantic teenage girl even to think of such a thing? If I had learned anything while being with Mrs. Brittany, it should be that such idyllic romance occurs only in movies. She was probably right. He would try to keep us both, with me on the side, the famous mistress French men were expected to possess, and his respectable, wealthy wife on his arm in public. I liked him. He was good-looking and sexy. I wasn't going to toss him off so quickly.

I considered the implication Mrs. Brittany had made that he would want me for a mistress. Why should such a possibility bother me, someone who was preparing herself for a life, at least in her youth, to be just that sort of woman for many wealthy and powerful men? If it did bother me that much, I certainly wasn't capable of being a Brittany girl, was I?

No, if he should ever propose such a relationship, I would smile and say, "Take a ticket." The idea brought a ripple of silent laughter across my lips. *Go play the game, Roxy Wilcox,* I whispered to myself. *Take the test, and prove yourself to yourself first and Mrs. Brittany last.*

Paul turned and saw me staring at him. He smiled and lifted an empty wineglass.

"Yes, please," I said, coming out onto the patio.

He poured me a glass and handed it to me. "Well, I didn't think it was possible," he said.

"What was possible?"

"For you to look more beautiful than you did before. The truth is, you look more and more beautiful each time I see you."

"Maybe you simply underestimated me," I said, and sipped my wine.

He laughed. "Compliments bounce off you the way rain bounces off an umbrella."

"Don't stop them coming, anyway. I don't mind being in the rain."

"Oh, I won't. Don't worry about that. Hungry?"

"Yes."

"Okay, we'll go after we finish our wine. I've called Norbert, by the way. He sounded relieved."

"Oh?"

"I think his partner was complaining about him not spending enough time with him. Looks like I came onto the scene just in time to save his relationship. And maybe," he added softly, "to start one of my own."

I didn't say anything. I walked to the railing and looked out at the sea. Someone was being pulled on water skis and doing well. Farther out, a rather large yacht was making its way toward Monaco.

"Is that your parents?"

"No," he said. "We don't have one quite that ostentatious. That has a helicopter on it. I believe it belongs to a prince from Saudi Arabia. He usually comes this way about now."

He stepped up beside me.

"I can't help feeling that when I say something or do something to bring me closer to you, you step back."

I turned and looked into his eyes. "What's your favorite gelato?" I asked him.

"Gelato? Boring to others, plain vanilla. But with a little chocolate on top. Why? What does that have to do with what I just said?"

"Don't you hate rushing it and hate it when you come to that final bite or lick?"

"So we're still walking?"

"Still walking," I said, and finished my wine.

He finished his, and we started out.

Margery stepped out of the kitchen. "Anything you need, Miss Wilcox?"

"Not at the moment, Margery," I said. "*Merci.*"

She stood there watching us leave. I wondered if she was a lot more than just a housekeeper and cook here. Maybe she was another spy for Mrs. Brittany. I couldn't resent her if she was. She and her husband probably were paid well and were comfortable. Why should she risk any of that for me?

Paul's restaurant in Beaulieu was delightful. The food was delicious, and like the people at the Café de Paris, everyone, especially the owners, knew him well. We sat at his favorite table in a corner by a window. The room was small but elegantly decorated. I liked the intimacy of it.

Maybe it was the excellent wine and the comfort of really good food, but I found myself becoming less defensive as the evening continued. Paul talked about his youth and his relationship with his sister before she became so distant from the family. I think he was being more open and revealing in the hope that I would reciprocate and tell him real things about myself.

However, hovering close to me the whole time was Mrs. Brittany's admonition not to do anything to destroy the mystery. I was tempted to tell him all about myself, nevertheless, as he prodded and pleaded.

"I want to know more about you. You fascinate me, Roxy. I feel at such a disadvantage."

"Maybe I wouldn't be so fascinating if you knew more about me," I said, half in jest. "I'm here. I'm who I am right now. Why change that?"

"But I don't know who you are right now."

"Sure you do. You keep telling me. I'm bright,

beautiful, fascinating. Think of me as someone with whom you have fallen in love on the movie screen. You don't want to know anything that would stain that image, do you? Who wants his goddesses to have feet of clay?"

He shook his head and smiled. "You are amazing." He leaned over to kiss me. Then, in a voice that vibrated with some fear and nervousness for the first time, he asked, "Will you spend the night with me in my family castle?"

"Family castle? Are you going to be my prince if I do?"

"I'd be anything for you."

Except a husband, I thought, but it didn't matter. I wanted to be with him.

I didn't have to say yes. He saw it in my eyes and asked for our check.

He was mostly silent on our way to his home. I sat close to him. I think he was afraid that if he talked too much, he might break the magic spell. I know I felt that way. It was time to put words back in a box and turn to kisses and caresses and the sweet hot breath that would slip out of his lips to mine and mine to his.

His housekeeper wasn't in sight when we arrived, but I had the sense that we were being watched. He took my hand and led me quickly up the stairway to his round bedroom. When we entered, he lifted me and placed me gently on his bed.

"I practice safe sex," I said.

"I do, too, only I'm beyond practice," he countered with that impish smile.

"We'll see," I told him.

He surprised me by getting completely undressed first. Then he knelt beside me and slowly, like someone unwrapping a precious birthday or Christmas gift, peeled away my clothing. He had what he needed beside the bed.

During one of our more intimate conversations, Sheena had pursued my descriptions of my sexual experiences, demanding more and more detail, especially involving my own reactions. I remembered telling her that it hadn't ever yet been for me the way it was described in her novels, the way some of the passages she read to me described it. She was shocked to hear that most of the time, I didn't even have an orgasm.

"Oh, I faked it sometimes when I knew the boy I was with might say something nasty about me. I wanted him to think he was quite the stud, even though he wasn't."

"I thought that was possible," she'd said. "I just didn't understand how or why."

"Good lovers consider each other," I explained. "Neither is really satisfied unless the other is, too."

"Oh."

I thought about that while Paul was making love to me, and I saw how much care he was taking to satisfy me first. He didn't rush anything, not a caress, not a kiss. Each one was as perfect and meaningful as the previous one. In one of Sheena's novels, the author had described the man making love as though he were playing a beautiful instrument. I had thought that was over the top until now. Paul strummed and touched me to bring me to one crescendo after another. We were composing a symphony. Did this extraordinary lovemaking stem from real passion or even, dare I say it, love, or was he just good at what he did?

Never had I felt so wonderfully exhausted afterward. My whole body was pleased, every part of me contented. We lay next to each other without speaking, listening to each other's quickened breathing as it slowed. He put his head softly against my shoulder, and, still naked, we fell asleep beside each other. Before morning, we woke and made love again. It wasn't as long as the first time, but it was just as sweet. Neither of us woke with the morning sunlight. We were too lost in the memory of each other soothing our dreams, keeping us floating in a restful repose.

When it was nearly noon, his phone rang, and we both woke, groaned at the interruption, and struggled to get up the energy and desire to rise. I turned over first while he talked. I didn't want to listen, but I could hear from his monosyllabic answers that he was talking to someone he didn't want to know about my presence.

"Yes," he finished. "I'll be there tonight. Yes, I'm looking forward to seeing you, too."

I heard him hang up, and then I turned to him. "You don't have to say anything," I said. "Just take me back."

"After breakfast, please. I'll call down and have it ready for us."

I hesitated, then shrugged. "Why not? I'll take a quick shower, then."

"So will I," he told me, smiling. "I'll wash your back if you wash mine."

"All right, but don't get too used to it," I told him. "I don't think it's something you'll experience too much."

He nodded. "Neither do I," he said.

I'd been half hoping he would disagree, but Mrs. Brittany's warnings sounded true and strong.

I just had to learn how to not care after I had convinced myself that I should.

16

I didn't see Paul for nearly a week afterward. He called once during that time to apologize for not being able to take me out on the family yacht. He described the various things he had to do. I read between the lines and understood that he was involved with his family and especially his future fiancée. Mrs. Brittany's words continued to haunt me. To her way of thinking, he would never be able to marry me, or even want to, but he wasn't above offering to keep me.

I suppose most people would wonder why that would continue to bother me even after I had convinced myself that it wouldn't. Here I was, training to be an escort for wealthy and powerful men, even women. What was the difference?

I guess, as hard as it would be for anyone to believe, especially my father, I saw my work with and for Mrs. Brittany as something that would give me respect and, most important, give me independence. To me, a kept woman was a plaything, something held on ice for whenever her patronizing lover had the time, inclination, or freedom to call for her. Even though I might have the same sort of worldly things, I wouldn't have an iota of self-respect. No, I thought, if Paul actually offered me such a relationship now, even after our time together, I would turn him down soundly. The longer I didn't see him, the more resolved I was about it.

Norbert stepped in and was there to escort me everywhere in the interim. The first thing we did, as he had first promised, was go to lunch up in Èze village. It was like being on the top of the world. He was right about the breathtaking views, the picturesque village with its cobblestone walkways and unique shops. We had pizza at a small restaurant and watched the parade of tourists from all over Europe, Asia, the U.K., and America stream by, some with guides rattling off details and information that seemed to float past them as their eyes went everywhere else.

I could sense that he wanted to talk about Paul but was hesitant. I pushed a little, since my curiosity was quite strong now, and he finally opened up.

"Paul has always had trouble being his own person. His father determined what would be his interests, who would be his friends in school, and, of course, who would be his fiancée. I keep waiting for him to cut that umbilical cord, which in this case is attached not to his mother but to his father. But don't misunderstand me. I love the guy and would do anything for him. He's essentially the brother I never had," Norbert told me.

"And how do you get along with Paul's father?" I asked. "Does he approve of the friendship?"

"Yes," Norbert said, smiling. "I know what you're implying, but with my love life the way it is, his father felt Paul was in safer company."

"Safer?"

"I wouldn't be introducing him to female barracudas who might pounce on his wealth."

"You introduced him to me."

He laughed. "You're a sunfish, Roxy, not a barracuda. At least, not yet."

"You might be surprised."

"Perhaps," he said. He had a wry smile. "I'd be glad to know that I underestimated you."

"Glad? I see. You half wish I *would* get between him and his father, don't you? That's why you brought him around."

"*Moi?*" he said, feigning innocence. "Heaven forbid."

"Do you really think there's any chance of that?"

He shrugged. "You're a remarkable young lady. He has to be very impressed with you. I know I am."

It was on the tip of my tongue to ask him what he really knew about me. How much did he know about Mrs. Brittany's company? Wouldn't he risk angering her if he was instrumental in ruining one of her girls by getting her good and married or involved with someone like Paul who might tempt her away? Look at how much she had already invested in me. I'm sure she would not be too happy with her godson if she knew that. I thought it best not to bring any of this up, however. It would, in fact, violate one of the stipulations of the agreement I had signed. A Brittany girl never talked with an outsider about the company, nor was I ever to mention what training I had undergone at Mrs. Brittany's Long Island estate.

Norbert sensed my hesitation and changed the topic of conversation to other things and the places I should visit while I was at Mrs. Brittany's villa. He volunteered to do as much of it as he could.

Later that week, when Norbert took me to the concert in Monaco, I met his partner, Caesar Ferrante, a handsome, dark-haired Italian man who was one of the assistant managers at the world-famous Hermitage Hotel in Monte Carlo. I saw immediately why Norbert was so fond of him. He had a great, upbeat personality and was just as tuned in to style and culture. At times, they seemed more like twins.

Afterward, we had a great time together at a club that catered to both gays and straight couples but favored gays. I danced with both of them and at one point with both of them at the same time. We were out until nearly three in the morning. I slept well past noon the next day, and Margery didn't attempt to wake me. Two days later, Norbert and Caesar took me to Sanremo, Italy, for lunch and some fun shopping. It was only an hour's ride, but they were keeping me so busy with these trips, lunches, and dinners that I had little time to pine over not seeing Paul.

And then, at the end of this week, Paul suddenly appeared one afternoon while I was lounging at the pool. Mrs. Brittany had just called to say she would be coming to the villa in two days. She said the media interest in my disappearance was waning.

"The magazine article appeared, but as far as I or any of my sources know, there isn't much follow-up expected," she told me. "I think this will soon be completely forgotten. There are too many young girls like you, anyway, for anyone to remember what you looked like or even care."

"Then I won't be here much longer?"

"No, not much longer," she said. "Unless you have some reason to stay."

"No, I have none," I said quickly.

I wondered if she knew any more about my parents, but I was afraid to ask and show too much interest. I couldn't help wondering how Mama had taken the failure of the media attention to produce any leads or result in my being found and maybe brought home. I imagined my father had berated himself for caring—or weakening, as he might think of it. I could just imagine him saying, "Well, that's that. We tried. She doesn't want to return. Don't bring up her name again."

Emmie would surely be terribly confused about it all. She had probably been right beside Mama, hoping the media attention would bring me back. Surely every time she saw her girlfriends with their older sisters, she thought of me. Young girls often idolize their older sisters and envy them for their freedom, their little love affairs, and their clothes. Whenever they can, they secretly put on their older sisters' things or use their makeup. They love listening in on their phone conversations or reading secret notes. I knew that Emmie's girlfriends who had older sisters surely mentioned these things and that she must have felt a great emptiness and envy. She'd had an older sister once, but that older sister had left without bothering to wake her up to say good-bye, an older sister who was probably more like a nasty dream.

I spent the morning thinking about all this and was heavily involved in my darker thoughts when Paul arrived.

"Hi," I heard, and turned to see him standing there in a white silk jacket and a black tie, with black slacks, hardly the attire of someone who wanted to spend the day lounging around a pool.

"Hi. What's up?"

"I'm on my way to Cannes for a business meeting and wondered if you would like to go along. It won't be a long meeting, and we could have dinner on the way back. We can spend some time there, too. Just walking on the Croiset in Cannes is fun for me, and I'm sure it will be for you."

The Croiset in Cannes, I thought, remembering my mother describing it to me. Her father had taken her family to Cannes for a little summer holiday when she was about my age. The Croiset, was just a long street that ran parallel to the ocean, but along the way there was so much to see, such as the shops that featured the major fashion houses and the art galleries, restaurants, and hotels that formed the backdrop. Many had been featured in old movies, and some were used in films to this day. My mother described the people who populated the Croiset in the evening as the "beautiful people," wealthy and glamorous people in their haute couture and their expensive cars.

"It was as if I had stepped into a movie myself," she'd told me. "Someday I'm sure you will go there and see what I mean."

Yes, I had thought. *I will go there, Mama, but when I do, I will be one of the "beautiful people."*

And here I was on the verge of making that happen. I would put on something expensive, wear the jewelry Mrs. Brittany had bought me, and drive into Cannes in Paul's $350,000 car.

"Okay," I said. "Let me get dressed. How much time do we have?"

"Whatever you need. They wait for me, not I for them."

"It's a mistake to tell a woman she has whatever time she needs. I might take hours."

"Something tells me you won't," he said.

I laughed and hurried in and up the stairs.

Of course, he was right. I didn't take hours. I was too excited and wanted to be with him. Besides, I had already been well schooled in how to look like a million dollars in a matter of minutes, not hours. It was practically written on a plaque above the salon at Mrs. Brittany's estate: *A Brittany girl is never ever at a disadvantage.*

On the way to Cannes, he told me how much he had missed me and how much he regretted not being able to do much about it. He knew that Norbert and Caesar were filling in. Despite their being gay, he sounded jealous when I described all the fun we had been having.

"Doesn't sound like you missed me all that much," he complained.

"Oh, I did. Occasionally," I teased.

"Thanks a lot."

"I like you a lot, Paul," I said in a very serious tone, "but I won't suffer because of any man."

He looked at me, my hardness surprising him. Any good psychoanalyst would probably say my attitude stemmed from my poor relationship with my father, but Paul knew nothing of that.

"I wouldn't want you to suffer," he said. "Ever."

It was all he came up with. I was disappointed but let it go.

While he had his meeting at one of the major hotels, I went shopping in the row of shops nearby and met him in the lobby afterward. He had my packages put in his car, and then, holding hands, we went walking along the Croiset. We window-shopped, listened to a street musician on an accordion, and then had a gelato and sat people watching for nearly an hour before we started back to Beaulieu, stopping for dinner in Nice at the famous Negresco Hotel restaurant.

I never asked him anything about his future fiancée or anything about his family the whole time, but I could feel it all hovering above us like a small but dark and angry cloud that constantly threatened to empty cold drops of rain on every warm smile, small laugh, or look of passion.

He mentioned going out on his yacht again. "I just have to clear the schedule," he said.

"Well, don't do anything yet. Mrs. Brittany is coming in two days, and I will have to wait to see what plans she has for us before agreeing to anything."

"Yes, of course. How long is she staying?"

"I don't know."

He was thoughtful. I knew he was wondering if Mrs. Brittany's arrival meant that my stay was coming to a quick end, but he didn't ask.

This time, when we returned, he spent the night with me. I knew that meant he didn't want me in his house while his parents were there. I doubted he had even mentioned me to them.

He was up early in the morning and gone before breakfast, telling me he had a breakfast meeting in Monte Carlo with his father to discuss a major European acquisition they were contemplating.

"Do you think rich people want to get richer out of greed or ego?" I asked him before he left.

He thought a moment and said, "Probably both. My father says when you're satisfied, you're ready for the long sleep."

"So he's always dissatisfied?"

"Let's say always hungry. Which reminds me. I want to take you to another of my favorite restaurants tonight, okay?"

"I can be hungry," I said.

He laughed, but I could see him looking at me a little askance, wondering why I was putting this new sharpness in my voice.

We had dinner again that night at a restaurant in Villefranche-sur-Mer down by the water. As it was everywhere else we had dinner, the staff, managers, and owners knew him and had a certain table reserved for him.

"Don't you ever eat at home?" I asked.

"When I'm sick," he replied. "How could I not want to take you out, Roxy? You make me look good."

"Thank you."

"You're accepting a compliment? No wisecracks?"

"Just this once," I joked. "Because this time, I'm sure it's true."

He laughed so hard everyone at the restaurant turned to look at us. I could fall in love with him, I admitted to myself. I wondered if he was considering any long-term relationship between us now as our time together was winding down quickly. Was I a naive fool to think that marriage wasn't impossible? I decided to test the water.

"I don't know how much longer I'll be here," I said, knowing what he probably had suspected. "It might be a matter of a few days."

"Oh?"

"Mrs. Brittany is coming tomorrow. I might go back with her."

"I see."

He was pensive a moment, and then someone he knew waved, and the moment seemed to float off like a balloon caught in the wind. He didn't voice any regrets or predict any terrible heartbreak if I should leave as quickly as I suggested. I didn't want to believe he wouldn't feel that. I concluded instead that it was too painful for him to talk about it.

The following morning, I woke up realizing that this was the day Mrs. Brittany was to arrive. No one had called to let me know when she would be here.

I hurried down to breakfast and was just sipping my first cup of coffee when the phone rang. Margery brought it to the table.

"It's Mrs. Brittany," she said.

"Oh? Thank you," I said, taking the receiver quickly, thinking she might be calling me from the plane.

"Hello, Mrs. Brittany. Are you close?"

"I'm not able to come over there just now, Roxy," she said. There was something in her tone of voice that was unusual. She sounded weak, her voice wobbly.

"Why not?"

"It's Sheena," she said after a short pause.

"What about her? Was she in an accident?"

"She's had a setback. I took her for her six-month examination, and the results of her tests . . ."

"What?"

"The cancer has returned. It's more aggressive than we had expected."

"Oh, no. Will she be all right?"

"I'm flying her to a new doctor and a new clinic tomorrow."

"I'd like to come back to be with her."

"We'll see," she said. "I'll call you in a day or so."

"I'm sorry," I said.

"Yes. I know. Watch yourself," she added, and hung up, leaving me feeling as if I was dangling in space. I imagined she had called Norbert, too, and then I thought, actually hoped, he had called Paul to let him know I was back to being free. It wasn't much more than an hour later when Paul called.

"I understand Mrs. Brittany has been delayed," he said, without mentioning why. Had Norbert told him the reason or just told him she was delayed?

"Yes."

"I'd like to take you onto the yacht for dinner tonight. I have my father's chef at our disposal. Will you come?"

I was depressed about Sheena, but since there was nothing I could do, I thought anything that would distract me from thinking about her and her situation would be good. Besides, perhaps this was going to be the night I dreamed of. Perhaps he was planning to propose to me, and what more romantic spot than on the deck of his yacht, sipping champagne and looking out at Monte Carlo all lit up?

What would I do and say if he did propose? Would I feel any sense of guilt? Surely something like this was always a danger for Mrs. Brittany with any of her beautiful and sophisticated women. Why wasn't it possible for a wealthy man to fall in love with one and woo her away? Had that happened in the past? She would never discuss any of her other girls in any detail. Anyway, we had risks. Why shouldn't she? Obviously, nothing like this had put her out of business, I thought.

"Okay," I said. "I have yet to be on the sea."

"Well, this might be more than just being on the sea. Maybe pack a little bag for an overnight."

"Just a little bag?" I teased.

"Pack a trunk if you want," he said. What did that mean?

I informed Margery that I wouldn't be home for dinner and maybe not breakfast, either. Less than an hour later, Paul arrived. I had only an overnight bag when I appeared.

"You look disappointed with my overnight bag," I said.

He laughed. "My mother's idea of an overnight bag is five suitcases and one bag just for shoes. It's not that she needs it all. It's that she likes to have the same sorts of choices she has at home."

"I didn't think we would need that much clothing on your yacht," I said, and he laughed.

"I gave the ship's crew the night off," he told me when we pulled up to the dock, "but we have some staff to help with our dinner."

There were so many yachts anchored, and I didn't know which one was his family's. He took my bag, and we started down the dock, passing one yacht after another, all luxurious and big to me, but when he stopped, I was shocked at the size of his.

"How big is this?"

"Only one hundred twenty feet," he said. "Sleeps ten, with a crew of five."

We boarded, and he showed me the luxurious living quarters with a big-screen television and the dining area with a table that could seat ten. There were two settings at the moment. Then we entered the galley, where his father's chef was preparing Lobster Fra Diavolo for our dinner. He introduced us and then showed me the owner's cabin. It was as big as the suite I had back at Mrs. Brittany's estate on Long Island.

I didn't want to sound like some country bump-
kin, so I didn't tell him how surprised I was to discover that rooms on a yacht could be as big as some
apartments, if not bigger than many.

"Do you want to change for dinner?" he asked.

"No. I'm okay. You?"

"I always go casual on the yacht. My parents like
to dress as if we were on the *Queen Mary* at the cap-
tain's dinner."

"Sounds like sometimes you're barely tolerated in
your family."

"Sometimes. Maybe more than sometimes," he
said, laughing. "C'mon. We'll have cocktails on deck."

A waiter was there already, fixing our drinks. We
sat looking up at the city, the lights just starting to go
on. From where we were sitting, it looked like a show
put on just for us.

"There's a special event tonight," Paul said.

"Oh?"

"I didn't know it until late today, but we're going
to have fireworks."

We were served champagne cocktails and some
wonderful hors d'oeuvres.

"I understand Mrs. Brittany has some family problems," he said after a while. "Her granddaughter is
very sick?"

"Yes."

So Norbert had told him some things, after all, I
thought. What else had he explained?

"And you know her well?"

"Very well. At the moment, she's my closest friend."

"Oh. I'm sorry. So you want to return to see her?"

"Yes."

He nodded. He was silent so long that I was convinced he was working himself up for some very serious proposal, but before he spoke, we were informed that dinner was ready. The sliding doors of the dining area were wide open to give us the feeling we were eating on deck. I couldn't imagine ever having a more wonderful gourmet dinner with expensive wines and impeccable service. A second waiter appeared to open the wine and clear the dishes as we ate.

I didn't know whether Paul talked out of nervousness or simply because he was afraid that pregnant silences would give birth to sad thoughts, but from the moment we sat until the moment we had our coffee on the deck, he never stopped. He told me more about his family company, the projects and plans they had for the coming year, the places he was going to visit in Europe and Asia, and then some ideas he had to innovate and expand even more.

I listened attentively and asked good questions as my training as a Brittany escort kicked in. I could hear the main points of Mrs. Brittany's lessons.

"Always give the man you're with the sense that you're with him, that you are attuned to everything he says and interested in everything he says.

"Don't let your mind drift, and never change the subject. He has to be the one directing word traffic in these tête-à-têtes, Roxy. You're there to be his audience, an admirer.

"Never bring up anything about yourself. Be polite when and if he asks questions about you, but always keep your answers general. It's part of the tease and the cachet, the mystery. Most of the men you escort will respect your privacy. Occasionally, you'll meet one who is more demanding. I'd rather you disappoint that sort and let him drift away than compromise yourself or our company in any way. Understand?"

It bothered me that I was putting on my professional persona with Paul tonight, but his avoidance of anything really warm and personal between us nudged me into it. Was he really happy with my phony smiles, my nods, my almost inane comments and praise? Couldn't he see through it, or didn't he want to see through it?

Afterward, when the fireworks began, I thought his passion for me was rushing back in. He had his arm around me. He kissed me and was more like a younger man again, filled with the same level of excitement I was feeling. The fireworks were elaborate, building to a crescendo.

As always, when I had a moment to stabilize myself and return to earth, I contrasted where I had been with where I was. Regardless of what happened between Paul and me, this was going to be my world now, and I was determined to succeed in it. I'd be nobody's poor, mixed-up, lost little girl again. I'd eat caviar and lobster in the most expensive restaurants in the world. I'd wear furs and jewels that would draw looks of envy. I'd fly in private jets and ride in limousines, be disdainful of budgets, and titillate the most powerful and wealthy men with my smiles, my gestures, and my promising kisses.

Paul and I made love in the owner's suite. With every kiss and caress, he told me how beautiful and wonderful I was and how much he enjoyed being with me, how grateful he was that he had met me. I kept waiting for that proverbial second shoe to drop, that next sentence, that proposal or idea to keep us together in some magical world of tomorrow, where neither of us would grow old or sick or tired of each other's company.

It didn't come.

I fell asleep with tears icing the lids of my eyes. He was up before me in the morning, and when I appeared, he was out on the deck having his coffee and looking at the sea like someone in a daze. His staff hurried to get me some breakfast. I had only *petit déjeuner*. Paul waited until I had something to eat and drank my coffee before he told me that Norbert had called.

"He said Mrs. Brittany wanted you to be at the airport this afternoon."

"Oh. Did he tell any more? I mean, anything about Mrs. Brittany's granddaughter?"

"No, nothing. Your things are being packed. I told him I'd drive you to Nice."

"Okay. Thanks."

"I don't know when I'll be able to get to New York," he said.

I nodded.

"But when and if I do . . ."

"Okay," I said, cutting him off. I didn't want to hear any promises. Right now, they were like flowers thrown on the water and drifting out with the tide.

"I want you to believe that I really care about you, Roxy."

I gave my best professional smile. Mrs. Brittany had actually taught me what that was.

"I . . ."

"Paul, please. Let's just—"

"No, you don't understand," he said. "I didn't see you this week because this was the week I got formally engaged. My father actually bought the ring for me."

I looked away. This would be the first and the very last time I would ever invest my emotions in a man, I vowed. From this day forward, I'd be the one who broke hearts. *As God is my witness,* I told myself.

"I'll see you again. I swear," Paul added.

Sure you will, I thought. *But it will cost you.*

17

Sheena went through a horrendous four months of chemo and radiation treatments. I didn't think anything I would ever experience would be as painful to watch. Through it all, she never lost her wonderful *joie de vivre*. She wouldn't permit me to feel sorry for her or be sad in her presence. On her good days, she wanted us to do "sisterly" things like shop and go to fun restaurants and movies. Mrs. Brittany arranged for everything. She didn't have to come out and say it. I could see in her face that the prognosis was not good. I knew she was putting me on hold so I could be with her granddaughter for her final days.

But I wasn't with her during the final days. Sheena was in and out of consciousness anyway, but as if she wanted to deny that it was happening herself, Mrs. Brittany had me remain at the estate, entertaining some of her important guests from Asia, CEOs of major companies.

"I know how upset you are," she told me, "but this is a good test of your own abilities. Pleasing these guests is your first priority."

I did what she asked. I hated it, but there was no question that the experience, the pain I had to hide, all of it, hardened me in ways that might otherwise have taken much longer. My first reaction was to hate her for forcing me to do it, especially when I thought Sheena needed me the most, but years later, I would find myself thanking her for showing me how to be stronger.

On the day after Sheena died, a day so heavy with gloom I thought we would all drown in shadows, I was surprised when Mrs. Brittany wanted to take a walk alone with me on the estate. Despite the heavy sadness we both carried, the sunshine gave us strength to talk about Sheena and rejoice in what we were able to share of her beauty and innocence. I realized that one other thing Sheena had done was to bring Mrs. Brittany and me closer, if only for a short while. I had the feeling that she was more revealing and intimate with me than she had been with anyone for some time, even her close companion, Mrs. Pratt. But she wasn't one to accept sympathy or pity for very long. She practically took my head off when I said I felt sorry for her loss.

"Sorry for me. Don't feel sorry for me. Feel sorry for Sheena. She's the one who endured the pain and suffering all her life, thanks to my miserable daughter and her good-for-nothing husband. I'll survive."

"I just meant—"

"Never mind what you meant. Look, Roxy," she said, stopping and turning that familiar hard, piercing gaze at me the way someone might aim a flashlight, "this is a very, very hard life for us, no matter how blessed we are with money or power. Turn everything into a life lesson. What you should understand is that you should never be ashamed of exploiting anything that will make life easier for you. I know that sounds bitter and cynical, but that's what's happening out there," she said, nodding toward the world beyond her property.

"You don't have to convince me of that anymore," I told her, her hardness bringing back my own. "I didn't exactly have the life of a little princess before I was brought to you."

She smiled. "Good. I'm glad you haven't lost your edge. It will keep you alive." She straightened herself, pulling back those firm shoulders and becoming the Mrs. Brittany I had known and feared as much as respected.

"I hope so," I said.

"I know so," she replied. "You have wonderful instincts and qualities, strengths and insights, Roxy. You're ready. I'm arranging for your apartment this week. Mr. Bob is on it all. I thought a great deal about your signature name, but in the end, it was Sheena who created it for you."

"Really?"

"She wanted that to be her final gift to you."

"What is it?"

"Fleur du Coeur, 'flower of the heart,'" she said.

I smiled, remembering that the fern-leaf bleeding heart was her favorite. "I'm proud to have that name, Mrs. Brittany," I said.

She nodded, and we walked on in silence. In a few short moments, she had resurrected the wall she kept tightly around herself. For a while, I had been her granddaughter's best and only friend. I was practically her surrogate granddaughter, but that had died with Sheena.

There was to be no doubt in my mind or hers. I was back to being her employee.

Two days later, Mr. Bob came for me in a limousine similar to the one in which he had first brought me to Mrs. Brittany. Mrs. Pratt had decided what I would take with me and what I would leave behind. What I would take was packed and immediately put into the trunk of the limousine. Both Mrs. Pratt and Mrs. Brittany walked me out to the car, where Mr. Bob waited.

"We want you to settle in for a while before you go to work," Mrs. Brittany said. "Bob will show you around your neighborhood, introduce you to the beautician and salon we've chosen for your coiffure and your manicure and pedicure. He will introduce you to the boutique I'm currently employing to provide you with wardrobe as it is required. He'll also show you the cafés and restaurants to frequent. Your physical trainer will come to you twice a week. The schedule is already set. Your masseuse will also come to you, and that is scheduled, too.

"Basic foods have been delivered and will be replenished as they are needed. If you want something additional, just leave orders for it, and as long as it's not something we disapprove of your having, you'll have it delivered. You can eat in anytime, any meal you wish. You just order it. Bob has arranged all that for you, too. The phone numbers are there."

"Your scheduled doctor appointments and dentist appointments will be posted in your kitchen," Mrs. Pratt continued, "as are all of your important phone numbers. When you need or want your chauffeured car, you will call down for it."

She handed me a leather-bound portfolio.

"In there," Mrs. Brittany followed, "you will find your credit cards, your banking information, and your passport. There is a wall safe in your apartment. Your place is ultra-safe, lots of security, but we never trust anyone or anything. I have known wealthy men who love pilfering, either out of some mental sickness or some sick need for a souvenir. From your past, we know that you're familiar enough with thievery to know how to prevent yourself from being anyone's victim."

"Yes," I said. "Don't worry about that."

"I won't worry. You worry," she snapped back at me.

I pressed my lips together and nodded.

"Finally, let us remind you of your agreement, your responsibility not to involve anyone in your business unless we arrange for him or her to do that. You cannot invite anyone you wish to your apartment."

"Whom would I invite?"

"I expect you will make some acquaintances, Roxy. Be careful," she warned.

"Okay."

"We'll be around to visit in a few days."

"When will I have my first assignment?"

"When I schedule it," she said.

She nodded at the chauffeur, who opened the door for me.

"We don't wish our girls good luck," Mrs. Brittany said when I started to turn to get in. I paused. "We don't believe luck has anything to do with anything. You make your own good or bad luck."

"Well, I have to disagree," I said.

Mrs. Pratt looked shocked. "What?"

"It was my good luck to have Mr. Bob notice me that day, wasn't it?" I asked, smiling at Mr. Bob, who smiled back. "At least, I hope it was my good luck," I added, and got into the limousine.

The chauffeur closed the door.

Mr. Bob spoke with Mrs. Pratt and Mrs. Brittany for a few moments, and then he got in on the other side. He still wore that little impish smirk as we started away.

"What is so funny?" I asked him.

"I was just thinking of the girl I brought here and the girl I'm leaving with today."

"And?"

"It feels so damn good to be right," he said.

I stared at him a moment, and then we both laughed.

The limousine turned out of the driveway. I looked back at the estate. In some ways, I did feel like someone who had graduated. I even felt a little affection for the grand place. Of course, most of the reason for that lay with my memories of Sheena, but in so many ways, it had become my home when I had lost my home. Mr. Bob once told me that Mrs. Brittany would replace my family. I never believed that fully in my heart, but for the moment, I had no choice. It was all I had. But sitting in this limousine, wearing clothes that cost as much as most people spent on their living needs for a month or two, and heading for an ultra-luxurious apartment with everything arranged for me, down to a bottle of orange juice, I had trouble feeling sorry for myself.

Maybe that was the ultimate lesson or power Mrs. Brittany had provided: Never feel sorry for yourself. That was when you became most vulnerable. And she was right, wasn't she? It was a hard, bitter, and highly competitive world out there. It was no place for weak sisters. I had vowed when I arrived and I was vowing now as I left. I wouldn't be a weak sister, ever.

The boutique hotel Mr. Bob brought me to was on the Upper East Side of Manhattan, a very upscale neighborhood of very expensive apartments in high-security buildings, with doormen and private garages, expensive classy restaurants and cafés, designer shops and boutiques, and probably the cleanest streets in the city. The hotel was called the Beaux-Arts and consisted mainly of luxury apartments. It didn't have a big or ostentatious lobby, and one look at the staff told me that discreetness and privacy were paramount. Mr. Bob had all the keys I needed before we arrived. No one was introduced to me formally, but I could see that everyone involved knew I was the new tenant. I wondered what name I was registered under and asked Mr. Bob when we stepped into the elevator, for which you had to have a key. My things were being brought up on another elevator.

"No name," he replied. "Just an apartment number, 3C. No one calling you will be connected through a hotel switchboard. You have your own private line."

"Mrs. Brittany doesn't own this hotel, does she?"

"Let's just say she has a majority interest. She usually does with anything and everything she depends on," he said.

"That's a careful woman."

"She wouldn't be where she is otherwise," he said.

Where was she? I wanted to ask him. She was a woman without a real family. She had lost her husband, her daughter, and now her granddaughter. The family she had was the family she manufactured. Of course, at the moment, I couldn't claim to have much more.

We stepped out of the elevator. I could see that there were only three apartments on the floor. Mine was the one on the right. It had a short marble-floored entry with a small but expensive-looking teardrop chandelier. There was a coat closet on the immediate right and a work of art on the opposite wall. It was a picture of a flower cut out of black velvet with pink cloth petals. There were artificial flowers everywhere.

Fleur du Coeur, I thought. The room was designed to fit my new image.

The entryway opened to a surprisingly large living room, with elegant leather and wood furniture. The centerpiece was a softly curved, L-shaped sectional that consisted of the sofa, corner back, and love seat. Directly across from it was a swivel accent chair with a round-bottom frame. Accent pillows were on everything. A matching coffee table and end table filled out the center of the room. To the right was a large panel window that looked east, and down from it was another, smaller panel window. A set of four different versions of what looked like the same flower was hung high on the far wall. The walls were faux-painted white with swirls of soft red and pink. The wooden floors were covered with a very large area rug that matched the furniture.

My eyes took in everything quickly—the sculptures, the lamps, and the bouquets of artificial flowers, and a fresh real plant at the center of the coffee table.

"They look like hearts," Mr. Bob said.

I laughed. "Don't you know my signature name?"

"Oh, right. Fleur du Coeur. Mrs. Brittany thinks of everything."

"I guess so. They're called *Dicentra* or bleeding heart."

He looked at me. "Well, aren't you the impressive one now."

I shrugged. It did feel good to have knowledge, to be confident about things. Why didn't I understand that when I was in school?

I continued to look at my new home. The floors were marble everywhere except in the living room, and the walls were faux-painted with the same white with pink swirls.

"It's a beautiful place," I said.

"Actually, it's the biggest apartment in the hotel. Mrs. Brittany saw to that."

"Are there any other Brittany girls here?"

"If there were and she wanted you to know, she would have told you."

"Right," I said. "We're the CIA love machine, on a need-to-know basis only."

He laughed. "Don't lose your sense of humor," he told me.

"Is that what it is?" I asked.

He shook his head. "Roxy, Roxy, Roxy," he chanted as we went through the hallway to the living room. He showed me the dining room and the kitchen, where everything important—numbers, my schedule of doctor and dentist appointments, even my first manicure and pedicure appointment—was pinned on a board. He glanced around at the very modern, up-to-date appliances.

"What a waste of machinery," he said.

"Why?"

"A kitchen is almost a vestigial organ for you," he quipped.

"Is that so, Mr. Smart-Ass? For your information, I can cook if I want."

He smiled skeptically.

"Maybe one night, I'll make you a special dinner."

"Looking forward to it. I love to be proven wrong when I benefit from that proof."

We went down another short marble-floored hallway to a double-door bedroom. The centerpiece was my blazing-red bed shaped like a heart. The walls were papered with depictions of beautiful gardens. There was a mirror on the ceiling above the bed. The area rug was a tight-threaded crimson. The wood in the dresser, vanity table, and nightstands was rich cherry. My en suite bathroom was very large, with a Jacuzzi, a large shower, and a second bathtub.

"Flowers and hearts," I said, looking at the bathroom. "Fleur du Coeur. Even here."

"Mrs. Brittany takes her themes very seriously. Okay, let Laura get you unpacked," he said, when my things were brought in followed by a middle-aged, slightly gray-haired woman in a maid's uniform. "Laura's here every day, of course. She'll make your bed and change the linens, the towels. We send everything out to be washed, dry-cleaned, whatever. There's a hamper in your bathroom. Laura will see to what has to be washed, and she'll also see to your basic groceries."

"So I don't do anything here?"

"I wouldn't say that," he replied with his charming smile. "C'mon, let me show you around the neighborhood and take you to lunch."

We left the hotel, crossed the street, and went up a few blocks to a salon, where I was introduced to the beautician Mrs. Brittany had chosen for me. After that, we stopped at one of the boutiques to meet the owner, who happened to be a woman from Lyon, France. We spoke in French for a few minutes, and then Mr. Bob took me to a delightful little café that happened to have the same name as the last restaurant Paul Lamont had taken me to, the one in Villefranche-sur-Mer, La Mère Germaine. For a few moments, memories came rushing back.

The delightful, flirtatious conversations, the passion that quickly had developed between us, bringing with it those long, demanding kisses, and the soft caresses that caused the sexual energy in me to turn my heart into a drum—it all seemed like a cruel joke now. They had nearly convinced me that I could fall in love and have a relationship in which he and I could grow old together, build a life together, with children and grandchildren.

When I thought back to all of that now, I couldn't help but wonder if it had happened by design, if the entire thing had been another lesson Mrs. Brittany had created to harden my heart and form the cynicism that would enable me to be the kind of woman I was about to become. Perhaps she wanted me to be disillusioned, to snuff out the last vestiges of illusions and romance.

What difference did the truth make? Even if she hadn't planned it that way, it was the way it was now. Whatever had remained in me that was still a young girl, with the dreams and fantasies young girls have and need to remain hopeful, was washed away. I was Fleur du Coeur in every respect, out for myself. There would be no false illusions, no disappointments. There would be no trust, no deep affections, and no deeply meaningful words or embraces.

And I wouldn't be pitied for that. I would tolerate no sympathy. My eyes would be dead to the sight of mothers and daughters, fathers and daughters, sisters, and families, especially on holidays. The only gifts under my Christmas tree, if I had one, would be gifts I had given myself, and I was determined never to shed a tear over that.

Maybe, in a very ironic and cold way, I had become more like my father and his father and brother. I would bury my emotions under the mountains of rules and regulations that now governed my life. I would take orders and fulfill missions. I would keep my body fine-tuned, my beauty exquisite. I would bring strategy, plans, and discipline to every assignment, and just as they could send thousands of young men and women into battle accepting the projected casualties, I would willingly die a little inside to plant my flag atop the hill of material comfort, luxury, and pleasure.

"You all right?" Mr. Bob asked as we sat at a table near the front window. He saw how silent I had become.

Outside, the sidewalks were filling with people off to lunch, many in suits and ties, designer dresses, and fashionable outfits. Some were the wealthy, who lived in the expensive apartments. Everyone had that look of success and contentment. There were no homeless in this neighborhood, no lost girls from the roach hotels.

I do belong here, I thought. *I've always belonged here.*

"Yes," I said. "I'm fine. Why?"

"Just for a moment, you looked more like that young girl I saw across the restaurant that first day, the innocent beauty who looked lost."

"She died a while back," I said, and reached for the menu.

"Miss her?"

"No," I snapped back at him.

"Don't lie to yourself, Roxy. Don't ever do that."

There were tears in my eyes, but I choked them back. When I was in one of my rages, Mama used to tell me that the worst lies were the lies you told yourself because you couldn't hide from them.

"Put on a false face," she'd said. "Rage, run away, be wild, do whatever to try to forget, but in the end, you'll remember. I can't guarantee anything for you in life, *ma chère*, but I can wish that my children don't have to lie to themselves."

What would I ever do now to stop? I wondered.

I lowered my menu and looked at Mr. Bob. "Let's just eat and stop talking. I'm hungry," I said.

He laughed and signaled for the waitress. "You'll be just fine," he said, nodding. "Just fine."

I looked away.

I would be fine.

That I swore to myself.

And so it was to begin.

18

My first client was an Asian man who was at least as old as my father. Later, when enough time had passed and I knew I had successfully established myself in Mrs. Brittany's mind, I asked her about my first assignment. I had some suspicions about why she had chosen him, which she confirmed.

"Because of how bad your relationship was with your father, I wanted to see if you could handle a man of, shall we say, that vintage."

Using the word "vintage" to refer to men wasn't an accident. On a number of occasions, Mrs. Brittany expressed her theory that men were like wine. They grew better with age, calmer and more self-assured. Successful men, that is. There were, of course, men who would always be boys, she told me, and if you were a true Brittany girl, you'd know which was which and handle each accordingly.

"When do I stop being tested?" I had wondered out loud. "Or have I?"

"Never, if you work for me," she'd replied, and she lived up to that.

Part of what made her escort service so successful was the follow-up. She didn't ask her clients to fill out a questionnaire. No, it was nothing as mundane as that. Instead, she personally interrogated each client the first chance she had, and based on that feedback, she decided how much work one of her girls would get.

Just as she had initially promised the young, wild, undisciplined, and rebellious Roxy (I could think like this because in my mind, I had become a different person), ninety percent or more of my assignments involved flirtation but not intimate sexual relations. I wasn't lily-pure by any means. There were men who were so charming, handsome, and sexy that it was inevitable I'd have them spend the night at my apartment or go off with them for a weekend on a private jet to some exotic Caribbean island home. Those men lavished more expensive gifts on me and were willing to pay almost any price Mrs. Brittany demanded.

My bank account and investments began to grow. Years after I had started, I fantasized about my father managing my wealth. It brought a smile but also a sense of loss, because thinking about him inevitably led to thoughts about my mother and Emmie, whom I had long ago nicknamed M.

However, it wasn't until nearly two years after I had begun as a full-fledged Brittany girl that I began to spy on my family. Naturally, I wondered if they still lived where we had lived together. I had kept close enough tabs on them to know they were still living in the same place. I would wander through Central

Park and make the turns onto the East Side streets that would bring me to the corners where I could look, hopefully unseen, at my family's town house. I really wanted to see what M looked like now. Did she resemble me at all? Did she look more like our father or our mother? What did they look like? Older? Had the years been kind to them, or had the loss of me taken some toll?

Sometimes I would stand for nearly an hour and see nothing, no one, but often, because I admitted to myself that I wanted to see them, I would plan the timing better and see M coming home from school or Mama arriving after shopping. I rarely saw my father, but when I did, I saw how slowly he walked. He had lost his perfect army-cadet posture, too, and he had become more gray-haired.

In fact, they all looked different to me now. It was as if I were watching them on television or in a movie, perhaps because I was observing them unseen. I tried to study the expressions on their faces, wondering if somehow, someway, I could discern any of them thinking about me, wondering about me, and being sad about me. I had no real way of knowing, but I liked imagining that they were doing just that, that it was why my father was so gray and stooped.

A few times, I saw Mama pause near the front stoop and look behind her. I pulled back to remain unseen, but I was able to peer at her and see the way she studied the street. Could she sense my presence? Was it true that mothers had a sixth sense when it came to their children, a sense they would never lose? When I saw her looking around in front of the house as if she was hoping to see me, I wondered if she often looked for me when she walked or took a taxi.

Invariably, after I had done one of these spying missions, I berated myself. Was I getting soft, regretful? This would only lead to terrible guilt and affect my work. I was afraid Mrs. Brittany would take one look at me and know. Maybe she always suspected I would do this and had someone following me. All of us Brittany girls were a little paranoid. We knew how closely she kept watch over us, over everything we did on our own. Surely she had some help.

My paranoia became so intense that I often stopped to look around to see if I could spot someone following me. Sometimes I would deliberately make a wrong turn or go into a store I had no interest in just to see if I could spot someone waiting out there, watching and tracking me. Of course, I expected that every phone call I received and every package delivered was scrutinized by someone at the hotel. It was, I imagine, like living in the world of Big Brother in Orwell's novel *1984* or some other type of dictatorship in which everyone spied on everyone else. I got so paranoid sometimes that I searched the apartment for hidden microphones and cameras. I never found any, but that didn't convince me that they weren't there.

Because of all this, there were often times, especially in the longer periods between appointments, when I would seriously consider leaving Mrs. Brittany. As if she could sense it, something more lavish would be done for me. I was sent on holiday with one of the other girls. No expense was too great. We had periodic retraining sessions at her Long Island estate, which always culminated with grand parties. I met some of the new girls and saw how they envied and respected me and looked to me for advice and guidance. If this was Mrs. Brittany's intention, it worked, because it boosted my ego and drove back any thoughts of resigning.

Where would I go, anyway? What would I do? What else was I trained to do? I didn't have enough to keep me in my high-living style for life. Everything I made was under the table, so to speak. Mr. Bob described it as being beneath the radar. The result was that I had no history. If I were to write a résumé for some job, it would be full of blank spaces. I began to realize that the effect was to make me invisible. It got so that I wondered if I would see myself reflected in a mirror.

The one love of my life had married and was on the verge of taking over his father's business empire. In the beginning, I often thought of Paul and wondered if Norbert had finally told him who and what I was or if he always knew and was indeed working for Mrs. Brittany right from the start. Whenever I asked her, she just smiled and refused to answer. She wasn't tormenting me. She simply wanted me to believe she was in control of everything that had to do with me.

Finally, nearly two years later, Paul came to New York specifically to see me. He went through the service, and Mrs. Brittany permitted it. No other assignment made me as nervous and insecure. I was practically trembling all over when he came to my apartment to take me to dinner and a Broadway show.

When I opened the door, we simply stood there looking at each other for a good ten or fifteen seconds, neither knowing how to start. Finally, he said, "You always surprise me with how much more beautiful you become, Roxy."

"You never surprise me with your compliments," I replied, and we both laughed.

I thought we would begin with a drink at my bar. He told me he had developed a liking for the Cosmopolitan cocktail. All of us Brittany girls could mix drinks as well as any bartender in the best clubs, hotels, or restaurants. There was one full weekend at the estate for just that training, and we had a great deal of fun getting a little looped in the process.

Usually, I had a nonalcoholic drink if I had cocktails first at my apartment with a client. Mrs. Brittany's admonition about getting drunk was frightening, first because of how angry it would make her for any of us to be at a very dangerous disadvantage. To be taken advantage of by a client was like ripping up your future, and for Mrs. Brittany, that was the loss of her investment in you. Besides, it cheapened the whole experience, and if there was one thing Mrs. Brittany guarded, it was the special elegant nature of her enterprise. Second, there was the real danger of embarrassing ourselves in public and therefore drawing more attention to the Brittany escort service. The more secret it was, the more special it was, and the more special it was, the more expensive it would be. More expensive meant it was more special, so it was a circle that rolled on, spinning great profit to feed the Brittany financial machine.

It was that night, however, when we both had something to drink, that I finally learned the truth. Paul confessed to having known from the start that I was one of Mrs. Brittany's girls.

"Of course Norbert told me, but it never made a difference to me. I also knew you were just starting out, a virgin, so to speak."

"Hardly that."

"No, but a virgin when it came to the Brittany escort service."

"Did you do what she wanted, become part of a test she had designed?"

"Yes and no. At first, Norbert brought me there for just that, but as I got to know you, I hated the idea of doing anything, saying anything, that in any way was a form of betrayal. Besides," he said, "I did fall in love with you. I'll always be in love with you."

"And how's your marriage?" I asked sharply.

He nodded. "I don't blame you for taking that tone. My marriage is a success as far as my father and our economic empire are concerned. It's easy to see, however, that it's a marriage of convenience. Most of the time, we go our separate ways. Lately, we don't even share coffee in the morning."

"Children?"

"None yet. It's a little troubling to both families. My father actually thinks I'm controlling my sperm or something. How does he put it? I'm 'psychologically depressing the little buggers.'"

I laughed. "Maybe you are."

He sipped his drink and looked around the apartment. "Very nice place."

"It serves its purpose," I said.

"And what is that?"

"To be a successful Brittany escort, what else?"

"Are you happy?" he asked.

"Comfortable," I replied.

"Is it enough?"

"I don't know," I admitted. "Is what you have enough?"

He looked down at his drink.

"Is it still true that ego and greed are at work for you?" I followed.

He took a deep breath and looked at me. "I'm not as much like my father as I thought I was. Feared I was," he added.

When we looked at each other now, neither of us turned away. He smiled. We drew closer, and when we kissed, it wasn't like any kiss I would give any client.

We didn't go anywhere that night. It was too hard not to reach out sensually, not to kiss, not to touch, and if we went anywhere, we'd be restrained. For a few hours, it was as if no time had passed, as if I had closed my eyes while I was at Mrs. Brittany's Côte d'Azur villa and then opened them to see him beside me just the way he had been, his handsome face in sweet repose and a feeling of wonderful satisfaction covering my body like a soft silk blanket.

When we parted in the morning, he promised to see me as many times as he could. I told him not to make promises.

"Make appointments instead."

"Yes," he said. "You're right."

"Besides, I'd rather that each time be a surprise, something unexpected, rather than something longed for. The ache becomes too painful."

"I understand. You'll take care of yourself, won't you?"

"It's part of the job description," I replied.

He laughed, but I really believed after a while that I could go on and on like this, employing Mrs. Brittany's beauty techniques, keeping up with my physical training and nutrition, slipping in and out of the latest fashions, updating myself with my cultural education. I even dreamed of someday becoming Mrs. Brittany, inheriting control of the company and having my own Wilcox girls. Was that pure ambition or pure stupidity?

Traveling, entertaining, socializing with the richest and most powerful people did insulate me and keep me from thinking about anything I had lost or sacrificed. I was exactly what I had told Paul: comfortable.

And then, one late afternoon, when my limousine had taken me to pick up a client after his dinner meeting, I looked out when the chauffeur opened the door for him and saw that the client was standing with my father. It was as if I had been shot through the heart with an arrow of ice. The look on his face seemed to shatter the very air between us. I pulled back, but it was too late. The client, a man not much younger than my father, got into the limousine. I didn't look back when we drove off, but I could feel my father's eyes on the back of my head. I was numb, speechless, and a terrible late-night date, as I would have been for any other client.

No matter what my client said or tried, I was unresponsive. Just the fact that he knew my father and had been standing there beside him brought my father into the limousine and into the remainder of the evening with him. When he spoke or looked at me, I could only hear and see my father. Finally, disappointed and disgusted, he cut the evening short. I knew this was my first serious failure, but I could do nothing about it.

The following morning, Mrs. Brittany came to my apartment. I was still in bed, feeling sick to my stomach and exhausted. I hadn't managed an hour of sleep. Every time I had closed my eyes, I saw my father's face, felt his surprise and his pain. I buried my face in my pillow to smother any sobs and instantly dry any tears. I didn't even hear Mrs. Brittany enter my bedroom. She slammed the door, and I sat up quickly. One look at her face told me she had heard more than an earful from my client.

"What happened?" she demanded. "Why did you treat that man so poorly? What got into you?"

"When we stopped to pick him up at the restaurant, he was standing with my father."

"Your father?"

"Yes, as it turns out, they're associates. He was at a dinner meeting."

She was quiet a moment, and then, nodding, she said, "I can understand it, but I can't forgive it. You know I don't tolerate failure. Ours is a business that depends on clients recommending the service because they've had an outstanding experience well worth the cost in their minds. Anything contrary hurts us all."

"I'm sorry. I can't imagine it happening again."

"It won't, or if it does, it won't," she said, making it clear.

She calmed down and decided to send me to Dubai on a week's holiday with Camelia and Portia. I knew she wanted me to see what I would be missing if I failed her again. We were all showered with expensive gifts, deluxe travel arrangements, and luxurious resort accommodations. It was a good antidote to what I had experienced, because the three of us had so much fun teasing and flirting with rich young Arab men who we knew would become new clients. One gave me a diamond bracelet worth fifty thousand dollars. He had it hidden in a bowl of whipped cream at dinner. I had never laughed so much or felt more relaxed and lucky.

When I returned, I was back to my successful Brittany girl self. I thought that was the end of my regrets and conscience. I had once again locked away my family memories in a keyless safe, stuffed into the deepest corner of my mind.

And then my mother managed to get a message over the wall of security that Mrs. Brittany had built around me. A relatively new receptionist at the hotel stopped me one morning to ask if I knew a Mrs. Wilcox.

"I'm not sure this is for you," he said. "I'm not even sure I'm supposed to ask, but from her description of the woman she wanted to contact, I thought immediately of you."

"You're not supposed to ask," I said. I was going to walk away, maybe even report him and get him fired, but I hesitated. Something stronger made me hesitate.

He held out a slip of paper and shrugged. "This is the message. Whoever it's for isn't going to be happy. I felt I should try, at least."

I stared at it, fighting the urge to take it from him, but it was too strong. I practically ripped it out of his fingers and opened it.

The words pounded through my brain and stole away my breath. I felt a weakness in my legs and an emptiness inside that I hadn't felt for years.

My father had died.

His funeral was in two days. The information was there.

I folded the paper.

"It isn't for me," I told the receptionist, and handed the paper back to him.

"Oh, that's good. Sorry to bother you," he said.

"It wasn't any bother, but if I were you, I'd throw that out and forget about it."

He nodded. "Sure."

I gave him a stern glare and walked away. At least, I thought I did. My legs were on their own. I got into the elevator and took a deep breath.

The general was dead.

I had expected that when I heard this news later in my life, I would feel nothing but relief. I didn't expect the cold, sick feeling of grief that crawled up from my stomach and surrounded my heart. I tried to ignore it. I ridiculed it, mumbling that now the beds wouldn't be made right, the house would go into disarray, and my grandfather's iconic picture would come down and be stuffed in a carton at the back of some closet. But nothing worked. My heart wouldn't lighten, and my laughter was more like sobbing.

Fortunately, I had no assignments the following day or the day after. I was certain I would have been a disappointment, and Mrs. Brittany had left no doubt about what result that would have. I did all I could to forget about my mother's message, but it wouldn't let go. I didn't go to the church service. I had the limousine take me there, and then I sat in it and watched the people go in and then come out. I had the driver follow far behind the funeral procession to the cemetery and park a good distance away. Then I walked to the very edge of the section and watched the burial from a distance, behind a tree, my gaze locked on Mama and Emmie, who both looked so small and lost to me. I thought that attending even from this distance might diminish the anger I felt toward Papa, but his dying made me even more furious. He was still hurting the people he was supposed to love, hurting them by dying.

I couldn't wait to get away, expecting that now I could put it all to bed and forget again, and I probably would have if it hadn't been for M. Little did I know that she had been spying on me and knew where I was and what I was doing, but it was Mr. Bob who stuck his neck out. I always knew he had a greater fondness for me than he had for any other Brittany girl. I was his special personal discovery.

I should have expected that Mrs. Brittany would know about my father's passing. She said nothing. It was, I assumed, another secret test. Since I had no assignments during the funeral or right after, I was fine with being tested. I did well with the first assignment I had afterward, too.

But then Mr. Bob was given a letter M had managed to leave for me at the hotel.

"I thought about just destroying it," he said. "But I have more faith in you now. Whatever it says, you'll handle it, I'm sure. However, let's leave this just between us, okay?"

I knew he meant never to mention it to Mrs. Brittany.

"Yes, of course. Thank you," I told him.

I didn't open it in front of him. I waited until he had left, and then I poured myself a glass of white wine and sat at the bar, staring down at the envelope. I couldn't help but smile at the way M had written my name. She was still doing what she did with the R, giving it a little curving tail. I opened it slowly, took a breath, and then read it.

Dear Roxy,

You and I haven't seen or spoken to each other for years. You knew Papa knew who and what you are now. There's no point in pretending anything. I don't care how angry you were at him and Mama. Papa died, and Mama left you a message with your service and at your hotel, and I know you are there. She tried to reach out to you, thinking you might have an ounce of decency left. I think it's horrible that you wouldn't even respond.

All I can say is that even with your rich possessions, you're someone I pity.

Your sister, Emmie

Inside the envelope was the charm bracelet I had once given her. It had a wonderful variety of charms that included the Eiffel Tower, a fan, a pair of dancing shoes, and a dream catcher. My mother's brother, my uncle Alain, had given it to me when my parents and I were in France visiting. This was before M was born. I had given it to her just a few weeks before my father ordered me out of the house.

My first reaction was sadness. Tears came to my eyes, but that was quickly followed by the familiar rage that had enabled me to put my family on a shelf. I resented M for pulling it off that shelf. I didn't want to resent her, but it was the safest reaction I could have. I hated myself for having it, but I needed it.

I left the letter and the charm bracelet on the bar for days and tried not to look at them again. But that didn't work. Finally, I put them both at the bottom of a drawer. I dived into my work, took on every assignment Mrs. Brittany sent in my direction, and came close to drinking too much with a French cabinet minister one night but managed to get through it. I knew I was off my stride, and those damn nights tossing and turning in my sleep as I agonized over M's letter and the charm bracelet were tearing me down.

Finally, hoping for some closure, I took the charm bracelet out of the drawer and called for the limousine. I had the driver park across from M's school just as the school day ended and the students emerged. When the first ones appeared, I got out and stood by the limousine. She appeared and saw me there. I thought she might rush off in the opposite direction, but she came to me. I had worked on hardening my heart, but as she approached and I saw how pretty she was and how much she looked like Mama, I felt myself softening. I did my best to fight it back, but it was like holding back a cascade of memories too heavy to be stopped. She got into the vehicle, and I had the driver take us through the park. I was hoping to turn her out of my life forever.

"You walk and hold yourself just like I do. It's the damn rod Papa had installed in us when we were born, that perfect military posture. Ironically, for me it's been an asset. So what are you, in tenth grade?" I asked, trying to sound as indifferent and bitter as I could.

"Yes."

"And I'm sure a good student," I said, making that sound bad or stupid.

"Not lately, although I'm doing better than I was."

I was interested in how she had found out where I was. She told me she had overheard the conversation Papa had with Mama after he saw me with his business associate. I told her I was at the funeral but too far away for her to notice.

"It would have pleased Mama to know," she said.

She had the same grit I had at her age, I thought, but I wouldn't tolerate her making me feel bad. "Would it? I doubt she would have shown it. He's gone, but his influence over her is probably as strong as it ever was."

"That's not true," she fired back at me, her eyes as big and as furious as mine could get.

"Please. There's so much you don't know. I suppose I shouldn't hold her as responsible as I do. She was a European woman from a family where the women were always subservient to their men, and when you were married to a soldier like Papa, you were trained and obedient."

"Papa wasn't a soldier, and he was your father, too."

"*Excusez-moi?* He didn't enlist or go to officers' school, but he was in the army from the day he was born. I remember our grandfather. You don't. Emotions like love and compassion are signs of weakness to the Wilcox men. I never had any doubt that if your father was in your grandfather's regiment, he wouldn't hesitate to send him to the front lines, and if your father was killed in battle, he'd write a letter to his wife and himself with the same official signature and stamp. That's how our father grew up, and that's how he wanted us to grow up, or at least me."

I hated how bitter I sounded, but I thought it was the right medicine to give her. She was speechless for the moment, so I had the driver take us to her home.

"Are you coming in to see Mama?" she asked.

"No."

"Why did you come to see me, then?" she snapped, whipping her words the way Papa could.

"I wanted to see what you were like, how you were doing. Now that I have, I think you'll survive," I said.

"But Mama—"

"Mama let me go, M. I can't forgive her for that."

"She loved you, loves you. She takes out your picture often, and she cries," she said.

"He let her keep a picture of me?"

"She kept it secret, but I think he always knew. If he hadn't died, maybe . . ."

"Maybe I'd get an honorable discharge?"

"You went to the cemetery service, you said."

"Not to ask him for his forgiveness but to see if I could forgive him. I couldn't," I said, and signaled the driver to open her door.

Then I handed her the charm bracelet.

"You should keep it," I told her. "It's better that I don't have reminders of family."

"No matter what you do, how far you go, you'll always have reminders," she told me. "It's like trying to get rid of your shadow."

I couldn't get away fast enough.

Because I knew she was right.

Epilogue

I didn't see M again until some time later, when she came to the Beaux-Arts to tell me Mama was very sick. She had gotten a bad result on an annual gynecological exam. In my heart, I knew that M was coming to tell me because she was terrified. My father's brother and his wife were not people with whom she could be close, and Mama's family was in France, Uncle Alain the closest to her. I liked him the best of all, too. He lived in Paris with his partner, a well-known chef, but I couldn't see M getting much help from him, either. Nevertheless, I resented her coming to me with more bad family news. I had hoped to shut it out, and I wasn't very sisterly or compassionate. I hated myself for it, but I thought I could live with it.

I couldn't.

Despite the hard surface I put on, I found out about Mama and went to the hospital to be with M while Mama was undergoing surgery. Unfortunately, I knew exactly what was going to happen. It had happened to one of Mrs. Brittany's girls, who, like Mama, was ambushed by cervical cancer. I didn't want

my sister to live in a world of fantasy, even though I
remembered too well that young people, especially
young girls, needed that world of illusion to help insulate them against the harsh realities of the adult world
that awaited them.

In this case, the harsh reality was that Mama's cancer was terminal. I tried to give my sister the truth in
little doses, first explaining how extensive and serious
Mama's operation was. I was deliberately cold and
demanding when the two of us met with her doctor,
forcing him to say the truthful things.

Despite my great effort to remain as aloof and
hard as I could, when I went with M to visit Mama
afterward, I felt like a little girl again. The tears fell
inside me, maybe, but they gushed as all my good
childhood memories with her came rushing back. I
knew the only thing I could do for her was to look
after M the best I could, which wasn't easy for someone like me.

Mrs. Brittany did not make allowances for family problems. We were never to bring any baggage
along with us as long as we were under her employ,
and too often, she had reminded me that I had come
to her with more baggage than she usually tolerated.
Nevertheless, I appealed to her, reminding her about
how dear Sheena had been to both of us. I think solely
because of that, she relented, giving me some time to
look after Mama's and M's needs as long as I fulfilled
the most important assignments, one of which took
me away for nearly a week at just the wrong time.
That did little to bond me with my younger sister,

who at times reminded me more and more of our father, condemning me with her gaze and her sharp tone when we spoke.

I made arrangements for Mama to have a private-duty nurse when she was home. I had no false hope or any illusions about it and tried to get M to understand, but she resisted right up to the day Mama had to return to the hospital. We were literally in countdown now. I made M go to school, but the hardest thing I had to do since I had left our home was to go there and get her the day Mama died.

Uncle Alain had flown over and was with us. Our aunt Lucy and uncle Orman descended like vultures to scoop M up and bring her back to their home. I could see what that was going to be like for her. She would be in an even worse situation than I had been in, because she had no ally, no one like Mama to be a buffer between her and our military uncle and our insensitive aunt. In the end, I couldn't let it happen. I went to see Mrs. Brittany. I was ready to quit, and she knew it.

"I want to be my younger sister's guardian," I told her. "I want her to move in with me."

"Do you know what you're proposing? That's ridiculous."

"I do. She'll live with me either at the Beaux-Arts or someplace else, Mrs. Brittany," I replied, with my eyes as steely as hers could be.

"It won't work. Do you actually want to expose a girl that young to our world?"

"I wasn't much older when Mr. Bob brought me to you," I said.

She shook her head and looked at Mrs. Pratt, who was in the office, too.

"She'll have to live by our rules," Mrs. Brittany said, showing me she was relenting.

"She will."

"I'll be there to make that clear myself."

"Good."

What I really wanted to say was that I wanted what was left of my family back. I wanted to be the older sister I never could be. Just as she had tried to hold on to some semblance of family through Sheena, I would through Emmie. But I didn't mention any of that. I knew she would see it only as weakness and another portent of disaster.

In the beginning, I thought I actually would enjoy being M's older sister, mother, and father wrapped up into one. I went to the school and met with the principal, who clearly wasn't happy about M coming to live with me at the Beaux-Arts. It was clear that the rumor mill had been running full-time at the school, but I thought we could endure it, or at least she could. I tried to be as stern and unyielding as Papa at times, insisting that M keep up with her schoolwork. On the other hand, I also enjoyed being her older sister, showing her how to look prettier, fixing her hair, teaching her about makeup, and buying her more attractive clothes. Little did I know that everything I did only made things harder for her at school. Dirty rumors were circulated more openly because of the things I had done for her. They were saying that I was turning my sister into another prostitute.

I didn't understand at first how this happened so quickly, and then M confessed and told me that before Papa's death, she and one of her girlfriends had been spying on me. Her girlfriend knew too much and, out of jealousy or just plain meanness, began to spread rumors about her after she had moved in with me. It all came to a head when Mrs. Brittany arrived one day to reveal that somehow her telephone service was getting nuisance calls. She was furious about it, and I knew that my days as a Brittany girl were numbered as long as M remained with me.

We might have survived for quite a while, nevertheless, if it weren't for a nightmare of mine coming to fruition. M was home, had just taken a shower, and, being upset with herself and everything else, poured herself a drink at my bar. She was sitting there in her robe when the door buzzer sounded, and unfortunately, she greeted a first-time client of mine who had arrived quite early. Things got out of hand, and he went after her, thinking she was another Brittany girl. She had locked herself in her bedroom by the time I arrived.

I managed to distract him, but he turned out to be my first and only vicious and despicable man. When I refused to bring my sister out for his sexual fantasy *ménage à trois*, he hit me. It was the only time any man had ever been violent, but it took only that one time to drive home the reality of what I was, what I was doing with my life, and where I would eventually end up.

Nothing reinforced my understanding more than

Mrs. Brittany's lack of sympathy or compassion. She blamed it all on me, of course, for taking M into my life in the first place, and then had the audacity to suggest that maybe I could turn it into an advantage. Her intentions were clear. She wanted me to develop M as a younger version of myself.

"You've exposed her to it. It's the only way to solve the situation. I know she must look up to you now. She sees how well you live and must realize she could live just as well."

I pretended to consider it, but I felt as if my father had returned from the dead, gotten into Mrs. Brittany, and wreaked his final revenge. I asked her for a little time off to think things over, and she gave me a few weeks. I told M we were going to have a vacation in Paris and called Uncle Alain immediately. He understood exactly what I was intending and was more than willing to take on the responsibility.

Ironically, M and I had never been closer than we were during those days in Paris. She loved Uncle Alain and his partner, Maurice, and they took to her immediately, too. I saw how comfortable she was with them and felt encouraged. I could leave her there and feel I had done the right thing. I didn't tell her my plan. I really didn't know how I would finally arrange it, but thankfully Uncle Alain was way ahead of me about it all, proposing a new school for her.

I had been back to Paris many times since I had begun working for Mrs. Brittany, but it never touched me or opened itself to me as much as it did when M and I toured it together, sat in cafés, listened to music, or just walked along the Seine. She tried many times to get me to give her more details about what my life was like. I held her off with promises to reveal more in time, but my intention was never to tell her any of it if I could help it.

I knew that when it came time for me to reveal what Uncle Alain had agreed to do—become M's guardian and take her in for her final high school years—she would resist and refuse. I really didn't know what I was going to do with myself, except that I would not return to Mrs. Brittany.

And then, late one afternoon, when I was alone at a café, musing about my future and all that had happened in my life, I felt his presence before I turned to look up and see him standing there.

"*Bonjour*," he said.

I was speechless for a moment. "How did you find me?" I asked him.

"You think your Mrs. Brittany is the only one with powerful friends?"

I kept looking at him, trying to convince myself that I wasn't dreaming. He laughed and sat next to me, ordering a café au lait and then taking my hand.

"Norbert," I said, nodding and realizing what had happened. "He must have had something to do with this."

"*Mais oui*. What are good friends for?"

"Do you have business here in Paris?" I asked him.

"Always, but that's not what brought me this time."

"Ah," I said. "Another free weekend?"

"All my weekends are free now."

"What are you saying?"

"The merger has dissolved," he replied with a smile. "The marriage one, I mean. Do you think there is any chance for us to pick up where we left off, to pretend that only a day or so has passed?"

"But you know it's been far more than that, Paul, and you know where I've been," I said.

The waiter brought his café au lait. He sipped some and nodded. "And I also know that if I had had any courage back then, you wouldn't have been where you've been and be where you are now. I don't blame you. I blame myself."

I smiled. "Okay. Then I'll blame you, too," I said, and he laughed before taking on the most serious expression I had seen on his face.

"Good, Roxy. That way, we'll both be able to live with it and go on." He reached for my hand, but I held it back.

"All my life, I've avoided illusions and fantasies, Paul," I said.

"Yes, but this isn't going to be an illusion, and this isn't a fantasy. This is us for real. I love you, Roxy. It was the epitome of stupidity to believe I could ignore it. And I hope it's the same for you."

I felt those stubborn tears come into my eyes, tears I had driven back so many different times for so many different reasons. But I couldn't hold them back now.

Now I would cry for my father, finally.

And for my mother.

And for myself.

He leaned over to wipe my cheeks and then kiss me. I gave him my hand.

Paris was lighting up. It was almost as if the whole city had been listening in on our conversation and wanted to congratulate us and wish us well.

"I have to return to New York," I said. "And bring a few things to a conclusion."

"My plane is at your disposal," he said. "That way, I know you'll return."

"I'll return," I promised.

Afterward, we walked together on the Boulevard Saint-Germain. I recalled my mother describing her life in Paris when she was a little girl and how she simply loved walking the streets, watching the people, listening to the laughter and the music that poured out of cafés or was played by street musicians.

She had said it all made up the heart of what she was.

"In the end," she'd told me as she brushed my hair and kissed my forehead, "you can't deny who you are. You can only embrace it, Roxy. I'm afraid it will take you longer to realize that, but I have faith that you will."

"Yes," I whispered as I held tightly to Paul's arm and then laid my head against it.

We moved in and out of shadows, but our silence wasn't born out of fear of our future. It was born out of hope and love and the knowledge that in the end, you will always come home and be forever with the people you love if you just stop to listen to the music in your heart.